To Christi

best wishes

THE BONE FLUTE

Daniel Allison

'Urgent drama and ancient magic… I loved The Bone Flute and devoured it in a single sitting'
Peter Snow, Author of The Shifty Lad

REVIEWS

CONTENTS

FREE DOWNLOAD OFFER

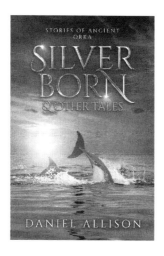

As the winter winds shriek and their family sleeps, Grunna and Talorc sit at the hearth-fire, telling the tales of ancient Orka. Stories of trowies, silkies and even the mysterious Silvers.

I'm offering Silverborn as a FREE ebook exclusively to members of the House of Legends Club.

Get my FREE ebook at www.houseoflegends.me/landing-page

In loving memory of John Martin, who made it all possible.

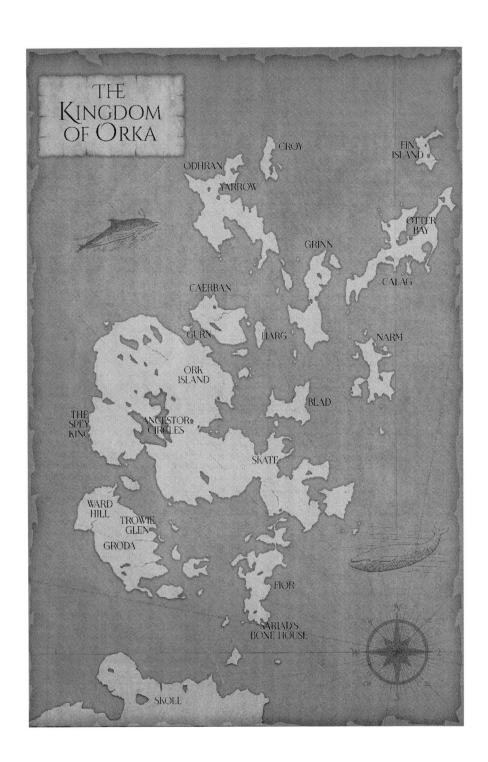

THE KINGDOM OF ORKA

ODHRAN
CROY
FIN ISLAND
YARROW
OTTER BAY
GRINN
CAERBAN
CALAG
GURN
HARG
NARM
ORK ISLAND
BLAD
THE SPEY KING
ANCESTOR CIRCLES
SKATE
WARD HILL
TROWIE GLEN
GRODA
FIOR
SARIAD'S BONE HOUSE
SKOLL

PART I

CHAPTER ONE

Orkney, circa 500BC

Talorc crawled through the forest of dune-grass, listening to the stranger sing. He couldn't see the singer yet, but it had to be a stranger. No-one he knew would steal out before dawn to sing up the sun, except Grunna, and she was dead.

The wind was fierce this morning, its howling covering the sound of his approach. Talorc wanted to see the stranger, but he didn't want the stranger to see him. Why not? Because this was Odhran, and no-one ever came here except in Grunna's stories, about marauders from the sea who stole away women and murdered men, or about finmen who came ashore at night to perform their secret spells.

Talorc reached the dune's peak and looked down.

Moonlight silvered the sand. Upon the sand stood the stranger. He wore a sealskin cloak and faced away from Talorc, north towards the sea, his arms spread wide as if he wished all the sea-creatures and the hidden stars to listen. His voice was deep and grating and his words made no sense. At his side was a skin-sack, and beside it a heap of seagrass.

The sack was moving.

Talorc noticed this but didn't dwell on it. Faint voices whispered in his mind as his gaze fixed on the scaled, blue-black skin on the stranger's hands, on his bare feet and on the coiled tail resting between his legs on the sand.

Talorc knew that he knew almost nothing of the world. He knew his village, half a mile south-east of the beach. He knew the beach, and the western cliffs where seabirds nested, and the rolling hills to the south and their scattered farmsteads. Not once had been to the south of the island, nor to any other island in Orka, nor out to sea. But he knew Orka's stories. He knew about finmen.

This was a finman.

The sack moved again. Something was alive inside it. The finman went on singing as he kicked it with the heel of his foot.

Whatever was inside the sack whined and fell still.

The finman ceased his rasping song. He walked around the sack, the hood of his cloak obscuring his face, and knelt over the mound of seagrass. Talorc watched as his long, scaled fingers arranged it into the shape of an arrow, complete with flight-feathers and barbed point. The arrow faced south-east, towards Talorc. Towards the village.

The sky was brightening. Talorc's family would be awake now and at the harvesting soon. He would be in for another skelping.

The finman now went to the sack. Was it really a finman? They were forbidden to leave their island, except to fish in the waters around it. Sometimes folk said they had seen one out at sea, but only ever for a few moments, and there was never any proof. But only finmen had tails, and blue-black glittering scales. It had to be a finman, which meant that this was the most exciting thing that had ever happened to Talorc. He had a story of his own to tell now. It also meant that he was in danger, for the finman was breaking the treaty, and if he knew Talorc was there...

Talorc's thoughts were interrupted as the finman pulled from the sack a fat seal pup. He held it aloft as it struggled, wriggling as it keened for its mother in sharp yelps. The finman let it struggle while he resumed his song. Though Talorc didn't understand his words, there was a feeling of finality to them, like the way Grunna had spoken when nearing the end of a story, or the way she had played the last few notes of a tune on her bone flute. The white-furred, black-eyed pup seemed to sense it too and writhed more desperately, keened more loudly.

The finman lowered the pup to his chest, out of Talorc's sight.

Day had come. The sand shifted from silver to white in the faint approaching sunlight. The wind howled like a bone flute played by a giant in the sky.

The finman reached into his skin-cloak, withdrew a stone knife and held it up high. Talorc's heart pounded as if trying to break free.

The finman's song reached its peak. The final note resounded.

The knife flashed down. Flashed up again.

Red blood poured from the pup onto the arrow as Talorc screamed.

The finman turned and looked straight at him.

CHAPTER TWO

They stared at one another. The finman's green eyes were bright against the dark scales of his face. In his hands he held the dead, bleeding pup.

The finman threw down the pup and Talorc turned and ran.

He ran as fast as he could but finmen were strong and quick – or so the stories said. Talorc would be caught and kidnapped or his throat would be cut. He needed somewhere to hide and there was only one possible place.

The bone-house.

He veered left, crashing through the dune-grass. Soon he saw it ahead; a cocoon of stacked slabs of stone, looking from the outside like any other house on Odhran. He raced around it, reached the doorway and dropped to his knees.

The entrance was a tunnel through the thick stone walls. You had to get down on your hands and knees and crawl to enter. Before that, the door had to be dealt with. Panting, Talorc took hold of the left side of the great stone slab and heaved, rolling it to the right and out of the way. He crawled into the tunnel.

Reaching the main chamber, Talorc turned and backed himself up against the wall. He sat still, sweating, panting, listening. The finman would see that the door had been rolled aside. He would know Talorc was inside. Trapped.

Talorc looked around. Light streamed in through the tunnel, enough to reveal the dark gaps in the stone which led to the bone chambers. Within, the skulls and bones of the ancient island people rested in never-ending darkness. They would help him, if only they could hear him.

'Ancestors,' he whispered. 'Men and women of Odhran. Ancient Orkadi, grandmothers and grandfathers. Protect me from the one outside who wishes me harm.'

Silence. Of course. How many times had he come here in darkest night, to sit and speak to the skulls in the hope of an answer? He didn't have the gift – he wasn't a spey.

Talorc heard a noise outside. A shadow fell over the entrance, cloaking the tomb in darkness.

If the finman came crawling through the tunnel Talorc could kick him, stamp on his hands. No good – the finman would be too quick, he would grab Talorc's foot and pull him out into the open, or bleed him right there in the bone-house.

Talorc waited.

Slowly it dawned on him that if the finman was coming in after Talorc, he would have done so. So what was he doing?

Light poured into the chamber. The finman had moved away from the entrance. Perhaps Talorc's speying had worked.

The light grew brighter, dimming at times as rainclouds passed overhead. Eventually he got down on his belly and crawled a little way down the entrance tunnel, ready to wriggle back. Daylight sang in the air. All the family would be in the fields, slicing the barley stalks with their heuk-knives. Today's skelping would be one to remember – if Talorc made it home alive.

Had the finman given up and gone? It wasn't safe for their kind to linger in the light; the bone-house was visible from the edge of the village. He must have left. It was time for Talorc to warn his family of what he had seen.

He crawled the rest of the way through the tunnel. Grunna's flute, which he kept in an inner pocket of his tunic, pressed against his ribs.

Talorc stopped just before the entrance, listening again.

Nothing.

He crawled out of the bone-house, stood up and looked around.

There was no-one in sight. The finman had left the island or was hiding deep in the dune-grass.

Rolling the door-slab back into place, Talorc ran as fast he could in the direction of home.

Jed saw him coming first.

There was no point in trying to avoid them. Jed called to Kellin as Talorc ran up the path to the fields and the cluster of stone-walled, grass-roofed houses and outbuildings that was the village of Yarrow.

They met him at the edge of the fields.

'Been down the beach, monster?' said Jed, using his favourite nickname for Talorc. Jed and Kellin both had Mam's raven-dark hair, pale skin and darting brown eyes. Jed was shorter and squatter, but he made up for it by being meaner.

'We've been working since before light. Had to work harder 'cos the monster was gone,' said Kellin.

'I need to speak to Mam,' said Talorc, his chest heaving. 'Now.'

'On you go then,' said Jed, smiling as he stood aside.

Talorc knew what was coming. He ran between his two brothers. As soon as they were behind him they shoved him, one hand each, knocking him to the hard earth; but Talorc twisted as he fell and grabbed Jed's arm, pulling him down with him. He rolled on top of his brother and managed to land one pathetic punch before Kellin pulled Talorc off Jed and pinned him down. Jed took his revenge with a series of well-practiced kicks, stopping only when he ran out of breath.

When he could move, Talorc stood, his cheeks burning and eyes stinging, and limped through the golden barley rows towards where his mother was working. He had promised Grunna before she died that he would stand up to his brothers more.

'Mam –'

'Not a word!' she said, pointing the little curved blade of her heuk-knife at him. 'Not a word!' She took a heuk from her belt and thrust it into his hand. 'The boys' lunch will be late thanks to you. Boys who work need their strength.' She strode off in the direction of the house.

Talorc looked down at the heuk-knife. He looked up at the figure of his Mam moving away through the waving stalks.

'Mam!' he shouted.

She didn't look back.

Talorc fell to his knees and punched the ground until his fists throbbed and shook. She wouldn't listen to him; she hardly even looked at him or talked to him. Just like the rest of his family. Even if he could make her listen, she wouldn't believe him.

Rising, Talorc set to work, taking hold a handful of stalks and slicing angrily at them with the iron blade of the heuk. Each clump was tossed into a pile that grew until it was time to begin another one. So the day passed as the sun rose behind the clouds and the wind moaned.

Every now and then he straightened up to rest for a few moments and ease the pain in his back. Not for too long; otherwise a warning shout would come from one of his brothers, followed by a quick, friendly visit if he didn't get back to work. Harvest was the busiest time of the year. All the crop had to be cut and left to dry in the wind before being collected and brought into the barn. There the family would gather for the winnowing, done in day after day of darkness, as winter won the battle of the seasons and took the island in her iron grip.

Maybe he could try telling Rillian? His oldest brother wasn't as bad as the other two. Rillian didn't like Talorc but he didn't seem to hate him either. But what would Talorc say? That he had seen a finman kill a seal pup and pour its blood on an arrow aimed at the village? What did that even mean? It sounded like magic. It sounded like nonsense. Rillian didn't like nonsense.

What about his father? Da was the headman on Odhran, answerable to King Anga on Ork Island. It was his duty to deal with problems. If the finmen were landing on Odhran then he would have to tell the king... which meant crossing the sea. Da hated the sea and only went on a boat when he had to. And besides, Da wouldn't believe Talorc either.

Noon came, the shadows of the barley stalks swinging to the east. Mam came out with cakes of dried barley for her boys. She looked towards Talorc for a moment then headed back towards the house.

Enough. Talorc threw down his heuk. He followed his Mam, catching up with her outside their home.

'Mam –'

'You heard what I said. Bannocks are for boys who work –'

'I don't care about the stupid bannocks!' said Talorc, though his stomach disagreed. 'Yes, I went down the beach this morning. I wanted to play Grunna's flute and think about her. But when I got there I saw a finman –'

At that word his mother's expression darkened. Looking at Talorc as if he was the monster, she turned, entered the house and closed the door in his face.

'I'm not lying!' he shouted. 'He did a spell, and he aimed it at the village...'

It was hopeless. He turned and trudged back to where his heuk-knife waited.

Grunna would have believed him. It was through her that he knew about finmen. Almost everything he knew about the world came from her and their days and nights spent at the fireside, his hand in hers. When Grunna was young she had been a senachai, traveling from island to island and village to village, telling stories and playing her flute. Grunna never hit him; she used to stroke his hair, saying it was the colour of the afternoon sunlight, just like his Grunda's had been. His eyes were as blue as his Grunda's, she said, as blue as the summer sea.

She had died on midsummer's day. Her body was given to the

Sea Mother; the Orkadi didn't put their dead in bone-houses any more. This winter, Talorc's fourteenth, would be her first beneath the waves. He didn't know how he would survive the dark fireside days without her.

Talorc's stomach was squealing like an angry pig when a shout made everyone in the field stand up.

Da was stood at the western edge of the field with their neighbour Rask, the low evening sun behind them. He was calling to Talorc's brothers to join him. They sheathed their knives and obeyed, disappearing with Da and Rask over the horizon.

Talorc followed. He reached the edge of the fields and looked towards the beach.

A dark mass lay at the edge of the water.

He ran.

CHAPTER THREE

Talorc covered his mouth as he took his place among the silent watchers.

The sea-wolf lay on the sand at the edge of the tide. Each lap of tide-water carried fresh blood away from it, yet more kept pouring from its wound.

Something had bitten off its tail. Not just its tail, but the rear of its entire body. Talorc knew the question on his mind must be on everyone's mind.

What did this?

He'd seen sea-wolves before, far out to sea. They moved like dolphins in the way they slipped in and out of the water, travelling always in a pack, on their way to hunt seals or walrus. He'd loved them for their beauty and mystery; hunters the size and shape of whales, black as midnight and white as the moon. Grunna told all kinds of stories about them. She said there was an island where they took off their skin-cloaks and were giant men. When he asked if that was true or not, she said it happened far away, where there was no such thing as true or false.

Talorc circled around it until the tide licked his boots. He glanced at his father, expecting reproach, as he wasn't allowed to put even his feet in the water, but his father wasn't watching him. He returned his attention to the sea-wolf. This one was no man in sea-wolf skin. It had the same stinking organs, flesh and bones that any creature had when you opened it up; only far, far bigger.

Rillian, Jed and Kellin stood with Rask and their father, holding their noses as they stared, silent and grim, at the dying hunter. Talorc circled back around it, looking for further signs of what had happened, but the only thing that caught his attention was the creature's eyes. They watched him as he moved and somehow Talorc could see its pain in its eyes, its fear... and something else.

'We'll have meat every night this winter,' said Jed. 'This thing'll feed the whole village until spring.'

'You're not cutting any flesh from this one, lad,' said Rask. Rask liked Rillian and Jed and Kellin; he took them out fishing since Da wouldn't go on a boat and because he didn't have any sons of his own, only daughters.

'Why not?' asked Kellin.

'Well, first off, we've nothing to kill it with. You'd need a long spear to cut to its heart, longer than any we have in the village. I don't know exactly where a sea-wolf's heart is, and I'm betting you don't either. And second...' he frowned, tugging at his greying beard. 'Second off, I don't know what creature did this, but whatever it was, I won't take its kill. I don't want anything to do with it. Because whatever did this isn't natural.'

'So what do we do?' said Rillian.

'This beast belongs in the sea,' said Da.

'We could use ropes, but we wouldn't have the strength to drag it,' said Rask.

'So what then?' asked Da.

'There's naught to be done but leave it,' said Rask. 'The gulls will feast and grow fat until there's only bones left. Good for roofing and carving, bones that size, but we'll let the sea take them.'

A keening sound rang out. They turned to look out over the darkening water.

Sea-wolves.

The entire pack was there. Some swam back and forth; others were still, their heads thrown back to the sky as they called out.

'They're singing,' said Talorc.

'Whales don't sing, idiot,' said Jed, shoving him but without much conviction.

'They do as a matter of fact, lad,' said Rask. 'So do sea-wolves, and that's what these ones are doing. They're not dumb fish. They're clever. These ones are calling to their brother.'

For a while they stood silently in the gloaming, listening to the grief-song of the sea-wolves. While they did, Talorc felt a strange sensation; like he wasn't alone anymore. These sea-giants felt what he had felt for Grunna, a deep sadness that one they loved was dying. He wanted to throw back his head and sing too, but he didn't.

The darkness thickened as the moon rose, faint behind the clouds. The sea-wolves quit their song and departed. Talorc felt a pain in his heart as they disappeared out of sight.

'It's time we were leaving,' said Da. 'This beast will be dead by morning. No-one is to come here until I say otherwise.' He turned and walked away up the sand towards the dunes.

'We can't just leave it here to die!' said Talorc.

'We can and we will,' said Rask, his voice thick with distaste, as if talking to Talorc filled his mouth with the taste of rotting meat. 'Like I said, we can't kill him. Unless you know a way?'

Jed and Kellin sniggered.

'No. But we could stay with him, so he doesn't die alone.'

Rask laughed. 'Found a friend, have you? If this thing found you in the water it would rip you to pieces. It's probably thinking that's just what it would do to all of us, if circumstances were different. Sea-wolves are no friend of man. Or you.'

Rask turned and followed Da. With final, lingering looks, Talorc's brothers followed them.

Talorc hesitated. He looked back at the sea-wolf. Now that they were alone, it seemed to be looking at him differently.

'Maybe you would eat me,' he whispered. 'I still don't think you should die alone.'

Talorc drew closer, slowly. He reached out and put his hand on its flesh, near where he guessed its nose was. He stroked it.

The sea-wolf let out a sound, sharp and rising, and for a moment Talorc saw in his mind the seal pup, the arrow, the finman... and something else. He couldn't quite see it, but he could feel its presence. Something big in the water that shouldn't be there.

'Talorc! Get back here!' Da roared.

The image was gone. Talorc drew his hand back, turned and ran up the beach.

On the way back up the hill, Da asked Rask to bring the rest of the villagers to his house for a meeting. Rask nodded and headed for his own door as Talorc's family entered their home.

The peat-fire was burning in the centre of the single room, the dried earth-bricks giving off their sweet smell and black smoke. At either side of the room were beds, made of stone slabs just like the walls and roof of the house - one for Mam and Da on one side, two that Talorc and his brothers shared on the other side. At the far end was the dresser, a set of stone shelves on which lay the family's clothes and other possessions. On the top shelf lay Da's sword, the iron gleaming in the firelight. It sat before the Sea Mother's altar: a bowl full of dried fish, precious stones and strands of hair from each of member of the family, lit on either side by seal-fat lamps.

Why hadn't the Sea Mother protected the sea-wolf? There was no pointing in wondering. *Only a fool would second guess the Sea Mother,* Grunna had always said.

Mam was cooking bannocks on slabs at the edge of the fire. In the corner between her bed and the door were the pots, bowls, spoons and everything else needed for cooking. The grinding quern, where stalks were ground into flour, almost seemed to be glaring at Talorc. On most evenings he sat and worked it until he fell asleep, and he was late to start now.

Talorc took a long drink from the water jug before sitting at the quern and setting to work, as his brothers and Da sat down around the fire. 'I've called a meeting,' said Da to Mam, before she could ask what happened at the beach. 'The others are on their way.'

'There's not enough food,' said Mam.

'The boys can have half. Talorc can have none. No work, no food.'

Mam turned to look at Talorc. Would she disagree, say that he needed to eat?

She nodded and turned away from them both.

Talorc's stomach growled again as his mouth twisted. He lifted the top of the two quern-stones off, set it aside and covered the lower stone with wheat from the pot. Putting the upper stone back in place, he set to work, grinding the two stones against one another. He didn't want them to see that he was angry. He'd worked almost the entire day, apart from a short while in the morning. Well, he could try telling them he'd been in the bone-house, hiding from a murderous finman. They wouldn't believe him, except perhaps about the bone-house – and he wasn't allowed to go in there.

The door-flap lifted as Rask entered, followed by his wife, Mab, and Mab's father, Jank. Toft and Mollick came last. There were no more adults in Yarrel, save for Mollick's mother, who never left her bed.

The family made space and their guests sat down around the fire, quickly refusing the offer of food. It was customary to offer a meal to guests but the offer was usually politely refused. Everyone needed to keep their strength up, particularly at harvest-time. Apart from Talorc, of course.

'Ale, boy,' said Da.

Talorc left the stones and went to the ale-pot. He removed the stone slab covering it and filled the cattle-horn jugs one by one before handing them out. Jank smiled and nodded at Talorc as he took his jug in thin-skinned hands that tried not to tremble. Talorc smiled and nodded back, then sat down again at the quern-stones. He liked Jank. His long white hair reminded Talorc of Grunna. She had liked Jank too.

'Rask tells us you have news, Torma,' said Jank to Da.

'Aye.' He swiftly recounted what they had seen on the beach. 'I'm no seafarer, as we all know, so I'd like those of you who are to tell me two things, if you can. What did this, and should we fear it?'

Those who had been at the beach sipped their ale; the others stared at Da.

'Well, in my days at sea I never saw anything so big it could prey on sea-wolves,' said Jank, breaking the silence. 'Except, of course, other sea-wolves. They're pack animals. Pack hunters. There may have been a fight between two packs, or a fight within a pack to decide who was leader. Whatever happened, this one lost.'

'I've seen enough sea-wolves to know how big they get,' said Rask. 'I've seen them leaping out of the water, smashing down so hard you can hear it a league away. They don't have a bite big enough to do what I saw down there.'

'A squid, then,' said Mollick. Mollick was bony and long-limbed, with wild eyes that reminded Talorc of a sheep about to get its throat cut.

'This wasn't a squid,' said Rask, trying not to sound irritated.

'Pem told a story once about a giant squid, one so big it could wrap itself around a whale and drag it down to the bottom of the sea,' Mollick went on. Talorc's heart skipped as Grunna's name was mentioned. It was rare for anyone to talk about her now that she was gone, but Mollick had always enjoyed her stories.

'Aye, a story,' said Rask. 'There's no such thing as giant squid.'

'Oh, so you've sailed the ocean end to end, have you?' Mollick replied with an arched eyebrow. 'And swum to the bottom as well?'

'It could have been the finfolk.'

Everyone turned to look at Rillian.

'What makes you say that?' said Da, in an encouraging kind of way. In Da's eyes, everything Rillian said was worth hearing. Rillian's snores and farts were worth hearing.

'Well, if it wasn't done by another sea-wolf, and there's nothing bigger than a sea-wolf, then maybe it was done with some kind of weapon. The finfolk hunt at sea. Maybe they've begun hunting sea-wolves?'

'They could have hunted it to the shore, then butchered it,' said Rask. 'It's possible. But why leave half of it? And why here? They don't hunt here, and if they did, they wouldn't do so in daylight when we can see them.'

'They're not supposed to hunt here,' said Mollick. 'Doesn't mean they don't. I saw one once.' Rask groaned. 'I did,' she continued. 'Out west towards the cliffs. There was someone standing on the cliff-edge. I looked away, and when I looked back they were gone. It must have climbed down the cliffs. I swear it by the Sea Mother.'

Da looked uncomfortable at the mention of climbing on cliffs. His own Da, Talorc's Grunda, had died that way. Loth fell from a cliff and drowned, leaving Da stranded on a ledge for a day and night before rescue came. He'd been afraid of the water ever since.

'They might not have needed weapons,' said Toft, Mollick's husband. 'They might have used magic. Everyone knows they have powerful sorcerers. Folk say that's where the speys got their powers from, thousands of years ago; they learnt from the fins.'

'There's a boy on Calag went missing, I heard,' said Mollick. 'He went to play on the beach and never came back. Bessa from Croy saw a boat sailing by with a tall figure and a child in it. They take children to use as slaves, or sometimes to eat...' Mollick fell silent, noticing at last the pained looks on the faces of everyone present. Mam's sister, Nosta, had gone missing when they were girls growing up on Luch. The wind probably blew her off a cliff, but that didn't stop other stories from being whispered.

'Well, one thing is clear,' said Da. 'We don't know what happened to that sea-wolf. And I wouldn't much care, except that it happened here and I need to know if whatever did it could do the same to us.'

'You're going to the king, then, Torma?' asked Jank.

'Aye,' said Da. 'If you'll take me, Rask, we'll start out in the morning.'

Rask nodded. Da could row a boat, and did so if he had to, but wouldn't go out on the sea alone.

'We should go now,' said Talorc.

All eyes turned to him as he stood up. 'We have to leave. It's not safe here.'

'What are you talking about, boy?' hissed Da.

Talorc didn't know what he was talking about. He hadn't known he was going to stand up or speak. His words were almost as much a surprise to him as they were to everyone else. Yet he went on talking.

'I went to the beach to play my flute this morning. I saw a finman. His skin was scaled. He did magic and spilt blood on the sand.'

'He's lying,' said Kellin, hatred in his eyes.

'I'm not lying! The sea-wolf spoke to me,' said Talorc. 'It showed me things. The finman has summoned something terrible and it's going to kill us all –'

'Quiet!' roared Da. 'Sit down, get back to work and keep your stories to yourself.'

Talorc didn't sit down. He stood, trembling, wishing he could stop shaking as he stared at his father. 'Please, listen to me, just once,' he said. 'We have to leave the village. I know it.'

There was no sound but the crackle of the fire as Talorc and his father remained in place, their eyes' fixed on one another.

Da stood up heavily. He walked around the fire and came to stand beside Talorc. Putting one arm around his son's shoulders, he pushed him to the ground. Talorc landed with a thud as Jed and Kellin laughed.

'Get. Back. To work,' Da hissed in Talorc's ear before going to sit back down.

They went on talking as Talorc set to grinding the quern-stones again, his limbs still shaking and his cheeks burning. He tried to take his anger out on the stones, but he could hardly see them for the visions that filled his mind's eye. The sea-wolf. The seal-pup. The keening pack, the finman's arrow and a great mass of scaled flesh, gliding through deep water.

It was coming. He had tried to warn them but they wouldn't listen to him, or the sea-wolf.

Was the sea-wolf dead yet? Maybe not. It was big. It had a lot of blood to spill before it died out there on the beach, alone.

No. Not alone.

Talorc looked up. His Mam glanced at him and glanced away quickly. She wouldn't even look at him.

If she didn't care about him, he didn't care about her.

Talorc stood and ran out of the door.

CHAPTER FOUR

'Are you alive?'

The sea-wolf didn't respond. Of course.

The night was clear, the moonlight bright. Looking about, Talorc saw that they were alone. He wanted to touch the sea-wolf, to lay his hand upon it and comfort it, but he would have to wade into the water to do that, and Talorc wasn't allowed in the water. For as long as he could remember, it had been the most important rule his parents, and even Grunna, had made him obey. It was only for Grunna's sake that he had never broken it.

Yet Grunna was gone now; and he had walked out of the house, away from his family, to be with the sea-wolf. They were only up the hill, but they felt so far away.

She would understand. She would have come down here, waded out, reached out and touched it.

Keeping his boots on, Talorc waded into the water.

It felt warm, perhaps from all the blood. It felt good. Just a few steps and he was in another world, one that pulled and tugged at him and swirled around him. But that didn't matter.

Walking around the sea-wolf, he couldn't see any change in it, although more gulls and ravens had gathered and were circling overhead or fighting on the sand nearby. They had scattered as he came running down the beach and now waited to resume their meal. He wouldn't let them. Not while it lived.

Talorc stood in view of the sea-wolf's left eye. He waved his hand. Did it move?

'I'm sorry you have to die this way,' he said. 'I know we all have to die sometime, but it would have been better if you had died in the sea, with your pack.'

The only answer was the soft beating of the tide on the sand. The waves seemed high, given how little wind there was.

'I don't know how I would want to die. I have a family, and they're like a pack, I suppose. Only I'm not part of it. So it wouldn't much matter to me if they were there when I died. One of them was different, my Grunna, but she's already dead.

'We gave her body to the sea, so maybe you ate her. I wouldn't mind that. I think she'd be happy to live on as part of you. Maybe her spirit would tell you stories and play you bone flute music.

'She liked to tell stories about your people, although I never knew if they were true or not. You would know which ones were true. Or maybe she's right, and there's no such thing as true or false, if you swim far enough away.'

The waves were higher now, and warmer.

'Were you trying to tell me something earlier? When I touched you I saw the finman casting his spell... and something else. In the water. Did it do this to you?'

The sea-wolf was as still as death.

Talorc reached out and put his hand to its flesh. It was cold. Yet Talorc didn't believe the sea-wolf was dead yet, though he didn't know why. Maybe there was a place between life and death, and that was where it was.

He imagined its spirit coming loose from its body. The tide pulling it under the water, where it would go searching for its pack, or perhaps down to the bottom, where the Sea Mother would care for it in her caves. Maybe it needed help to get there.

Reaching into his tunic, Talorc withdrew his flute. He put it to his lips, put his fingers in place and blew.

He didn't play any tune that he knew, instead letting his fingers move themselves across the holes as he watched the sea-wolf, lying still amid the rising, bloody tide. When it became too much to bear, he closed his eyes and focussed solely on the breathy sounds of the flute.

The music washed over him steadily, just as the rising water washed over his calves, his knees. He noticed the water less and less as he went on playing. The sounds of the flute became a sea in which he swam, gliding as quick and agile as a seal, bright-eyed in the murk.

Thoughts came to him, clear and bright like shards of moon-light dancing on water. He imagined the sea-wolf's spirit swim-ming back and forth in the shallow water, unsure where to go. It could see into his mind, so he told it the story of the flute. How his Grunda, Loth, had met Grunna when she was a senachai and she came to his village to tell stories. Loth played his flute for her and she knew she wanted to marry him. She did so, and they had a son, Torma, but then Loth fell from the cliff, and Torma grew up hating the sea. Grunna was gone now too, but before she died she gave Loth's flute to Talorc and taught him to play it. She said that Loth lived in its music, and so would she.

You'll live on too, he told the sea-wolf, *so long as your pack re-member you and sing of –*

Talorc cried out, dropping the flute. Bright light and a pier-cing wail tore through his mind. He couldn't open his eyes, so he felt for the flute, amid the waves that were up to his chest now. The water was so warm that a fire might have been lit beneath it…

Another wave of pain, this one burning a picture into his mind. A dark mass lit with veins of fiery light, coursing through the water.

At last, Talorc understood.

It was coming. It was coming now.

He opened his eyes. The flute; he had to get the flute. The rest-less sea growing ever hotter, he took a breath and plunged his hand in. The sea-wolf went on screaming in his mind to get out of the water, but he had to find it. He tottered around the sea-wolf, pressing his hand against it for balance, the waves grow-ing wild as if in the grip of a midwinter storm. He grit his teeth against the pain as the sea began to scorch him.

There!

Roaring with pain, he lurched out of the water, the flute in his scorched hand. He collapsed on the sand then crawled further up the beach as the waves reached him. Talorc crawled until he was safe and lay down again, closing his eyes.

The sea-wolf was gone from his mind.

It was dead.

Talorc felt it as if something had been pulled from him; an eye or an arm. It was worse than the pain of his scorched skin. For a brief time they had been companions, like he and Grunna had been, their spirits intertwined. Now he was alone again. But its terrible suffering was over, so he was glad.

He got to his knees and turned to look at the sea-wolf. Its ruined body was being quickly submerged within the sea that had been its home.

But the sea had changed.

Nothing hunted sea-wolves. They had lived without fear ever since the Sea Mother gave birth to them. No longer. For the waves were wild now, and the sea was bubbling and hissing and Talorc's skin was red and broken. The sea was no longer the sea.

It was coming. Talorc found himself backing away as a sensation filled him, perhaps the last whisper of the sea-wolf's spirit.

It said to him, *it is here.*

He saw it.

CHAPTER FIVE

It rose out of the water and into the night air. More came, and more, until its head was higher than an eagle would dare to fly.

Talorc heard Grunna's voice in his mind, clear as a rock-pool in spring.

There's all manner of monsters in the sea, lad, though a monster is just an animal that frightens us so much that it needs another name. Of all the sea monsters I ever heard of, the most terrible are the Azawans.

She'd said that Azawans were as green as grass. This one wasn't. It was black, scaled like a fish or a finman, with a web of glittering, flame-coloured veins covering its scales. Patterns of light shot back and forth across them, from the sea up to its great head and its mouth that yawned open, making Talorc wonder for a moment if it was going to swallow the moon.

Azawans are like snakes. You remember I told you about snakes? The way they hunt?

It didn't swallow the moon. Light streamed across the veins towards its mouth, where a torrent of fire erupted. The Azawan waved its head back and forth, lighting up the night sky, and Talorc feared the stars would catch fire.

They didn't. The stars weren't in danger. He was. Talorc backed away... and the Azawan's flame-spear vanished as it turned its head, quicker than a diving hawk, to look at him.

Talorc stood motionless.

The Azawan was still.

Snakes don't see, or so a man over the water in Catness told me.

They only see what moves. They lie still, a mouse walks by, and –

The Azawan shot down from the sky. It landed in the water with a smack that caused a wave of boiling water to cover the beach, almost up to where Talorc stood. Talorc barely noticed the deadly wave as the Azawan shot out of the water, weaving from side to side up the sand and halting once it was face to face with him.

Its head was twice as tall as Talorc's house and twice as wide. Each golden eye glittered like the heart of a fire. The heat it gave off felt like it would melt the skin from Talorc's bones.

The Azawan opened its great mouth, revealing fangs that made his father's iron sword look as deadly as a barley-stalk. Fire danced within its throat as its tongue shot out.

The tongue flickered back and forth, creating a tickling breeze. It was forked at the end, and came close to Talorc but did not touch him. He got the feeling that flicking its tongue towards him could tell the Azawan all about him; his name, his memories, his forgotten dreams.

It was no good being still now, hoping it wouldn't see him. The snake had tasted him. It knew him.

It was time to die.

But the Azawan turned and shot away as quick as it had come. Up the beach it went, over the steep bank of the dunes without slowing, towards the bone-house. Towards the hill.

Towards the village.

'No! Stop!' Talorc watched almost as if he were a bird looking down on himself as he ran after the Azawan. It was hopeless; an ant might as well chase a bear. Still Talorc went on running, to the dunes, up and over them and through the long grass. He wasn't so much chasing the Azawan as running alongside it, for its tail had not yet come into view. Did it have a tail? Did it go on forever?

No-one can tell you how long an Azawan is. Some say they are never-ending, like the sea, but who can know?

Talorc went on running up the hill until he could run no longer. He bent over, his hands on his knees, heaving for breath, his head spinning as the Azawan coursed endlessly by. Dimly he remembered that he hadn't eaten all day. Even if he hadn't been hungry, he was weak. He had been born weak. His legs trembled, his skin burned from the touch of scalding seawater.

Another voice came. Jed's.

I remember when you were a baby. Da wanted you drowned. Did you know that? Said you were a runt, said we should do to you what we do to weakling pigs that waste their mother's milk. More milk for the strong ones that way, see? You were white as flour, blue in places like bad cheese, and you smelt like bad cheese.

Talorc shook off the memory and went on running. The crest of the hill was in sight when flames lit the horizon. Screams rent the air.

He reached the hill's crest and looked down towards the village and the harbour beyond.

The Azawan had encircled the village within its massive, glittering coils. Though every home and storehouse was made of stone, the storehouses were full of grain and the houses of the village were roofed with wood and thatch.

All were burning.

The Azawan held its head high, dancing back and forth, surveying its work. Its tongue flickered in and out.

Something caught its attention. It turned its head and shot a devastating wreath of fire in that direction, before lunging with open jaws, so fast that it didn't seem possible. A scream that Talorc had barely been aware of, amidst all the others, was silenced.

He had to do something. What could he do?

The answer was clear. Nothing.

Yet he had to try. This was his village. Though the people

there hated him, they were the only people in the world he knew. They would all be dead soon if he didn't help them... and perhaps he could help them. Because the Azawan, for some reason, hadn't killed him when it had the chance.

Talorc dashed through the field, trampling the barley. He crossed the mound that separated the field from the grazing grounds at the edge of the village and stopped as he realised two things at once.

The screaming had stopped; and the Azawan had seen him.

It was looking down at him. Its head waved slowly, like barley in the breeze.

'Go away!' he shouted. 'You don't belong here! Go back to the sea!'

The Azawan's tongue flickered in and out.

It lunged at him. Talorc dived into the grass, roaring with pain as it streaked by him, even hotter now than it had been before, making his skin sizzle. He rolled away from it, over grass and stones and bare earth, until at last the heat receded.

Talorc stood and looked towards the hill. He could see the light the Azawan gave off, but not the Azawan.

The light faded. The Azawan was back in the water, swimming out to the deep sea. It was gone.

Talorc turned back to the burning village.

CHAPTER SIX

It didn't take long for the fires to die.

Talorc stood motionless, watching the light of flames give way to moonlight.

Could there be survivors? It was possible. They might have run out into the fields or beyond, far enough away from the Azawan so that it couldn't spot them. They might have figured out that it couldn't see them if they were still. The fields would be the best place to look, then, rather than the smouldering ruins of the village.

Yet Talorc wasn't moving. Instead, he stood staring at the blackened ruins of the houses and storehouses, inhaling the odours of burnt grass, burnt grain and burnt flesh.

Move, he told himself.

He turned and walked away from the village, making a circuit through the surrounding fields, his feet like rocks.

'Mam?' he called out, stopping.

'Da?'

'Rillian?'

No-one answered. Maybe he just needed to shout louder.

'Jed! Kellin!'

He went on shouting. He called out the name of everyone he knew.

No-one answered.

Water. He needed water. He hadn't drunk anything since he ran out of the house to be with the sea-wolf. Rolling up his sleeves, Talorc saw that the skin on his arms was an angry red.

His legs and torso - every part of him that had been submerged in the scalding water - was in the same state. Somehow he had hardly been aware of the pain. No longer. It surged through him as if seeking revenge for being ignored. He had to drink and to bathe his blistered skin. The only source of fresh water nearby was the well in the village.

He had to go to the village.

Slow as a walking corpse, Talorc crossed through the fields to the broken buildings that were once the village of Yarrel.

The ground was warm beneath his feet.

How long had there been a village here? Grunna would have known. It was a senachai's job, as well as knowing stories, to know the names of all the islanders, who married whom and who their parents were, back and back into the mists of time. She would have known who the first man and woman were to break the soil at Yarrel, to lay stone upon stone and a roof upon the stones.

The stone walls of the houses were blackened and broken. The roofs were gone altogether. The air with thick and dark with smoke that burnt his already burning throat.

No-one would live here again. No-one would be born, grow up, grow old and die here ever again.

Where was he going to live?

He pushed the thought from his mind. Water. He needed water.

Talorc came to his family's home.

Destroyed.

There was no door in the doorway. Burnt. Like all the other houses, the roof was gone, the walls were mounds of rubble.

Water.

Talorc turned and crossed to the opening in the ground that led to the well-house. Down the steps he went into the underground stone chamber, finding his way in the darkness by memory. At the bottom was the pool. He took a bowl, scooped up water and drank, over and over again, then removed his clothes and washed himself from head to toe.

When he was finished Talorc dried himself with his tunic, dressed, climbed the stairs and emerged into the moonlight. The winds had come, carrying the smoke away east. He retraced his steps until he stood once more at the doorway of his home.

Talorc closed his eyes. Opened them again. Nothing had changed.

He passed through the empty doorway.

Only stone had survived the Azawan-fire. The quern stones sat where he had left them. The slabs that had bordered their beds lay collapsed on their sides, the shelves in a heap at the far end of the room.

No bodies.

No bones.

Only ash dancing in the wind.

He was screaming. Roaring, howling, on the floor now, beating his burning fists against the hard, ash-coated earth, coughing as ash got into his mouth and throat.

He was still.

It was their fault. All of them. He warned them about the finman. They were ready to listen when Rillian talked about finmen, but not Talorc. Of course not; why would anyone listen to him? He was the monster, so how could he possibly know anything? Well, they were in the Azawan's stomach now, or burnt to ashes, and it served them right.

No, it didn't. But they were cruel and deserved to suffer as he had suffered. That was the way it was in Grunna's stories, or some of them anyway; bad things happened to bad people. In other stories bad things happened to good people, and good things happened to bad people, and Grunna would just shrug and say the world was like that.

He should have made them leave. If he'd stayed longer he might have found a way, but instead he had run away to be with the sea-wolf. He should have found a way to make them leave, or stayed and died with them.

When Grunna died he felt alone. When the sea-wolf died he felt alone. Now he really was alone.

Talorc woke up in the ruins of his home.

He sat up. Daylight had come and he didn't feel sad anymore. He didn't feel anything except hunger and pain. The food was all burnt, but there were rock pools down by the harbour where he could gather mussels.

Then what?

There was only one thing to do. He had to warn the other Orkadi.

The trouble was, they wouldn't believe him. But there were other villages on Odhran, to the south, where people might have seen the Azawan. What would they do? Would they come here? They might do, or they might go straight to Ork Island to warn the king. King Anga could send messengers out to all the islands. Of course, what the Orkadi were to do, should the Azawan visit them, was another matter. But people had to be warned.

So he could go south, to the other villages. The problem was, no-one who hadn't seen the Azawan with their own eyes would believe him. They might think he was mad and try to take him home. In the meantime, the Azawan could strike again.

No. He wouldn't waste time in the southern villages. He would go to the king himself.

How to get there? By boat, of course. The only problem was that he'd never sailed a boat. He wasn't allowed in the water or on it. Well, there was no-one to tell him that now. He'd spent enough time watching boats go by to have an idea of how it was done. There were curraghs at the harbour, ready and waiting for him. Their owners were dead.

So all he had to do was sail to Ork island, find King Anga and convince him that a fire-breathing Azawan had destroyed his village and killed everyone he knew. What would the king say to that?

   He would know soon enough.

CHAPTER SEVEN

Talorc pushed the boat out onto the water, grabbed the side and heaved himself in.

At least, that was what he tried to do. The curragh leapt out of his grasp as he jumped, and he landed with a splash in the water.

Thankfully the harbour was shallow. Seaweed covered the sea floor, so there was no risk of tearing the boat on sharp rocks. Talorc surfaced, spat out salty water and grabbed the end of the boat, pulling it back and readying himself to try again. This time he was prepared when the vessel slipped away as he put his weight on it. He kept one leg in the water and hooked the other over the side before clambering in. Not very graceful, but he was aboard.

Talorc had walked the short distance from the village to the harbour. After scouring the rock pools for mussels he turned his attention to the curraghs. The little boats, made from skins stretched over a wooden frame, sat overturned on the sand. He chose Rask's boat, the one he had watched his brothers sail out in so many times. What would they say if they saw him now?

A pang of guilt struck Talorc. He shouldn't think such things. He wasn't glad they were dead. But he liked being free to go in the water. Talorc sat himself down on the bench. He had saved a few mussels to offer to the Sea Mother; after dropping them into the water with a whispered prayer he slid the oars into the hoops and into the water.

Now, time to see if he could row.

He had watched men rowing so many times; he had imagined rowing his own boat so many more times. It looked easy. It wasn't. Soon his feeble muscles were aching, his arms were trembling and he hadn't yet made it out of the harbour. Well, at least in the shallow water there was no danger of drowning when he fell out of the curragh. He still didn't know if he could swim.

Talorc pulled the oars in and allowed himself a rest before trying again. This time he tried a longer, slower stroke. The curragh groaned its way through the water but he felt it pick up speed. This must be the right way to row. Talorc suppressed a smile as he left the harbour and entered the open water.

The wind was mercifully weak as he rowed south, following the coast of Odhran as the sun rose behind a wreath of grey clouds. Soon they released their rain and Talorc sighed in relief as the drops cooled his burning skin.

He had no choice but to give his muscles regular rests, pulling in the oars and looking about him as the curragh bobbed on the waves. Talorc was astonished. He had lived his whole life by the sea, but had never known how different the world looked when upon the water. On land, everything was still; on the sea, everything was alive and moving, shifting and bucking beneath you and around you. Gannets dove into the water, cormorants skimmed over the surface; flocks of terns cried out as they dipped and dived over the waves. In the distance a sunshark, a giant, harmless fish that loved to bask in the heat of the sun, swam in lazy circles. The land belonged to people; the sea belonged to sea creatures. People were visitors who needed luck and skill if they wished to make it home alive.

Talorc had little in the way of skill, and he'd never thought of himself as lucky. Yet slowly, in fits and starts, whispering prayer after prayer to the Sea Mother as he went, he made his way south, passing all the cliffs and coves on the east coast of Odhran. Here they were, not half a day's row from where he had lived his whole life, and he had never seen any of them.

Eventually Talorc reached a stretch of water that lay between Odhran and another island to the south-east. Other islands were visible to the south. Which was Ork? He didn't know, and didn't want to go stopping on every island to ask, but he needed directions. Talorc went on following the coast of Odhran and as the sun reached its zenith he saw smoke rising from a house by the shore. Should he stop in there?

His stomach growled. Yes, he should.

The little cove was empty when Talorc hopped out of the boat and onto the sand, pulling the curragh up onto the shore behind him.

Grunna had said the houses across Orka were much the same. Over in Skoll, they were made of wood, as there were trees everywhere in Skoll, while in Orka trees were rare, so houses were made from stone. This house looked just like his own had done, before the Azawan came. Beyond it lay fields and wild, uncultivated land.

Smoke was rising from the smoke-hole. Talorc went to the door.

'Hello?' he called out.

'Who's that?' said a woman's voice.

Talorc went in.

It took Talorc a moment to adjust to the darkness in the house. Once he did, he saw a thin-faced woman bent over the hearth-fire, baking bannocks on stones. The bannocks filled the house with a smell that made Talorc's mouth water. She had a baby wrapped up in a fur at her chest.

'I don't know you,' she said, with surprise in her voice but no hostility.

'I'm Talorc,' he said. He had thought about what to say while he rowed his boat into the cove. 'I'm from Yarrel, north of here.'

'Are you now? Well, I'm Arryl, and I've never been to Yarrel,' she said, laughing at her rhyme. 'Neither has Grag, but he knows the headman, Torma, he bides in Yarrel. You'll know Torma, then?'

Talorc swallowed. Time to start lying. 'Yes. He's my Da. He sent me here.'

'Sent you here?' she said, inspecting the bannocks as she turned them over. 'And why did he do that?'

'There was a fire in Yarrel. One of the storehouses burned down. That's how I got burnt, trying to get the grain-sacks out. He wanted me to tell the king. They couldn't go, my brothers I mean, they're too busy at the harvest, I'm the only one that could be spared...' Talorc trailed off as Arryl stared at him. He wasn't used to lying and he got the feeling he wasn't very good at it.

'Your father didn't tell you the king bides here, did he?'

'Here? No,' said Talorc, 'I mean he sent me to the king, and I stopped here because I forgot which way it is to Ork Island.'

'Right,' said Arryl. 'Well, I don't know either, so I'll go and get Grag, he's out at the heuking. Keep an eye on those bannocks.' With that she left him alone in the house.

Talorc leaned over the fire. Its heat made his tender skin itch. The bannocks looked close to being ready; maybe he could take one? No, he mustn't. But he was tired from rowing and nothing had ever smelt so good to him...

Arryl returned, followed by a straw-haired man with blue eyes which widened when they saw Talorc. 'Look at you, lad,' he said. 'Those burns can't be painless.'

'They're not so bad,' said Talorc.

'So you're Torma's son? Which one are you? I think I mind the names; Rillian, Jed, and Kellin, is that right?'

Talorc looked at the floor. So his father knew this man, had told him the names of his sons but hadn't mentioned his youngest. A wave of hatred for his Da washed over Talorc. He had more important things to think about, though, like getting to Ork and warning the king about the Azawan.

'I'm Talorc,' he said. 'He might not have mentioned me because I'm small and weak, and he was - is - ashamed of me. That's why they sent me to Ork, because I can be spared. That's why I was sent into the storehouse, because I can be spared.' He could feel his anger rising, even though he was lying. 'Please tell me the way to Ork.'

'Of course,' said Grag. 'Follow the shore until it turns away westward, but keep the course you're on. You'll come to Caerban. Follow the east coast of Caerban, then ahead you'll see another island across the sound to the south. That's Ork.'

'Thanks,' said Talorc. He saw that Arryl had taken the finished bannocks off of the heat-stone. 'Da... Da said I was to ask you for food for the journey.'

'There's no need to be asking that,' said Arryl. 'We wouldn't see you away from here hungry. You take that,' she said as she handed him a bannock. 'Now, we'll need to get back to work,' she said. 'Look in on your way home.'

Out on the open sea the water was wilder, forcing Talorc to work harder. Brown-eyed seals watched him pass before disappearing underwater. His muscles seemed to have accepted that their punishment wouldn't end soon and did their work without complaint.

The sun was sinking into the mouth of the west. Talorc guessed he would make it to Caerban before darkness fell but not beyond. He would have to spend the night on Caerban.

Pulling the oars in, he stopped to rest and eat. He was trying to make the bannock last, since he didn't know when he would next eat. As he chewed a thought crept into his mind that he had tried to ignore all day.

Why Yarrel? Why his village?

The finman had performed his spell in order to send the

Azawan to attack Yarrel; that seemed clear to Talorc. There had to be a reason he had chosen Yarrel, but Talorc couldn't think of one. But then, what did he know of finfolk?

Grunna had avoided telling stories about them, because of Talorc's mother-sister. She had disappeared when she and Talorc's mother were girls, taken by the finfolk, people said. Stories of the finfolk thus weren't welcome in Yarrel, but Grunna had told some to Talorc all the same, in the dark, slow hours while the others slept.

The finfolk lived on an island in the north-east of Orka. They had come to Orka many years ago in peace, and the Orkadi allowed the fins to make a home for themselves. But the finfolk were deceivers, and it turned out they wanted the islands for themselves. They made war on the Orkadi, back in the time of hunger, when the sky turned black.

That was when the first king, Valdar, united the people and drove the fins back to one island. He allowed them to live there, so long as they never went beyond its surrounding waters. Some said he was bewitched, for the fins were great sorcerers. If he hadn't been under a spell he would have destroyed them, but they remained, and the Orkadi were under oath to let them remain so long as the treaty wasn't broken. Meanwhile, folk told stories of fins that came to their islands in secret, to steal their children away or wreck their boats, but nothing was ever proven.

Talorc knew a fin had broken the treaty. He would swear it, and if the king believed him, it would mean war. Words from his mouth could start a war; a war that could be the end of the fins.

Unless the Azawan killed all the Orkadi first. Orka would then belong to the fins. That must be what they wanted.

The king had to be warned, but what could he do about the Azawan? The king knew about war, he had heard his father say. Anga had lived in Skoll when he was young, where war was a way of life. But what good was that against an Azawan?

That wasn't for him to decide. He only had to tell the king

what he had seen. He finished his bannock, took up the oars and rowed.

Dusk descended. Talorc had passed several villages but had chosen to continue on since reaching the coast of Caerban. The further he travelled tonight, the less time it would take to make it to Ork in the morning.

Talorc was squinting through the rain, looking for a cove to beach his boat in when he spied a dark figure, watching him from the shore.

CHAPTER EIGHT

Talorc froze.

The mist was too thick for him to make out anything other than the shape of a man – or finman – wearing a cloak.

It was the finman. Somehow Talorc knew it. He imagined his scaly face under the hood, his tail flicking against the sand.

'Hoy there!'

The shout didn't come from the finman. It came from further south along the shore. The finman stood a moment longer before melting into the mist.

Another figure appeared out of the mist. This one was waving.

'It's safe to land here,' called the figure. 'Come in towards me.'

Talorc did as he was bidden and soon he was hopping out of the curragh and into shallow tidewater. He pulled his boat in as his rescuer came forward to meet him.

'It's late to be making port,' said the man. He was thin and white-haired, not quite as old as Grunna had been but getting there, Talorc guessed.

'The fog came in, I didn't know where to land,' said Talorc. 'I'm on my way to Ork. Is this Caerban?'

'It is that. You're not far from Ork, but you won't be getting there tonight; you'll need to bide with us until morning. Come away in.'

Talorc gratefully accepted the old man's help, following him from the shore and looking about as he did so. The finman was out there; but he was secretive. He wouldn't attack Talorc so long as he had company, or so it seemed. If Talorc stayed the night here he should be safe.

Unless the Azawan came.

The man introduced himself as Criff as they walked up the path to the house. Inside sat an old woman roasting fish on skewers over her fire, the smells of peat and haddock thick in the air.

'This is my wife, Gwynn. Put another fish on for Talorc here.'

Gwynn looked at Talorc for a few moments before smiling, revealing a mouth full of broken brown teeth, and pulling a pot towards her from which she scooped out another haddock. Talorc noticed as she did so that her head had an unusual shape underneath its greasy, thinning hair; it was narrow at the top like an egg.

'Gwynn doesn't talk much these days, but she's as good a wife as a man could ask for,' said Criff, gesturing for Talorc to sit down as he did so. 'Now, you've a story to tell.'

Talorc nodded. 'I'm from Yarrel, on Odhran,' he said. 'My father sent me to see King Anga on Ork.' So he repeated the story he had told Grag and Arryl. 'We're hoping the king will have some food to spare for us,' he finished.

'Well, that's a terrible tale if I ever heard one,' said Criff. 'And your skin must be dreadful sore.'

Talorc nodded. 'It's better than it was yesterday. I...' he was interrupted by Gwynn slapping her hand on the dusty floor. She caught Criff's eye and began to make gestures with her hands. Talorc didn't follow but Criff watched and nodded as if her miming were as clear as speech to him.

'Gwynn talks with her hands,' said Criff when she had finished. 'She's saying she knows a plant that will soothe your skin. She'll away out and get it in the morning.' Talorc looked at Gwynn, who gave him a satisfied smile before tending to the fish.

They ate in silence, Talorc trying not to eat so quickly that he would give away how hungry he was. The feeling of hot food in his stomach soothed him, and he found himself relaxing in the company of the kindly old couple. They had believed his story without asking a single question. If only his family had done the same.

After they had eaten, Talorc offered to sit at the quern-stones awhile, an offer they eagerly accepted. Criff said the work was hard on their ageing bones. Talorc went over to the stones, packed them with barley and set to work, grinding them against one another while the ears slowly softened.

It felt good to repay the kindness they had shown him. But in no time at all Talorc felt his mind drifting and his head nodding, snapping back, nodding again.

'You're exhausted, lad,' said Criff. He flicked his head at his wife and Gwynn stood, pulled back the furs from their bed and took two handfuls of straw from within it. These she spread out by the fire before collecting more. 'That'll have to do you for a bed,' said Criff, 'though I fancy it'll be enough. You'll be asleep before you're sideways. On you come now, the stones will be there tomorrow.'

It was no good resisting. Talorc stood, crossed the room and lay down on the warm straw as Criff put another peat on the fire. 'We'll be awake awhile yet, but we'll be quiet,' he said.

Talorc closed his eyes. He was safe. The finman wouldn't come in here. What about tomorrow?

He didn't have enough energy to be frightened. The knots of his mind were loosening. He was drifting away already, only dimly aware of Criff's voice.

'His boots are soaked through, he'll catch his death of cold if they're not dried out. I'll slip them off, you fetch some more straw to stuff them with. They'll be dry in the morning if we keep the fire going.'

Talorc felt Criff gently pull at his boots. He smiled. It would be good to have dry feet at last.

Feet…

Talorc sat bolt upright, his heart pumping. It was too late.

Criff and Gwynn were backing away from him. He followed the direction of their horrified stares, towards his feet.

His long, finger-like toes were revealed in the firelight, as were the webs between them.

'Fin-feet!' hissed Criff. 'You're a fin-child!'

How could he have been so careless? How many times had he been told never to show his feet to a stranger?

Criff and Gwynn stood across the fire from him, hunched and tensed, their eyes wide with fear and hatred. He had to get away from them.

Criff's eyes went to the corner of the room where there lay two fishing spears and two heuk-knifes. Talorc realised that he had lost his own heuk-knife at some point, though he didn't know when. He could try to go for the weapons himself, but Criff and Gwynn were much closer. He would need to escape by different means.

'That's right,' said Talorc, twisting his speech so his words came out in a kind of growl. 'I'm a fin-child. I was looking for children to steal, but you have none.'

'Monster,' stuttered Criff. 'We… we should kill you.'

'My people are down at the shore, waiting for me,' said Talorc in his finman-voice. He'd never heard a finman speak, but he guessed they hadn't either. 'If you harm me they will take you away as slaves, or kill you if you are lucky.'

It tore Talorc's heart in two to see the effect of his words on his hosts. They believed him. Criff gestured to Gwynn and the two of them circled around the fire until they stood before the stone chest opposite the door. As they did so, Talorc grabbed his boots and circled the room too, until he stood before the door.

'Don't follow me, and don't tell anyone you saw me,' he said, 'or I will return.'

'We won't,' said Criff. 'Now get out of our house.'

Talorc turned, lifted the door-flap and escaped out into the night.

The rain was falling in torrents, soaking Talorc before he reached his boat. Once there he stopped.

Where to go?

He could crawl under the curragh and shelter the night there, but Criff and Gwynn might come for him. Criff and Gwynn were the least of his cares, though. What about the finman?

Talorc stood shivering, looking up and down the beach. The moon was still full but the clouds were too thick to allow much of its light through. The finman could be anywhere, could come at him at any time and he would have no warning. Should he return to the house, force Criff and Gwynn to harbour him until daybreak? If he fell asleep they might kill him. If he stayed under the boat, he would be sheltered, and would at least have some protection between him and a knife. And the finman thought he was safe indoors for the night; he might have gone elsewhere.

It seemed he only had one choice. Talorc lifted up the rim of the boat and crawled into the shelter it offered.

He lay there, listening to the sound of the rain beating on the boat-hide, listening for footsteps. Criff and Gwynn might come after him but probably wouldn't. The finman had probably gone elsewhere but might return. He wasn't safe, that was for sure. But there was no way to make himself safe, so what could he do? Sleep? No. He would have to stay awake, if he could. No, he had to stay awake. Otherwise, if the finman came…

Time passed, however, without the finman coming. The only sounds were the rain and the ceaseless music of the tide. Slowly, slowly, Talorc felt himself relax.

As he began to believe himself safe, Talorc's mind wandered.

He was sat alone with Grunna by the fire, talking about his feet.

'There's nothing wrong with your feet, Talorc. They're just different.'

'But Jed says I'm a fish-boy. A monster. He says I should be drowned.'

'Jed is a cruel little boy who makes you feel small to make himself feel big. You know I don't lie to you, Talorc, so let me give you the truth, plain and clear. You're not the first child of these islands to be born with webs, or fin-feet as some say, and you won't be the last. Like many things, it happens, but it isn't talked about, because folk don't understand it and folk fear what they don't understand. So some mothers who have a child with webs will drown it, or leave it out on the hill at night. Others let the child live, as your parents have done, but make them keep their webs secret.'

'What happens if people find out?'

'I think you can guess.'

Talorc had kept his fin-feet secret for so long that he was hardly aware of it. At home he had never taken his boots off except when alone. But he had been careless, and now his secret was revealed...

The crunch of feet on stones broke through his thoughts.

CHAPTER NINE

The footsteps grew louder until whoever it was stood right beside the upturned boat.

Talorc listened for the sound of breath but couldn't hear anything over the drumming of the rain on the hull. Was there anything he could use as a weapon? Only stones. Quietly he cast about for one large enough and took hold of it.

It could be Criff or Gwynn, but whoever was out there hadn't approached from the house; they had come from along the shore. It had to be the finman.

Well, Talorc wasn't a seal pup. The finman wouldn't take him without a fight.

He waited.

Nothing happened.

The finman didn't attack. He didn't leave either. What was he doing?

Talorc could lift the boat a sliver, take a look at his feet. What good would that do? Or he could lift it suddenly, swing an oar, knock the finman off his feet and run. No good, there wasn't enough room and the oar was too big to swing one-handed. Knocking the finman down wouldn't stop him. But what was he waiting for? Maybe he wanted to slit Talorc's throat at sunrise, like he did to the seal pup?

Time passed, and more time. Nothing happened. Talorc couldn't help it; he relaxed his guard, let his grip on the stone go loose. He judged half the night had passed and still the finman hadn't moved; and he was sleepy again.

He couldn't fall asleep. If he did he would never wake up. The stone knife was waiting.

But he was falling asleep.

Talorc woke up, his head jerking back.

How long had he been asleep? Was the finman still there? He would have to lift the boat to see. He couldn't do that.

At least he wouldn't fall asleep again; the knowledge that he had done so while at the mercy of the finman sent terror coursing through his blood. But it was still dark, and his bones told him the night was far from over.

Talorc was bored. If the finman wanted to kill him, couldn't he just get on with it?

He knew how to deal with boredom, though. All he had to do was the same thing he did while working in the fields, minding the sheep or grinding the quern-stones. He told himself a story.

Grunna had told him so many; one for every wave on the sea, it seemed. She always knew the right story to tell, whether it was a funny one, a sad one or a scary one. Since she died he had enjoyed telling himself her favourite ones, thinking that if her ghost was listening it would make her happy.

Talorc told himself the trowie wedding story. A senachai was walking home from a wedding when the little people of the hills and caves surrounded him, put him on a horse and took him underground to tell stories and play the flute at their wedding. Talorc had always wanted to see a trowie; when he was small he had peered in every hole in the ground he came across, expecting to see a family of them inside, sat at their dinner. Now he wasn't sure if they were real or not, but he liked the story. Grunna always finished by hinting that she had been that senachai, but Talorc never believed her.

He spoke the story in his head, and as he went on he grew bold, whispering the words that passed between the senachai and the trowies. He grinned as he did so. Lying there under the boat, telling himself a story instead of cowering in fear made him feel good. Brave. If he was going to die at dawn, he might as well enjoy his last hours.

Talorc reached the part of the story where the senachai played at the wedding. He reached into his shift and took out his bone flute.

Putting it to his lips, Talorc played. He kept his eyes open, watching to see if the finman would suddenly upturn the boat and attack him. But the finman, if he was still there, did nothing. So Talorc went on playing, faster, louder, tapping his foot on the stones, watching in his mind as little bearded men and women spun and flung one another around a torchlit underground hall.

He went on playing as he spoke the remaining words of the story in his mind. *And when he came home to his wife, thinking he'd been gone a day and a night, he found out he'd been gone fourteen days and fourteen nights. She cried, and laughed, and kissed him, and that was the last time he ever played for the trowies.*

Once the story was over he still went on playing, slowly, and it made him feel peaceful. It was as if the flute knew which notes he needed to play to put his mind at ease, even to give him strength.

Talorc no longer imagined himself in the trowie cave. Now he was underwater, in the deep blue darkness. He couldn't see but he could feel what was around him. Tiny fish swimming in shoals, as graceful as birds in flight. Lobsters crawling along the seabed beneath. He played on, hardly knowing he was playing.

A strange sound. Another and another, all around him. From out of the darkness they came, shining with their own light. Talorc's heart leaped. Dolphins!

Around and around him they swam, speaking to him in their alien language. As they spoke he felt his skin hum and thrum and tingle.

They left, with sounds that seemed like laughter, and Talorc's eyes opened.

Day's first light had come, penetrating his little boat-cave. He didn't know if the finman was still there, but hiding wouldn't do any good if he was.

Talorc put his hands to the hull and lifted.

There were no feet beside the curragh. He was alone.

Quickly he overturned the curragh. Looking about, he saw no sign of the finman or anyone else.

It was time to go.

The day dawned cold and grey as Talorc rowed from Caerban to Ork. Looking over his shoulder, he saw a sight he had often imagined but never believed he would see. It was sat atop a cliff, growing steadily larger as he drew nearer.

The broch of Gurn.

King Arta the Inventor was the eighth king of Orka. We remember him as the second great king, after Valdar the Uniter. It was Arta who designed the brochs; stone towers that scores of men, women and children can enter and stay safe inside, should invaders come.

Talorc guessed that the round stone tower stood three times as high as any ordinary dwelling, and three times as wide. Grunna had told him of times past when invaders had come and then left again, their efforts to break into the brochs fruitless. There were brochs all across Orka, but the one at Gurn was where King Anga held court.

He was nearly there.

It already seemed so long ago that the Azawan had come, though only two nights had passed since the attack. Had the Azawan struck elsewhere last night? If so, someone might already have come to the keep with news. If not, Talorc was going to have to convince the king that the Azawan was real and that he wasn't mad. That might be difficult. His burns might serve as proof...

It was only then that Talorc realised his burns had gone.

He pulled in the oars, lay them on his lap and stared at his hands. It was as if they had never been burnt. He rolled up his sleeves; the skin which had been red and hard was almost healed. The skin on his face had healed too. How?

It didn't make sense, but then nothing that was happening made sense. He only knew for sure that his parents and brothers and the people of Yarrel had been eaten by an Azawan, and he had to tell the king about it.

After that?

He didn't want to think about after that.

After rounding the cliff Talorc sighted a beach and turned his craft towards it. He landed, pulled the boat up onto the sand and headed up the hill.

A high stone wall surrounded the keep. Talorc skirted it until he came to the gate. Through the gateway he could see the broch at the far end of the enclosure. A path led from the gate to the broch between two rows of dwellings, three houses on each side. Talorc observed all this as he walked up the path to the gate, which was guarded by a brawny man who glared at Talorc from beneath bushy eyebrows as he approached.

'What do you want?' said the man.

'To see the king,' said Talorc.

'He's busy.'

'My father is Torma, headman of Odhran. I have urgent news.'

The guard laughed. 'Urgent news from Odhran, is it? Have you lost a lamb?'

This wasn't working. Talorc considered what he knew about the king.

Anga was brought up over in Skoll, at Bradach's court in Varaness, where kings make war on one another as a way of life. He misses it, they say, and wishes invaders would come to Orka just so he can be the one to beat them back.

Talorc sniffed. His lower lip trembled. The guard frowned.

'We didn't see them coming!' he ran at the guard and wrapped his arms around the man's waist. 'They were huge, and they spoke words we didn't understand, and they burnt our crops and they killed people and... and...'

'Get off!' shouted the guard as he wrested himself away from Talorc and waved him through the gate.

Talorc wiped his eyes and ran past the guard, trying not to smile.

The door of the broch was open. Firelight flickered inside. Talorc approached, took a deep breath and entered.

A stairway led upwards on his left, while a doorway led to a dark recess on his right. Passing these, he came through another doorway to the main chamber. A peat-fire burned in the hearth in the centre of the chamber, just like at home, though this fire was larger. Around it sat five people. One had to be the king; he was tall and broad, with arms as thick as Talorc's waist, and wore a boar-skin draped around his shoulders. Beside him sat a girl who had something of the king in her face, though her hair was brown where his was black and her features were narrower and sharper. His daughter, then. There was also a sharp-faced, white-haired man, a heavily muscled man with a ponderous look, and a fair-haired woman with blue eyes and a round, kindly face who sat close beside him, whom Talorc guessed to be his wife.

'What else?' said the king.

'More of the same,' said the white-haired man, whose face and frown reminded Talorc of a gull. 'Bad fishing. Boats disappearing, crops being stolen. Children crying through the night for no reason.'

'The same old stories then, Derran,' said the king.

'Yes,' said the girl whom Talorc took to be the princess. Grunna had told Talorc her name: Runa. 'It's the same stories we've always heard,' Runa continued, 'things going wrong and people saying it's the finfolk. But all at once, and on nearly every island. This isn't chance. Something is going on.'

'But is it the finfolk?' said the woman sat with the big, ponderous man. There was something calming about the way she spoke. 'How can we know? People have been telling stories of how they or their brother or their mother-by-law's friend's son saw a finman ever since the treaty was made, but when has there ever been proof? Without proof we can't act.'

'That we can't,' said the king. 'For if the finfolk are breaking the treaty, and coming into our territory, it will mean war. You all know I'm not afraid of war, but I won't start one on the back of rumours. I need proof.'

'You'll find proof on Odhran,' said Talorc.

Everyone turned to look at him as he walked forward into the firelight.

'I don't know who you are, boy, and I don't recall inviting you to join our counsel,' said Anga.

'My name is Talorc. I'm – I was – the son of Torma of Odhran.'

'And what is Torma's son doing walking unbidden into the king's chamber?' said Derran.

'Bringing you news that couldn't wait,' said Talorc.

'If the news is so urgent I wonder why Torma sent a scrawny boy like you,' said Derran, frowning more deeply. 'Someone bigger would have got here faster.'

'My father didn't send me,' said Talorc. 'My father is dead.'

The company listened as Talorc told his tale in full, from his first sighting of the finman to the moment he stepped through the door of the broch.

Silence followed.

'Get this idiot out of here,' said Derran eventually, dismissing Talorc with a wave. 'Take your lies elsewhere, runt. Bring them here again and I'll have you thrown off a cliff. We have serious matters to discuss –'

'I'm not lying!' shouted Talorc. 'Would you lie about your whole family being murdered? I saw what I saw, and if you go to Odhran you'll see my village. There's nothing left of it but scorched stone. If you think I'm a liar, you come to Yarrel with me and tell me what did that if it wasn't an Azawan –'

'Enough.'

They turned to the king.

'I'm sorry for whatever happened to you to make you say such things,' said the king. 'I know Torma. He only ever mentioned three sons, none of them called Talorc. I see he was ashamed because you're soft in the head. Not your fault, but not my problem either. Be gone with you. Your parents will be worried.'

'I –'

'Go.' Anga's voice and look made it clear that he would not suffer any further words to leave Talorc's lips. Talorc looked about at Anga's companions. In their eyes he saw a mixture of curiosity, pity and scorn.

It was over. He had failed.

Talorc stood on the cliff's edge, looking north. It was mid-morning, the low autumn sun casting long shadows as it revealed itself between quick-moving clouds. Behind him Ork Island stretched out far to the west, south and east, while in the north-east he could spy the summit hill of an island whose name he didn't know.

He had never expected to see the islands. Most people only left their home island for a wedding. Talorc was never going to marry, for who would marry him? And he had always been left at home on wedding-days. But all the same, he had dreamed of one day being free. Building a boat, setting off to see the islands of Orka, though Grunna said they looked much the same as one another, but for Groda. He would see all the islands, then go further, exploring the vast and mysterious land of Skoll; he would see the bears and wolves of Grunna's stories, visit the courts of the warring Skollish kings. The sea went on forever, Grunna said, because there was no such thing as nothing. Maybe Talorc could row his boat as long as he lived, searching for the place where there was no such thing as true or false.

Maybe that was where Azawans came from. Maybe he could become a hunter of Azawans, killing them when they were new-born in their nests. Or maybe he could go back to Odhran, re-build his home, live alone and fish and try not to starve.

What was he thinking? There was only thing that could happen. The Azawan would burn him and devour him, as it was going to do to every person in Orka. So what if the king didn't believe him? He would believe soon enough; and very soon afterwards, he would be dead. There was nothing the king could do. There was nothing anyone could do.

'You're quite a storyteller,' said a voice from behind Talorc.

CHAPTER TEN

Princess Runa approached him, her eyes burrowing into his.

Talorc looked her over. Runa and he were the same age, Grunna had said, and now he saw that they were the same height. She wore a finely-cut deer-skin jerkin and matching trousers, fur-rimmed sealskin boots and a necklace of five triangular stones of a kind Talorc had never seen. She had no heuk-knife at her belt; maybe princesses didn't work the harvest.

'Trouble is,' she went on, 'my Da doesn't like stories.'

'Doesn't matter if he likes my story or not,' said Talorc, meeting her gaze. 'It's true.'

'Would you believe a boy who showed up in your house and told you his village had been destroyed by a sea monster?'

'If he was telling the truth.'

'And how would you know that?'

'My Grunna said ghosts live in our eyes. If you look closely enough you can see them.'

Runa stared into Talorc's eyes. He tried to think about the finman, the Azawan and scorched stones, but his memories melted away under her brown-eyed stare. His mind felt as empty as if he had been born that morning.

'Come with me,' she said.

Runa led Talorc south from the cliff-top, through fields of barley and open grazing land. At the far side of a field Talorc stopped and stared.

Grazing on the grass were creatures he had never seen before except when Grunna sketched them in ash and sand. Horses.

There were seven in total; two white, three brown and two black. At Runa's whistle, one of the white horses raised its long head and came trotting towards her.

'Good morning, Farla,' she said with a laugh as the horse nuzzled her face. 'Farla, this is Talorc. He's going to come for a ride with us.'

Runa took hold of Farla's mane and swung herself onto her back with the ease of a seal riding the waves. She extended a hand, Talorc took it and he clambered onto the horse, seating himself behind her.

From Runa's snorts of laughter Talorc guessed he hadn't been so graceful. He didn't care. He was sat astride a white horse with Orka's princess sat before him, wind-whipped strands of her hair tickling his nose. He had landed in another story; one he liked better than the last.

'Hold onto my waist,' said Runa. Talorc did so and all of a sudden Farla was bouncing up and down as she walked, Runa guiding her southeast.

'Where are we going?' he asked.

'To visit some ghosts,' said Runa.

Ork Island was disappointing. It was the largest island in Orka; the Island of Kings. Despite what Grunna had taught him, Talorc half-expected it to teem with battling warriors, deep lochs and knife-sharp mountains. Instead it looked much like Odhran. He had plenty to occupy him, though, in the form of Runa and her horse. Talorc wasn't used to being so close to anyone. Since Grunna died no-one had touched him except to punch, kick or shove him. Now here he was, his arms around Runa's waist, her horse rising and falling beneath him like the sea. Horse-riding was like being at sea; it was a new world, except in this world he wasn't alone. Runa was right there with him. Farla was right there beneath him. He hoped the ride wouldn't be over soon.

They rode through the morning as a fog blew in from the

west, cloaking the land around them. As the sun reached its peak and Talorc's stomach started to growl again, he saw a hill rising out of the mist before them. At the foot of the hill were a series of mounds that looked to Talorc as if a family of giants had gathered in a circle, lain down and then fallen asleep for so long that grass had grown all over them.

Runa halted at the edge of the mounds and bade Talorc dismount before doing so herself. She stroked Farla's face and whispered a few words before the horse ambled off.

'Sore?' said Runa.

'A bit,' said Talorc.

'You get used to it. You might find it hard to walk tonight, though.'

Talorc nodded, unsure what to say.

'Do you know what these are?' said Runa, turning to the nearest mound.

'They look a bit like bone-houses,' said Talorc. 'Only they're narrower.'

'Right and wrong. They are bone-houses, yes, but not like the ones you know.' She gestured for Talorc to follow her as she walked between them. 'In the ancient days, before the time of the kings, everyone on Ork was buried in a bone-house. Not every bit of them, of course, or the bone-houses would have filled up fast. Maybe a rib-bone, maybe a thigh-bone. Maybe their skull.' She paused. 'You probably haven't heard of the dark days.'

'I have,' said Talorc. 'My Grunna was a senachai.'

'What did she tell you?'

'She said that there was a time when Ork was covered in trees. Deer and boar lived in the forests and it was warmer than it is now. That was when people used to get buried in the bone-houses, and everyone would visit them to honour their ancestors. There was a spey in every village, and the speys would sit with the dead in the bone-houses, listen to them and pass their messages on to the living.'

'And then what happened?' said Runa.

'The sky turned dark. No-one knew why it happened, but after that Ork grew colder. The crops failed, and people hunted the deer and boar until there were almost none left. Forests and farmland turned to bogs, so people started stealing land and food from one another. Raiders came from Skoll and other places, killed Orkadi and took their land. People blamed the speys and attacked or killed them, saying they must have turned the sky dark with their magic. Those were the dark days.'

'And it was thanks to this man that the dark days ended,' said Runa, stopping at the doorway of a mound. 'King Valdar lies here, as do all of my family that have lived since that time. It was him who ended the dark days.'

'That's what Grunna said. She said the finfolk took advantage of our weakness, making war on us and trying to take all of the islands for themselves. Valdar united the clans and together we fought off the invaders and the finmen. Ever since then we have been one clan, the Orkadi, and the finmen have been bound to stay on their island and fish only in its waters.'

'And now here we stand,' said Runa. 'Me, the descendant of Valdar the Uniter and you, a boy who claims that Valdar's treaty has been broken.'

'Do you believe me?'

Again Runa searched Talorc's eyes, and again he had the curious sensation of his mind going empty, as if time stood still.

'Do you know why I brought you here?' asked Runa.

'No.'

'I come here a lot. Every Sevenday. I come to remind myself that my ancestors have ruled this land since the dark days. My mother is buried here, my father will be buried here, I will be buried here and my children will be buried here.

'If I am to lie here as a ghost among my ancestors and descendants, until such time as the sea dries up and the islands crumble to dust, I want to know that in my time I did everything for Orka. That I gave everything I have. Everything I am.'

'I understand,' said Talorc. Runa took a step closer to him.

'Then you understand why I would do far more than throw you off a cliff if you are lying to me,' she said. 'For if we believe what you say, it will mean war with the finfolk, not to mention the Azawan. The finfolk are strong and cunning. Many, many Orkadi will die in such a war.'

Runa stepped closer to Talorc. He could feel her breath on his face.

'Talorc, son of Torma, did you lie to my father?'

'No,' said Talorc.

Runa looked at him for a while longer. She nodded.

'I believe you.'

Talorc tentatively smiled. Runa did not.

'So what happens now?' asked Talorc.

'We ride back to Gurn. Fast.'

'Your father will believe me if you believe me?'

'Lets find out.'

Runa whistled for Farla, who soon appeared over the horizon. 'Hold on tight,' said Runa as Talorc mounted the horse. He wrapped his arms around her, she kicked Farla's flanks and they were off. Farla gained speed quickly, and soon Talorc was digging in desperately with his thighs as he tried to stay on, the misty fields and farmsteads streaking past them.

When they reached Gurn it was almost dusk. A group of people were stood at the cliff's edge where Runa had approached Talorc earlier. Runa turned Farla to join them, and as they rode up they saw why the group stood so still and silent.

In the water, stretching from the western horizon to the east, lay the Azawan.

PART II

CHAPTER ELEVEN

Faint afternoon sunlight shone on its black scales. Steam rose from the water around it.

Talorc looked around. Everyone who had been in the broch was there, silently staring. He knew what they were thinking; that their own eyes must be deceiving them. Such a thing couldn't be real. But it was. Why did people always insist that some things were real and some weren't? If the sea went on forever then everything must exist in it somewhere.

'Is that its head?' said Runa, pointing east.

Straining, Talorc thought he could make out the shape of its head in the far distance. 'I think so.'

Anga turned to Talorc and looked up at him as if trying to decide if the Azawan was an apparition of Talorc's creation. 'Derran,' he said to his old gull-faced guardian. 'Blow the horn.'

'Which signal?' asked Derran.

'Invaders,' said Anga. 'All guardians to muster at Gurn.'

Derran nodded and went running in the direction of the keep.

'Council meeting in my chamber,' said Anga to the rest of them. 'Now.' He looked at Talorc. 'You as well.'

Runa and Talorc dismounted and walked with the rest of the group to the keep. As they walked a low, moaning sound rang through the air. Talorc thought he could hear a similar call coming from somewhere to the south.

'That's the signal horn,' said Runa.

'I know, said Talorc. 'My father has one. Had one. He never

used it.'

'When it's blown like that it means invaders are coming,' said Runa. ' ` Everyone has to go to the nearest broch. Guardians have to muster at Gurn.'

'My father was a guardian.'

'I know.'

They entered the broch. In the central chamber the fair-haired woman, whom Runa told Talorc was named Kretta, carefully stoked the fire as Anga studied it, as if an answer to his predicament might be revealed in the flames. Talorc felt a pang of sympathy for the king. Anga knew an attack was coming. He wanted to defend his people; but how?

The first families began to arrive. Kretta left the chamber to attend to them, speaking in a quiet, soothing voice as she guided them up the stairs to the rooms above the king's chamber.

'Brochs are built so that whole villages can live in here for weeks if they have to,' whispered Runa. 'We have stores of food and water upstairs and throughout the keep.'

Talorc knew she was thinking the same thing as him. That was all very well if human invaders came, or finfolk; but what use were stone walls and supplies against the Azawan?

A man entered and bowed at Anga. He carried a dagger on his belt, a bow on his back and an iron sword in his hand. 'Sire,' he said and went to stand straight-backed at the edge of the room. Others followed one by one. As they did so, Talorc took his chance to study the room. On the walls hung artworks woven, he guessed, from plant-stalks. On some of them, intricate patterns of myriad colours wove in and out of one another like living things, while others depicted animals and birds. Between the hangings were symbols, Talorc guessed, of the old clans of Orka that Valdar had united: a pair of deer antlers, an otter skin and a necklace of teeth, a boar's head and a pair of sea eagle's wings. At the very rear of the chamber was an altar, the bowl full of dazzling stones as well as fragments of tusks and claws.

Once a dozen guardians had arrived, the blowing of the horn ceased and Derran appeared in the chamber. Anga cleared his throat and the murmuring of the men ceased.

'Guardians of Orka,' said the king. 'You have all seen what lies in the water to the north?'

'We've seen it, sire,' said one man, 'but we don't know what it is we've seen.'

'It's an Azawan,' said another.

'No such thing.'

'What do you call that then?'

'Silence,' said Anga. 'I'm not interested in whether or not you believe in Azawans. Whatever you call that thing, it is in our waters and I have reason to believe it will attack us tonight. There is only one person here who has seen such an attack before.' He turned to Talorc, as did everyone else. 'Boy, tell these men what you told us this morning.'

Again, Talorc told his story. Sometimes he would catch a man looking to his neighbour, as if seeking permission to disbelieve Talorc and mock him. He stumbled and lost track of his words when that happened. Yet the king's face remained deadly serious, and most of the men followed his example.

'When I got here I told the king what I'd seen,' finished Talorc. He left out that he had been disbelieved; that was a given, and he didn't want to embarrass Anga.

'So there you have it,' said Anga. 'If what the boy says is true, we can expect the Azawan to attack tonight.'

'It attacked at night last time. One attack doesn't make a pattern. It could strike anytime,' said Derran.

'True,' said Anga. 'In either case, I don't want to give it a chance to reveal its routines. I want it dead tonight.'

'How?' said one of the guardians.

'We all know as much as one another,' said Derran. 'If anyone has an idea, speak it.'

'The first thing we have to think about is getting to wherever it attacks in time,' said the guardian who had spoken first, a man with a long red beard.

'It entered the channel of Gurn from the west,' said Runa. 'You can see its head to the east. There's no way of being certain but it will probably attack somewhere to the east.'

'We can assume that,' said Derran. 'But we can't assume it will attack Ork Island. It could strike at Grinn, Blad, Namh, or any of the northern islands.'

'Maybe we'll be lucky and it will eat the fins,' said another guardian. There were murmurs of assent.

'That doesn't seem likely,' said Anga, 'since it is the fins we have to thank for this. We can't do anything if it strikes another island, as the waters around it are boiling hot, according to Talorc here, and we can't cross a boiling sea. But if it strikes Ork in the east, we can be ready for it.'

'We could ride to Herder's Hill,' said Runa. 'From there we could follow its movements and try to predict which village it will attack.'

Anga nodded slowly. 'Good,' he said. 'So we ride to the hill and watch it for movement. When it moves, we ride hard and meet it where it strikes. So we only need to decide one thing. How do we kill it?'

The only answer was the crackle of the fire.

The door-flap opened. Kretta entered.

'It's moving,' she said.

CHAPTER TWELVE

The guardians mounted horses that stamped and brayed as darkness descended.

Runa led Talorc to Farla. They mounted before joining the circle of riders awaiting instructions. King Anga sat atop a thick-muscled black horse whose eyes rolled back and forth as its hooves scraped the ground.

'We take the Norbarrow Road,' he said. 'Ride hard and be ready to fight at the end. Runa, keep back and keep the boy and yourself safe.'

'I need a weapon,' said Runa.

'Anyone who sees her with a sword is to put their own sword through her,' said Anga. 'Stay back. You're coming so the boy can observe and advise. Ride!'

Anga kicked his heels and his mount surged forward, the guardians following. Runa fell in at the back of the line, leaning in close to Farla as they gained speed. Talorc tried to mimic her as he bounced up and down, landing hard on Farla's back with each beat of her hooves on the hard earthen road.

The road led south-east, away from the coast at first, which meant the Azawan couldn't be seen. But it was out there. It was moving. Anga must know they had no hope of outpacing it, yet they had to try. What were they going to do when they met it? A sword would be no more than a needle to the Azawan.

'Halt!' cried Anga as they crested a hill.

The riders formed a row, Runa and Talorc fell in line and they saw it.

The Azawan had left the sea. Its great bulk arose from the waters of a bay no more than five hundred paces from the foot of the hill, encircling a coastal village that glowed in the light of its scales. Its head danced far above the ground, weaving from side to side as it watched and waited. Steam rose from the bubbling water of the bay and even atop the hill, the air felt warmer.

'It's attacking Skate!' called one of the guardians.

'There's a broch there,' said another. 'The people will be safe.'

Sure enough, a stone tower sat at the centre of the village. Like the broch at Gurn, its roof was of timber and thatch, its high walls of thick stone. If any other invaders were to come, the broch would keep the people safe. But this was an Azawan.

'How many people can a broch hold?' said Talorc.

'Almost a hundred,' said Runa.

Talorc's heart sank.

Just then the Azawan drew back and opened its mouth wide. Talorc gripped Runa's waist.

The Azawan spat a blast of flame. The broch disappeared among the torrent while the riders cried out in dismay.

'Guardians!' called Anga, riding out in front of his men and turning to face them. 'You, you, you and you, circle to the beast's south. You to the north. Attack its flanks. You might not pierce its hide but you need only distract it. Get it away from the broch.' He pointed to the remaining guardians. 'Ride directly for it, then fan out. Use your bows; aim for the eyes and throat. I'll take the centre.'

'You can't fight it –' began Runa before Anga silenced her.

'Runa, stay here. Keep the boy alive and stay alive yourself! Guardians, do your duty! Ride!'

Anga turned, raised his sword and spurred his mount on with a roar. The grim-faced guardians gave an answering shout as they followed, the horses braying with them.

Looking back at the broch, Talorc saw that its roof was gone yet the light of flames still shone from inside it.

'The roof must have fallen in while it was still burning,' whispered Runa. The upper floor is wooden. It must be alight. The whole place will go up.'

'So the people will have to run or burn,' said Talorc.

He was right. From their viewpoint they watched as the Azawan turned its head suddenly, tensed and shot forward, so fast that it had fallen still again before Talorc could cry out. It lunged again, and again, and Talorc knew it was picking off villagers fleeing the burning broch.

The light from the Azawan's scales illuminated the guardians as they fanned out around it. Farla paced back and forth and tossed her head, Runa absently stroking her neck as they watched the scene unfold beneath them. A steady stream of villagers was pouring from the broch now and the Azawan was in a frenzy, lunging left and right, devouring as many as it could.

The guardians took their chance. Talorc saw one rider approach the Azawan from the east. He came in close to its flank, turning his mount and striking with his sword as he wheeled away.

Was the Azawan wounded? Talorc couldn't tell. But it must have felt the prick of the guardian's sword, for it turned suddenly, shot towards the rider and swallowed him and his horse whole.

'Look!' cried Runa. Another guardian had taken advantage of the Azawan's distraction and struck at it just as the first had.

He met the same fate.

Talorc hadn't believed that swords would defeat the Azawan, but still he had hoped. Now hope died in him as the guardians died, one by one. At least the villagers were given a respite; Talorc saw them disappear into the fields around the village, to hide there or keep running.

But it wasn't over. As the Azawan reared up over its attackers it threw back its head, writhing back and forth. Talorc spotted a guardian watching the Azawan, a bow held in his hands. So he had scored a hit. An eye maybe, or inside its mouth. Would the

Azawan retreat?

It didn't retreat. Instead it did something new.

It screamed.

The Azawan screamed and Talorc screamed. Runa screamed. Farla reared and they were thrown to the hard ground and Talorc didn't care; all he cared about was that it stopped. Every nightmare he had ever dreamed was in that scream, and all the pain ever felt on Orka and everywhere else. He thrashed and screamed, pounded his fists on the ground and threw up on the grass.

It was over. The Azawan had stopped screaming. His head still ringing and with vomit sticking to his clothes, Talorc stood, lurched forward and joined Runa, who was staggering forward, her arms outstretched. It seemed she was trying to run but she only made it a few steps before falling down, getting to her knees and standing again on trembling legs. She was mouthing words she couldn't speak.

Talorc looked to the Azawan and saw why.

Anga stood before the Azawan. His horse gone, his sword held aloft, Orka's king stood before the monster that terrorised his kingdom.

The Azawan saw him. It lowered itself to the ground and slithered forward, slowly.

The Azawan stopped, face to face with the king. Talorc remembered standing just as the king had stood, two nights ago. It didn't matter that Anga was bigger than him, or stronger. It didn't matter that Anga was the king. He was going to die.

The Azawan opened its mouth. Its tongue flicked out, so close to Anga it might have touched him.

Then it screamed again.

Talorc forgot Runa. He forgot Anga and the world and everything he had ever known. There was only the Azawan, its terrible screeching and the devouring horror it released in him.

Then it was over. The taste of vomit stung his throat again and he was pulling himself to his feet as the world spun around him.

The Azawan was gone.

CHAPTER THIRTEEN

'Da?'

Runa waved her hands in front of Anga's face. His eyes flicked back and forth.

Talorc and Runa had raced through the fields to the king's side after the Azawan departed. The five surviving guardians had one by one appeared and now watched in silence as Runa tried to communicate with her father.

'Da, speak to me.'

It was no good. Anga's body stood before them but his spirit was somewhere else. Had the scream of the Azawan driven it from him? Would it come back? Did Orka still have a king?

'Da, speak to me!' Runa was shouting now. She gave his cheek a backhanded slap, making Talorc wince. He knew how that felt.

It was no good. Anga simply stared at her, the way a ghost might stare at its own dead body.

By the shore, the broch burned.

Runa pursed her lips. The look of fear vanished from her eyes. She turned to the men.

'My father is unwell,' she said. 'I will stand in his stead until he is ready to rule again.' She looked around as if giving the men a chance to challenge her. None did, though Talorc saw a few of them glance at Derran. He said nothing, but watched Runa intently as she spoke.

'Lerrick,' she continued, 'go and find anyone hiding in the fields. Tell them to head inland and spread the word. Every survivor of an Azawan attack may remain in their home or take shelter inland, wherever they find it. They are to be given food and whatever else they need, by my order.' The guardian nodded, turned and disappeared into the darkness. 'The rest of us will return to Gurn.'

'Sorry, Princess Runa,' said one of the remaining men, 'but is that the best idea? The Azawan could attack Gurn, and we know now that the brochs aren't safe. We could head inland too.'

'No. News of the Azawan will spread fast after tonight. People will be afraid and look to their king for leadership. Will it give them courage to hear he has run for the hills?'

'She's right,' said Derran. 'The king must be in his keep.'

Runa gave the white-haired guardian a slight nod. The others seemed to look to him as their leader, though his best fighting days were long behind him; his approval would make life easier for her until Anga was himself again.

'Lets go,' said Runa, taking her father's hand. She tugged on it and after a moment he allowed himself to be led, peering from side to side and stumbling like a newborn calf taking its first steps.

Cloud covered the moon, extinguishing its light as rain began to fall. Anga tripped, fell to the ground and lay there, unmoving.

It was going to be a long walk.

The moon was halfway across the night sky by the time they reached Gurn. Kretta was waiting at the gates, a burning torch held in her hand. Her eyes were fixed on the king.

'Kretta,' said Runa as they approached, 'the guardians will lodge at the keep tonight. Light a fire and bring them food and ale.'

The woman nodded. She turned away and the weary soldiers followed her through the gate and into one of the houses. Runa led her father and Talorc up the path and into the broch, where a fire was already lit in the king's chamber. Perhaps a fire always burned there; Talorc didn't know why but he liked the idea.

Runa guided Anga into his chair before stoking the fire. Talorc stood across the fire from her, unsure whether to sit or stand, talk or stay silent. Did he have a right to sit with the king? Was the strange, wordless creature sat in front of him the king?

Finished with the fire, Runa turned to her father again. She knelt in front of him and took both his hands in her own. 'Father,' she said. 'Can you hear me?'

Nothing.

'If you can hear me then listen carefully. We need you to come back. You are Anga, son of Barda, of the house of Valdar the Uniter. You are the king, and Orka needs its king now more than ever. Wherever you have gone, come back.'

The burning peats crackled and hissed, their light dancing off the stones in the altar-bowl. Was the Sea Mother angry with the Orkadi? Was she allowing this to happen?

'Come back!' Runa shouted and slapped her father. He didn't respond; she grabbed his shoulders and screamed the words again, rocking him back and forth, his head nodding like wheat in the wind. She punched him in the chest, over and over until her strength failed her. Talorc stood and watched.

Runa collapsed at her father's feet, clutching his hands.

'I've lived my whole life in a keep,' she said eventually. 'Around weapons and defences and talk of war. I know how iron is forged and how a sword is kept sharp. But you can't really understand it all, my father told me, until you've slain an enemy. I've never done it. I've never killed.'

Talorc guessed she was thinking about the finfolk, and revenge.

She turned to face Talorc. 'Do you think I could do it?'

'I don't know,' he replied. 'But what I know doesn't count for much.'

'Sit down,' said Runa. Talorc sat.

'I could do it for Orka,' she continued. 'I would kill anyone I had to kill. Derran and my father taught me how to ride and use a sword and bow while other girls cut barley and ground out flour. I knew it wasn't a game. Orka has been invaded before, many times. We've always won, but if we fail just once, Orka will be lost to us forever. And if she falls now, it will be me that lost her.'

'Your father will get better,' said Talorc. 'And even if he doesn't, you're strong. You'll find a way to defeat the Azawan, just like Valdar and Arta would have done.'

'You don't know that,' said Runa, standing and pacing back and forth. 'You don't know what that thing is. Azawan is just a word. Where did it come from? Why is it doing this?'

'The finman is controlling it, I think. He's using his magic to make it attack us. Otherwise, why would it bother? I doubt its stomach would be filled even if it ate everyone on Orka.'

'How could you know that? How many of our islands have you visited?'

'Three,' said Talorc, 'including Odhran.'

'I've been to all of them. Many times. I know the name of every headman and every harbour. I know how many-'

'And I know nothing. I understand. You've seen the Azawan yourself now, you don't need the advice of an ignorant farm boy.'

'I didn't mean that,' she said, looking into her father's empty eyes again. 'I just mean... it's frustrating. I know this kingdom as well as anyone, I want to defend her, I would kill for her but I can't, because I don't know what we're facing.'

'Well, lets forget about the Azawan for now. The fins summoned it. They're your enemy. What do you know about fins?'

'No more than most people,' she said. 'My father taught me about them. He said they came to live on the islands not long after we did, back in the days of the clans. They claimed they had been men until a spey in their homeland cursed them to look like monsters. They were cast out by their people, so they came here and asked to be given land. The clans agreed and made space for them. We were fewer back then and the weather was kinder.'

'My Grunna told me the same,' said Talorc. 'She said the fins were good neighbours at first, sharing their food with us when we had lean harvests, so people came to trust them.'

'Then the sky darkened,' continued Runa. 'And when the crops failed, and people were starving, the fins attacked us. They came at night, creeping into houses and striking with spears in the dark. They waited in the water, launching themselves at boats and dragging the fishers into the sea to drown, so that people were too scared to fish.They wanted Orka for themselves.'

'But then your father brought the clans together, and made us one clan,' said Talorc. 'We united against the fins and drove them to Fin Island, where they agreed to stay.'

'And we warned them that if they ever left their island and its waters, we would kill them. We would kill them all,' said Runa.

She took a length of iron and poked the fire with it. Talorc knew what she was thinking: if her father didn't get better, would she have to fulfil that promise? Would she be the one to lead the Orkadi to war?

'The problem with going to war,' said Runa, 'is that it could well achieve nothing. The finman was on Odhran, then on Caerban, according to your story. He moves fast, so he could be anywhere now. If he is the one summoning the Azawan then he is the one we have to kill.'

'It could be worse than that,' said Talorc. 'Going to war could be just what the finman wants.' Runa frowned at him. 'Think about it,' said Talorc. The finman must know the terms of the treaty, so he must know that breaking it would lead to war. If you attack their island, how will you get there?'

Runa frowned.

'By sea,' said Talorc. 'All of Orka's guardians, not to mention Orka's king, bobbing about on the water. Along comes the Azawan, the war is over and Orka is defenceless. The fins have won.'

'You're right,' said Runa. 'Except that we're already defence-less. The Azawan could attack us right here in the keep, right now.'

'But it hasn't,' said Talorc. 'Why not?'

Runa had no answer to that.

Kretta entered carrying two bowls of broth. She gave them to Runa and Talorc and looked at the king. The fear in her eyes was clear to see. 'He'll eat later,' said Runa. Kretta nodded and left without a word.

'I don't know how we'd manage without Kretta. She's kept this keep going ever since my mother died,' said Runa.

'When did she die?'

'She died giving birth to me,' said Runa. 'While I was still inside her. Kretta had to cut me out.'

Talorc watched Runa as she drank from the steaming bowl. She was the king's daughter, as fierce as an angry boar. She made decisions and commanded men as easily as a gull flapped its wings. Her name was famous; his was unknown. Yet they were united in one thing: the world had hurt them before they drew their first breath. It had taken her mother; it had given him fin-feet.

He could see in her eyes the question he had asked the fire, the sea, the Sea Mother and the skulls. Why? Why must fate be so cruel? Perhaps because the sea was endless; there had to be a place where everything was wrong, as well as a place where everything was right. Where there were no fins, no Azawans, and where parents lived and loved their children.

'The dead are dead,' said Runa. 'We are alive and we need to act, which means either going to war or finding the finman.'

'How?' said Talorc.

'I don't know.'

They slurped their broth.

'There might be a way,' said Talorc.

'What?'

'My Grunna told me a story about a man who fell in love with a woman whom he saw dancing on a rock by the sea. He tried to talk to her, but when she saw him she put on a sealskin, dived into the water and swam away. He realised, then, that she was a silkie. Silkies are people who can put on sealskins and swim in the sea as seals, yet when they take off their skins they are men and –'

'I know what silkies are,' said Runa.

'Sorry. Well, he looked for her everywhere, he longed for her but couldn't find her. So he went to a spey-wife.'

Runa's eyes narrowed.

'He'd heard that spey-wives could find missing things and missing people by talking to skulls in bone-houses. Maybe… maybe we could find a spey-wife and she could ask a skull where the finman is,' finished Talorc, his voice trailing off under Runa's unblinking gaze.

'It was the spey-wives,' said Runa, almost spitting her words, 'that caused the sky to go dark. It was my ancestor, King Valdar, who outlawed their magic and closed the bone-houses. And now you want me to ask their help?'

'It might work.'

'We know there are spey-wives still,' said Runa. 'Gurn is not blind. Herb-women offer spells as well as medicines. They perform their rituals in Groda's glens. We can't stop it, but we won't condone it either. Even if we asked them to perform a spell for us, by law we would have to kill them afterwards. I don't see many coming forward.'

'You could send out messengers. Have them announce on every island that any spey-wife who comes to Gurn to help defeat the Azawan won't be punished.'

Talorc watched as Runa's mind worked. He knew already how important the traditions of her family were to her. Could she go against them?

'Very well,' she said through gritted teeth. 'I see no other choice. We will call in the speys.'

'No,' said Anga, making Talorc jump. 'You won't.'

Anga drank down the last of his broth and addressed his daughter. Runa was trying to look serious. She had hardly stopped grinning since her father awakened, and had fussed over him like a mother hen until he snapped at her to stop.

'I heard everything you said,' said Anga. 'You acted wisely at Skate but your words are misguided. I will not allow magic to be done on Orka. It is because of magic that we are in this mess.'

'We're in it,' said Runa, 'and we need to get out of it. I don't want to involve the speys either, but do you really think swords are going to stop that thing?'

'No, I don't. But arrows might. Fifty in each eye might. Besides, I said nothing of striking at the Azawan. We are going to strike at the fins.'

'But if the guardians try to sail to Fin Island –'

'We will be in no more danger than we are in while we sit here,' said Anga. 'The fins began this war. I am going to end it.'

'Why didn't you say anything?'

Anga looked away from his daughter, lowering his eyes as if ashamed.

'I couldn't. I heard you, I saw you, but only half of me was here. The other half was somewhere else.'

'Where?'

The king hesitated before answering. 'Somewhere that should not exist. When the Azawan screamed at me... I fell into its scream. It was everywhere, all around me like the air we breathe, and it was inside me too. It took my thoughts and twisted them into the shapes of demons. I saw my father rise from the dead and strike my mother. I saw the people of Orka slaughtered by finmen. I saw you...' Anga shook his head.

'Enough of this evil. Where is Derran?'

'With the other guardians.'

'Bring them here. We must discuss the invasion.'

Runa was turning to go when Talorc spoke up. 'King Anga. May I speak?'

Anga nodded.

'Runa says magic is already practised in Orka, even though it is outlawed.' Anga nodded again. 'So if it is being practised, why not turn it to your advantage? Why not enlist the help of the spey-wives?'

'I do not trust spey-wives.'

'Then have them do their magic here, or somewhere you can watch them.'

'Why are you so keen on speying, boy?'

'My Grunna was a senachai. She couldn't spey herself but she knew speys, she told me. She said that though some of them did harm, most of them did good. They were just ordinary women who had been born with a talent, the way some are good with net-mending or flute-playing. If they were treated kindly, they would use their talent to help people. If they were hated and despised, well, then they might be tempted to use it to hurt. If you show kindness to the speys, show them you value them, they'll want to help. It's their kin that are suffering and dying too.'

'They want the Orkadi to suffer and die,' said Anga. 'Why else would they darken the sky?'

'How do we know they did?'

'Because that is our learning, handed down from our ancestors. You deny our ancestors?'

'We make mistakes now. People must have made mistakes then too,' said Talorc. 'And if you enlisted the speys, we could speak to our ancestors rather than arguing about what they might or might not have known.'

'You mean the speys could speak to our ancestors.'

'Yes. I know no-one trusts them. But my Grunna said there must have been a time when the speys and the rest of us lived happily together, whatever might have happened in the dark days. They have power. You can find a way to use that power, or ignore it.'

Talorc waited as the king considered his words.

'You speak well, boy,' he said at last. 'You could be a senachai yourself.' He sighed. 'Very well. Runa, send out the messengers in the morning.'

Talorc grinned.

'And send in Derran,' continued the king. 'If the Azawan lives four days from now, we are going to war.'

CHAPTER FOURTEEN

'Next.'

At Anga's word the next supplicant pushed his way forward out of the throng that crowded the king's chamber.

Anga sat leaning forward on his chair, his face supported by his palms. Talorc thought he could see the king pinching the skin of his cheek; whether to keep himself awake or to control his visible irritation, he couldn't say.

'Wellyn of Stort at your service, sire,' said the man that came forward.

'Thank you for coming. Please speak,' said Anga.

'I thought you might be needing help dealing with the Azawan, sire. I know a thing or two about such creatures. My Da was a whale hunter, he sailed north of Orka to the Teeth and to the Fire Isle, and he taught me everything he knew. He said that the thing to do with Azawans is to lure them with gold. They can't resist it, they swallow it up, but the thing is, it poisons them and sends them dead to the seabed. So all I need is gold and a good boat and I'll –'

'Next.'

'I know it sounds –'

'Next,' said Anga, putting his hand on his sword hilt. The man scurried from the chamber.

Talorc shook his head in disbelief. It was the third day since they had ridden to Skate. Tomorrow Anga would declare war. The trickle of supplicants arriving at Gurn since that night had become a wave, and now there was scarcely room to move for them. Most were simply scared villagers and farmers, looking for protection from the monster that every tongue now spoke of. Others were those who had lost their homes and relatives; a few, like this one, seemed to think the whole thing a joke.

Talorc glanced at Runa. She stood beside him, chewing on her lip as she watched her father. That meant that she was trying to concentrate on what she was seeing and think about something else at the same time. Runa was concerned for her father. After recovering from the Azawan-scream he had stayed up until dawn discussing the invasion with Derran, or so Runa told Talorc. Talorc had been given a house of his own to sleep in, one normally reserved for visiting headmen. He had imagined his Da sleeping where he slept. Since then, his waking hours had been spent trailing behind Runa as she saw to her duties, which now involved managing the tide of fearful visitors to the keep.

At times he would wonder at the strangeness of it. Him, accompanying Princess Runa as she went about her duties. Standing beside her in the king's chamber. He understood why; he had been the first person to see the Azawan, and was the only person who had seen the finman that summoned it. Yet why did Runa keep him so close by her side? Did she think he might run away?

He was glad she kept him close, whatever her reasons were. It stopped him thinking about his Mam and Da. He missed them; he even missed his brothers. It had been hard to sleep beside Kellin, shoved into a corner of the bed, woken up with an elbow to the ribs; but it turned out it was harder to sleep without him. There was an emptiness in him since they died, and it ached to be filled. Being busy helped, and he could see it helped Runa too.

But her father was always on her mind. Every now and then his eyes would go distant and Talorc knew he had left them; he was back among his nightmares. At other times he would trail off mid-sentence, or get up and walk out of the chamber and out of the keep to stand on the grass, staring up at the sky. Kretta knew a little about herbs and had been brewing teas and making poultices for him. Nothing seemed to work.

'Skelda of Groda, my lord,' said the woman that now stood before the king. She was old, her skin as craggy as the cliffs of Odhran and worn like leather; her waist-length silver hair was tied back but seemed to wish to burst free. Her clothes were goatskin and she carried a herder's staff. Though she was short, she stood tall and straight, looking at the king as if her green eyes could see through his skin and into his soul.

'Thank you for coming. Please speak,' said Anga.

'I am here about the Azawan,' said Skelda.

'So is everyone else.'

'I am a spey-wife.'

The chamber fell silent. Talorc shivered and tried to mask his delight. A spey. This was a real spey.

'You say you are from Groda?' said Anga, eyeing the woman as if she were a wolf that might suddenly leap at him with bared teeth.

'Yes.'

'Yes, sire,' said Runa. Skelda turned and looked at her, and Talorc thought he saw a flash of recognition in her eyes. Perhaps Runa had met the spey-wife on one of her trips to Groda.

'Yes, sire,' said Skelda, turning back to the king, a smile hovering about her lips.

'I am told there are many spey-wives on Groda,' said Anga.

'There is more than one, my lord.'

'Yet only you have come.'

'I come as a representative of the council of speys.'

'I did not ask for a representative, nor did I know there was a council. I asked for all the speys that would help me to come forward.'

'Spey-wives have learnt wariness the hard way, sire.'

'I swore that all who came forward would be protected, by law, for life. You do not believe I would keep my oath?'

'Quite the contrary. You are known as a man of honour, and what I see before me confirms that. You are haunted by ghosts,' she said, narrowing her eyes and stroking the wispy white hairs on her chin, 'but not by broken promises. Yet it is not your wrath the speys fear. If we survive this, they shall have years of life ahead of them, and can you promise that in all those years they won't be persecuted? Can you speak for the goodwill of every man, woman and child among the Orkadi?'

'Very well,' said Anga, waving his hand. 'Speak.'

'They say the Azawan has struck twice so far. First at Odhran, then Ork. Is this correct?'

Anga nodded.

'And it is being said that a finman has been seen summoning the Azawan, and you wish to find him.' Again, Anga nodded. 'Very well,' said Skelda. 'We may be able to help you with this.'

'May?' said Anga, raising an eyebrow.

'I would have said certainly, a moon ago. But our work has been challenging of late. The skulls who grant us our knowledge have been... reticent. Yet we will try, sire.'

'Good,' said Anga. 'Send for your people and have them gather here. We will find a place where you can do... whatever it is you do. Under supervision and under my protection.'

The spey-wife shook her head. 'No, sire.'

'No?'

'We will work on Groda. The currents of magic are strongest there, and we know the places where they are strongest of all.'

Murmuring broke out among the crowd, with many a dark look aimed at the spey-wife.

'Sire,' said one man, 'we can't let them do that, out where no-one can watch them. They might put a spell on us.' Heads were nodding.

'We know our art, sire. You have asked for our help. Let us give it,' said Skelda, ignoring everyone but the king.

'She's helping the finman!' came a cry from the rear of the chamber. At that Skelda's head whipped round.

'Who said that?' she hissed. 'Who spoke?'

No answer came.

'A ghost, was it? Well, listen to me, ghost, you and all the other fools in this chamber. I am a spey, yes. An Orkadi spey. My blood is the blood of these islands. My sisters and I risk the law and our lives every time we speak to the skulls, and we do so for you. All of you! Finding your lost livestock, blessing your crops, reading your miserable futures. I see more than one here whom I have helped in the past, and do they speak up for me? Ha! I expect no better.

'But say that I am in league with the fins,' she spat on the floor, 'who summoned the Azawan that attacked Skate, where my sister-daughter and her family lived, and who are now in its belly; say that I am in league with them again and I'll sail from these islands, glad in the knowledge that you'll all soon be dead.'

Talorc guessed from the looks on the assembly's faces that Skelda had not won them over with her words. Her hand was trembling where she gripped her staff; one more word she didn't like and she would be gone.

'Sire,' said Talorc, stepping forward. 'I have an idea.'

'Speak it.'

'If you want the speys to help, you have to trust that they know the best way to do it. If they say they have to work on Groda, they have to work on Groda. People are worried about letting them meeting in secret, so why not send Runa there to oversee them?'

He turned to Runa and saw that she had gone as white as a gull's wing.

'My daughter is heir to Orka. She is not going out on the water,' said Anga.

'She's in no more danger from the Azawan at sea than she is here, sire,' said Talorc. 'You said so yourself.'

'Someone must go to observe, though,' said Runa. 'We can send one of the guardians.'

'By all means,' said Skelda, 'if the princess is frightened, send another in her stead. It is all the same to us.'

Runa stepped forward. 'I'm not frightened of you or your kind, spey-wife,' she said, her lip curling as she spoke. She turned to her father. 'The guardians are busy training. If you won't let me fight then I can be spared. I should go.'

'Would this be acceptable to you?' Anga asked Skelda. The king didn't look happy about Runa going to Groda, but he obviously preferred it to the thought of her fighting in a war against the fins.

The spey-wife nodded. Again, a slight smile played about her lips.

'Very well,' said Anga. 'Return to Groda. Do your work with my protection. Runa shall go with you.'

'And you,' whispered Runa into Talorc's ear as she grabbed his arm, 'are coming too.'

Talorc grinned. He had always wanted to see Groda.

'Ow!'

Talorc was vaguely aware that he had just squeezed Runa's waist, hard enough to make her yelp. He would say sorry later. Now, all he could do was stare.

They had left Gurn almost immediately after Anga's exchange with the spey-wife was concluded. Kretta had packed a bag of provisions for them which now hung off Talorc's back as they rode again from Gurn. They had taken the road that led to the tombs of Runa's ancestors, but instead of turning off towards the tombs, they had continued south.

Skelda rode behind them, on a horse loaned to her by the king. Talorc recognised it from the night at Skate; Farla and all the other horses that survived had come back to Gurn of their own accord in the following days. Those who saw the spey-wife mount the king's horse looked far from happy about it; to ride, Talorc had learnt, was a great privilege.

The day was clear, the autumn sun low in the sky, when Talorc first saw them shining in its light. Runa tugged at Farla's reins and she halted.

The Ancestor Circles.

Between two lochs, two giant circles of stone pillars – one on flat land, the other on a low hill – towered from the ground and glittered in the light. Looking at them, the world seemed to fall silent and still, as if time did not pass in their presence.

'Never seen the rings before, lad?' said Skelda, stopping beside them.

Talorc shook his head. 'My Grunna told me about them. She drew them in the sand. But I didn't...'

'It's one thing to hear about them, another to see them,' said the spey-wife. 'There are other circles, many of them, in Skoll and Aira, even in Gaul I hear. But these were the first ones. The first anywhere. They were never surpassed.'

The stones pulled at him. He wanted to put aside the mission, ride to the stones and sit in silence at their feet, as if they were ancient people who knew all the secrets of the sea and sky. It seemed as if they knew his thoughts; they wished for him to join them. They called to him, sang to him. Grunna's story must have been true.

'My Grunna told me that they were an ancient race of people,' said Talorc. 'Giants who came to Orka and wanted the islands for themselves. They were huge, and strong, but they turned into stone if they saw daylight. So a senachai went to their camp and played his flute for them, and he played so well that they danced all night until the sun came up and turned them to stone.'

'Rubbish,' said Skelda.

'It's not rubbish.'

'No disrespect to your Grunna, lad, but it is. Stories like that are told because people want to forget the truth.'

'And what's the truth?'

'That the stones are stones, brought there and put up by men and women, by the order of the speys.' Talorc frowned. 'Sounds strange, doesn't it? Speys ordering people about? But that's how it used to be in Orka. Speys weren't just accepted, they were respected, even revered. We ordered whole villages to put their work aside and come together to move the stones, and they did so gladly. They trusted us.'

'But what are they for?' asked Talorc.

'Many things,' said Skelda. 'Many, many things. Even the great speys of old believed that they knew only a little of the power of the stones. A spey-wife would sit with them, learn from them all her life and only begin to know their secrets. They could be used to measure the passing of the seasons and to learn when the sun would hide behind the moon. Weddings were blessed at the stones, chiefs elected. A person who swore an oath at the stones and then broke it would always meet a terrible end.

'But there was so much more. Some speys, it is said, could glimpse far-away lands through the stones. They even talked to other speys who lived in those lands; speys with skin as dark as the earth, and spey-kings and queens who rode on the backs of giant creatures and were worshipped by their people as gods.'

'But not anymore,' said Talorc.

'No,' said Skelda. 'For speying is outlawed now, and speys risk their lives by visiting the stones. So knowledge has been lost, and our speying is weak, and Orka is weak. Kings and headmen took over the midsummer and midwinter rituals, yet the rituals are ill-remembered and empty of power.'

'Enough gossiping,' said Runa, sounding annoyed. 'We need to get to Stort.' She dug her heels in and Farla ambled on. Talorc glanced over at Skelda and again saw her watching Runa, her gaze as intent as that of a kestrel about to swoop upon a mouse.

CHAPTER FIFTEEN

'Put your back into it, girl!'

Talorc couldn't see Runa's face from where he sat on the bench behind her, but he could imagine it. Beyond her, Skelda sat watching them work with a twisted grin on her lips.

They had ridden in silence the rest of the way to Stort, where Skelda's curragh was laid up at the harbour. Talorc kept looking back, towards the Ancestor Circles, until something else caught his attention.

Groda.

Witch Island, Grunna had called it, using the Skollish word for speys.

The islands of Orka were a family of giants once, great stone giants from the Fire Island. They came to Skoll to visit their friends, got drunk, and on the way home they fell into the sea and drowned. A group of speys called the Spey Kings, who were looking for a home for their people, heard about the fallen giants. They rowed out, turned the corpses into stone and their people came to live on them. That is how our people, the Orkadi, came to live on Orka. The Spey Kings are now stone themselves, pillars of rock that stand in a circle around the islands, guarding the fallen giants. The giant that became Groda was a spey, and Groda is full of speys to this day.

Unlike all the other islands that Talorc had seen, Groda shot from the sea up into the sky like a breaching whale, its hilltops higher than he had thought possible. *The hills of Groda are a sight, lad, but not compared to the mountains of Skoll. Those hills are like molehills compared to the Seat of the Hag.* Talorc craned his neck as he rowed, turning again and again to watch the mist-shrouded isle draw closer.

'Stop gawking and row!' said Skelda. 'Groda isn't going anywhere. You could say the same for this boat, mind. Have you two never rowed before?'

'My brothers are – were – better fishers than me,' said Talorc, which wasn't exactly a lie. 'I worked in the fields.'

Skelda snorted. 'What about you, my lady? No rowing for royalty?'

'No-one ever lets me,' said Runa. 'Everywhere I sail, men insist on rowing for me.'

'Well, insist back next time. Orkadi who can't handle a boat are like fish that can't swim. Your arms are shaking. Straighten up. Let your back do the hard work.'

Talorc saw Runa follow the spey-wife's instructions and felt the curragh respond immediately. He did the same and soon it felt as if they were flying over the water.

'Better,' said Skelda.

'You look like a herder,' said Runa.

'I am.'

'So how do you know how to handle a boat so well?'

'Like I said, lass, a real Orkadi can handle a boat as well as she can walk. Not many goats at sea, of course, but I use my curragh to get around the isle for my other work.'

'Speying?' said Talorc.

'Aye,' said Skelda, 'and herbcraft. Teas, ointments and poultices for pains, broken bones, sickness. Herbcraft and speying were once seen as one and the same, mind. Now we call them different names, and use one as cover for the other.'

'So people send for you, saying they need herbcraft, but really they might be wanting you to spey for them?'

'That's right.'

Talorc looked round again. Groda still seemed far away.

'How do you do it?' he asked.

'Do what?' said Skelda.

'Spey.'

'Why do you want to know?'

'I don't know.'

'But you're curious. So is everyone.' She gave a snorting laugh and spat in the sea. 'Folk say they hate us, but everyone leans in close when a senachai tells a spey story.'

'My Grunna was a senachai. She came from Groda.'

'So I hear.' Skelda laughed again at Talorc's frown. 'You think the whole of Orka hasn't heard of you, lad? You're as famous as she is now,' she said, nodding at Runa. 'Pem was her name, yes? From the village of Burra. I knew her. I still remember the first time I heard her tell a story, back when I was a girl and she was learning from her mam, who came to our village. The old man and the trow's pig, that was it. She had us all squealing at the bloody bits.

'Then she married Loth, of course, your Grunda, and they had their boy. Torma was your Da's name, wasn't it? I remember hearing the news about Loth, after he fell. Pem never travelled after that. I never saw her again.'

Talorc realised tears were welling in his eyes. He was glad Runa couldn't see. It had never occurred to him that the people he had met since he left home might have known his Grunna. She had told him all about her journeys across the islands, how she had continuing going out as a senachai each summer even after she married Loth, but never again after he died. He remembered the winter night when she told him that story, about an old man who was asked by one of the little people to look after his pig, and the price the trowie demanded when he lost it. There had been a time when stories about the little people who lived under the earth were his favourite; he loved that they could be cruel and kind, which meant that you never knew where the stories might go.

'Did she tell you spey stories?' asked Skelda, her voice softer.

Talorc shook his head. 'She said people only wanted to hear stories about evil speys, and she didn't believe that speys were evil.'

Skelda nodded approvingly. 'A wise woman. To answer your question, speying isn't something you just do. It is learnt over many long years. There are different ways of learning, but the result is the same. You learn to listen to skulls. Get better, and you learn to converse with them. Get even better than that, and you learn spellcraft.'

'What's spellcraft?' asked Runa, who had been quiet since they got on the boat.

'That's when you and the skulls work together to make things happen.'

'Like what?'

'Like making sick people get better.'

'What about making them get worse?'

'You can do that too,' replied Skelda after a few moments, 'but that's not my trade, lass. Nor that of my sisters.'

'How did you learn?' asked Talorc.

'My Mam taught me. She had the gift too, or the curse as some call it nowadays. The skulls told her even before I was born that I had it, so she started me straight off, leaving me in bone-houses to sleep as a baby.'

'And the skulls spoke to you?' asked Runa.

'How should I know? I was a bairna. No doubt it helped, though, when my time came. I was ten winters old; it might have been the same year I saw your Grunna tell that trow story.'

'What happened?' asked Talorc.

'My mam was getting old. Said I was too young but she couldn't risk dying before she'd initiated me. So one evening, when the moon was full, we rowed over to Ork. She had a long length of rope with her. I knew initiation was tough, but I didn't know what I was in for. If I had, I would have run.'

Talorc and Runa waited for her to continue.

'We sailed up the west coast of the island until we came to one of the Spey Kings. It rose out of the sea like a sword of rock thrust at the sky. I noticed a gap in it, a little way up.

'The sea was calm. We tied the boat at its foot, climbed onto the King and up to the gap. There my mother bade me stand still, and she tied me fast to the King. I couldn't move. After that she tied a skull so that it sat atop my scalp. She told me that it wished to be my initiator, and left me.

'The wind took up, the waves crashed against the King and the tide began to rise. I watched it rise and rise until it was up to my feet. My waist. My neck.

'The whole night I was there, gulping and spitting out seawater, wanting to scream for my mother, but she had forbade that. Instead I was to stay silent, and speak to the skull, praying and praying for it to talk to me. If it did, I was a spey.'

'And if you drowned?' asked Runa.

'Then I wasn't a spey.'

'That's obscene,' said Runa.

'That's how it's done,' said Skelda with a humourless grin. 'Few have so much of the gift in them that they can spey without going through an ordeal to crack them open. Very, very few.'

'But the skull spoke to you?' said Talorc.

'She did,' said Skelda. 'And she's done so ever since. Until recently, that is.' The spey-wife's expression darkened.

'What happened? Did you lose it?'

Skelda slapped her thigh and crowed with laughter. 'No, lad, I didn't lose my skull. I'm not the greatest spey but I'm better than that. The skulls have all stopped talking, or rather, we stopped being able to hear them.'

'When?' asked Runa.

'Since the last moon.'

'Why?'

'Why do you think?'

'Because of the finman,' said Runa.

'Aye,' said Skelda. 'That's what we think, and that's why we're meeting tonight. If we work together we have a chance of breaking his spell and using the skulls to find him.'

'So why haven't you met until now?' asked Runa

'It takes time to arrange a meeting without the help of the skulls. And, of course, we didn't have your father's permission,' said Skelda, her tone mocking.

'That wouldn't have stopped you,' said Runa.

'No, it wouldn't. But it's nice to have it, all the same,' said Skelda. 'Look about, lad. Time to guide her in.'

Talorc turned and saw that his rowing had indeed improved; the rocky shore of the Witch Island was visible through the deepening mist. With Skelda's guidance they brought the curragh in close before climbing out and pulling her ashore.

'Where now?' asked Runa.

'Now, my lady,' said Skelda, 'we go to meet the sisters.'

'Where?' asked Talorc.

'Where magic is strongest,' said Skelda. 'The Trowie Glen.'

CHAPTER SIXTEEN

Runa was looking increasingly unhappy.

Skelda had led them up a narrow winding path that took them away from the shore and deeper into the mist. Above the mist, Talorc could see the peaks of the hills. The path led towards a gap between two hills that he guessed must be the Trowie Glen.

The old spey-wife walked ahead of them with surprising speed for one her age, her pack swinging on her back. Sometimes Talorc heard her muttering to herself. Runa, on the other hand, was as silent as a stone, and made no effort to disguise her discomfort. What was the matter? She had been to Groda before, but not in the company of a spey-wife; and soon they would meet a whole council of spey-wives.

Runa hated speys because they had darkened the sky, or so she believed. Grunna hadn't thought so, but neither of them could know. How would the speys treat Runa? They must all know that it was her ancestor, Valdar, who outlawed their art and closed the bone-houses. It was her father's law that forbade their art still, and by disobeying that law they had all risked their lives. They might have had friends who were executed as speys. So it was understandable that Runa would be nervous about meeting them. Should she be frightened? Might they try to harm her?

No. The king himself had sent her here. The speys must know what would happen to them if they harmed her. But what if one of them harboured a grudge, and put a spell on her in secret? So that she took ill and died, not today but on some distant day?

Talorc didn't even know if Skelda could be trusted. Several times he had caught her looking at Runa strangely, at the audience in the king's chamber and on their journey to Groda. The finman had used the blood of a seal pup to summon the Azawan. What if the speys' spell needed royal blood to work?

It was no good guessing. All he could do was trust no-one, and be ready for trouble.

A wind blew in, dispelling some of the mist as the path led them into the Trowie Glen. Talorc still couldn't see far, but all there was to see was trees. There was one cove on Odhran where trees still lingered. Grunna used to take him there; it reminded her of Groda. They had once covered Orka, she said, but most had either perished or been cut down during the dark days, leaving Orka as bare as a dolphin's back. That was why Orka's houses were made of stone, rather than wood as they were in other places, and why peat was burned on her hearth-fires.

On Groda, though, there was no shortage of trees, or at least not in the Trowie Glen. Why? Maybe it was because Groda had once been a spey-giant; her blood must be thicker, stronger.

Talorc had always liked the idea that the island he lived on was once a drunken giant. Walking upon a dead spey-giant, though, made him uneasy. He realised that he had been feeling uneasy since arriving on Groda. Was it because he would soon meet a group of speys who might want to kill Runa? Or was it the giant beneath his feet, or the endless ranks of trees?

The deeper they walked into the glen, the denser they grew around him. The wind whistled as it pried their dying leaves loose, sending them to join the damp, spongy mass beneath his feet. Talorc couldn't shake the feeling that there were people among the trees, watching them pass. Perhaps the trees themselves were watching them.

Talorc realised the path had disappeared. Skelda was leading them down some route known to her but not discernible to him. What if they lost her? Would they find their way back, or wander lost among the trees until they perished?

No. They wouldn't die of starvation. Something more awful would happen to them first. Whoever was watching them would see to that.

Skelda abruptly turned round, giving Talorc a piercing look. 'How do you like the Trowie Glen, lad?'

Talorc shook his head. 'I don't,' he said.

Skelda grinned and laughed, showing her teeth. 'I'd be worried if you did. It's not a place that anyone but a spey would choose to come.'

'It feels like… like we're being watched.'

'That's because we are,' said Skelda, laughing again as Talorc spun round, imagining a spey sneaking up behind Runa and knocking her on the head with a skull. There was no-one there, only Runa, who was standing and glaring at Skelda.

'Who is watching us?' asked Runa.

Skelda ceased smiling and lowered her voice to speak. 'The trowies,' she said.

Talorc looked round again. He saw no-one, but still felt eyes upon him.

'You won't see them lad,' said Skelda. 'Not unless they want to be seen.'

'Do you see them?' asked Runa.

'No,' answered Skelda, 'but I feel them, same as you. They're following us, watching us. They wouldn't bother if it was just me on my own, but they don't know you two, and they're curious.'

'My Grunna told me stories about this place,' said Talorc. 'She said a senachai entered the Trowie Glen by accident, long ago, and was kidnapped by trowies who made him play the flute at a wedding. He didn't come back for half a moon, though it had seemed only half a night to him.' As he spoke Talorc felt for the flute beneath his jerkin. Would the trowies think he was a senachai if they saw it?

'That didn't happen long ago,' said Skelda with a snort. 'And Reck wasn't gone for half a moon. He was gone for forty years. I was a girl when he disappeared, and old when he returned. His wife was dead, of course, but he had grandchildren still alive, so they took care of him.'

'Took care of him?'

'Of course. You think forty years playing for the trows doesn't leave a mark on a man? He was simple when he came back. Played fine music, don't get me wrong, finer than I ever heard before or since. But he couldn't feed himself, couldn't wash or go to the waste-pit without help. They had to tie a rope on him in the end; he kept wandering off to the Glen to look for the way back into the caves. One time he got away and never came back, so maybe he found it. Anyway, enough about trowies. Help me gather wood.'

Talorc and Runa obeyed, gathering a bundle of sticks each as they descended deeper into the glen. It was a good thing they had set off in the morning; dusk was coming and Talorc had no idea how long it would be before they reached their destination. Whatever was going to happen, he hoped it wouldn't happen in the dark; but that seemed unlikely...

Runa halted in front of Talorc. He looked over her shoulder and saw why.

Among the mist-wreathed trees ahead stood a tiny figure, watching them.

The figure turned, ran and disappeared into the mist as Talorc realised it wasn't a trow. It was a girl.

Skelda went on walking in the direction the girl had taken. They crossed a stream, leaping from rock to rock before coming to a faint path that led them uphill.

Waiting for them at the end of the path was the council of speys.

They were gathered before a gigantic rock that might have been stolen from the Ancestor Circles; only it lay on its side and looked far bigger. He spied a doorway hewn into the rock near the far end. Did someone live in there? He didn't think so; the place felt like a tomb. Whatever it was, he didn't like it.

The spey-wives had been talking in groups, or sat alone, as was the case with a fair-haired man who sat leaning against the fallen stone, eyeing Talorc and Runa with a mixture of boredom and suspicion. The girl whom they had seen on the path sat atop the giant stone.

As Skelda approached, the speys fell quiet and gathered around the newcomers.

But for the fair-haired man, the speys were all women. Some were older, some were younger; some were dark and some were fair, but there was nothing about any of them to suggest they might be a spey.

Except for one of them.

She stepped forward, leaning on a staff as Skelda did. The staff was not made of wood but of bones. At its top was a collection of skulls, human and animal, woven together with cord and intermingled with knives, arrowheads and carved stones.

Talorc guessed the spey who carried it must be the oldest person he had ever seen. Her thin, blue-tinged skin hung from her face and neck; blue veins crisscrossed her pockmarked, ancient hands. A few strands of hair hung from her head like ancient cobwebs and she looked at Talorc with a single eye; the hole where the other eye should have been held nothing but crusty skin.

'What has Skelda brought us?' she said, her eye roving over Talorc and Runa.

'Everything I promised, Brog,' said Skelda.

'Anga has given us his protection?'

'Yes.'

There were satisfied noises and grins among the speys. Talorc could understand why; the threat of execution for speying had hung over their heads all their lives.

'Today is a good day, sisters,' said Brog, addressing the group. 'For as long as this king lives, we may spey freely. A dark time has ended.'

'It's wonderful,' said the young man who still sat with his back to the tomb. 'The only problem is, the king will be dead soon. But then, so will we.'

'You have no faith in speying, and wonder why your speying is weak,' was Brog's reply. She didn't bother to turn her head to speak to him. Her eye was now fixed on Runa.

'There is royal blood in this one,' she said.

'I am Princess Runa, daughter of King Anga, of the House of Valdar the Uniter,' said Runa. Talorc noted a slight tremor in her voice. 'My father thanks you for agreeing to help us. He has sent me here to oversee your speying.'

'We do not spey for you or your father, Lady Runa. We spey for Orka. But you are welcome, as is the friendship your father offers us.' She carried on eyeing Runa, a smile spreading wide across her wrinkled face. Talorc found his hand going to where his heuk-knife used to sit.

'And who is this?' asked the old spey, abruptly moving to stand before Talorc. 'I did not know Orka had a prince.'

'This is Talorc, son of Torma,' said Runa. 'He-'

'Talorc!' said Brog. 'We know of Talorc.' She moved closer to him. Her smell made him think of bone-houses. 'All Orka knows of Talorc.' She lowered her voice. 'Everyone is asking, but no-one is answering. Why did the finman let you live?'

'I don't know,' said Talorc, his voice quavering.

'But you will,' said Brog, nodding slowly as she spoke. 'You and he shall meet again. The web will bring you together before this is finished.' She turned to Skelda. 'We work atop Ward Hill tonight.'

'Good,' said Skelda. 'The further we are from the sea, the further we are from the finman's power.'

The speys dispersed, retrieving packs and bundles of wood

from under trees or by the tomb. They walked back down the path to the stream, the young man following with a reluctant look on his face. Skelda nodded at Talorc and Runa.

'Follow me,' she said.

The speys were busy preparing for their ritual as Talorc and Runa stood side by side, silently drinking in the view from Orka's highest hill.

To the north lay the islands, shimmering like bronze in the sun's dying light. To the south and south-east, Groda's hills rippled into the distance, concealing glen after glen in which Talorc imagined trows creeping beneath the trees. Beyond Groda, distant but not nearly so distant as Talorc had always imagined, was Skoll. All that could be seen of it was the dark shape of its cliffs, yet to see it gave Talorc a satisfaction he had never known until a few days ago; that of a dream coming true. If he were to die soon - as he most likely would - he would die having sailed the sea, ridden a horse, stood among speys and looked upon a foreign land.

All because his family had been roasted alive.

He glanced at Runa. On the way up the hill he had asked if she had ever climbed it; she had replied with a curt shake of her head. Now she was chewing her lip as she looked towards Skoll. Should he say something? Reassure her that he would protect her if the speys tried anything? No; she knew as well as he did what such words were worth. Nothing.

He turned back to look at Orka again. The sun had sunk into the sea; the horizon was dark.

Skelda approached, torch in hand.

'It is time,' she said.

CHAPTER SEVENTEEN

Skelda led Talorc and Runa across the hilltop and down to a hollow where the speys were waiting.

Beyond where the speys had gathered was a wide circle marked with small, conical stacks of wood. In-between each stack was a carved wooden figure atop a wooden stake driven into the ground. At the centre of the circle was a wide, shallow, wooden bowl, which sat atop a circle of skulls.

The skulls faced outward over the bones arranged on the grass before them. Talorc guessed there were two or three skulls for every spey present. He had seen skulls before, of course, in the bone-house on Odhran. He used to crawl into the tiny chambers where they lived, gaze at them and, sometimes, pick one up. He would trace his finger over its contours, the smooth surfaces and rough joins, before closing his eyes, imagining its owner appearing out of the darkness and speaking to him. He had made up names and stories for many of the skulls in the bone-house, and always liked to believe that at least some of them came not from his imagination but the skulls themselves.

But he didn't really believe it. Deep down, he knew he was a dreamer, not a spey.

I never had the gift, much as I wanted it, Grunna had said one night. *I never would have been a senachai if I could have been a spey. Feels ungrateful to say so, ungrateful to my Mam and to the stories and songs, but it's the truth. You might have it, though. You might.*

Maybe tonight, finally, the skulls would speak to him?

'The ritual will take place within the circle,' said Skelda, her face lit up by her torch. Talorc was grateful for its warmth. 'We will light the fires, fill the bowl and close the circle. After that we will speak with the skulls, and hope they answer.'

'How long will the ritual last?' asked Talorc.

'As long as it lasts,' said Skelda.

'What are those wooden figures?' asked Runa.

'What do you think they are?'

'Do they represent the Spey Kings?'

'Yes,' said Skelda. 'Like the fires, they give protection. You cannot see from here, but the bowl has a spiderweb marked upon it. It stands for the web of fate, upon which we shall pour seawater, soil and feathers.'

'*For all knowledge is in the sea, earth and sky,*' said Talorc. 'My Grunna used to say that.'

'Sounds like your Grunna fancied herself a spey,' said Skelda. A smile hovered around her mouth again.

'Where will we be?' asked Runa.

'Yenna and Jarren have made a protective circle for you within the main circle,' said Skelda, gesturing towards the girl who had been watching them and the bored-looking young man, who were listening to their conversation, along with the other speys. Were they brother and sister? 'You will remain there and observe. And fall asleep, likely. I doubt this will be over quickly.'

'I won't fall asleep,' said Runa. 'I am here to oversee this ritual on behalf of my father.'

'Of course you are,' said Skelda, as if Runa was a petulant child who needed calming.

'Don't talk to me –'

'This isn't right, Skelda,' said Brog, shuffling over and pulling her sealskin cloak close about her as the wind began to pick up.

'This is my will,' said Skelda coldly.

'What's not right?' said Runa.

'The ritual, little queen,' said the ancient spey-wife. 'Skelda here would have us ask the skulls how to find the finman. That is all. I am trained in battle magic,' she said, rattling her skull-staff. 'When we find him, I could destroy him.'

'Or you could destroy us,' said Skelda. 'No other spey here has your training, and we do not know the finman's strength. If he hits back, and you are not as strong as he is, we will be defenceless. The entire council could be killed.'

'And if we tell your father how to find the finman, and he finds him,' said Brog to Runa. 'How does he plan to kill him?'

'I don't know,' said Runa.

'He doesn't have a plan,' said Brog. 'Anga cannot fight a foe steeped in dark magic. I can.'

'Maybe you can,' answered Skelda. 'But we can't, and the only hope we have of getting the skulls to talk is by working together. I was voted head of this council, Brog, and I have decided how we shall work. Maybe in time we can look at other courses, if this fails.'

'I offered you the training,' said Brog. 'I hope you see now your folly in refusing.'

'Battle magic breeds battles,' said Skelda. 'There are enough skulls in Orka. Let us begin.'

Talorc stood alongside Yenna and Jarren as the speys began the ritual.

Skelda went to the nearest wood stack and knelt over it, murmuring for a while and waving her free hand before lighting the fire from her torch. She went to stand inside the circle, and another spey came forward and lit the next fire from the first, and so on until all the fires had been lit and all the speys stood within the circle. Talorc understood now why they used the hollow beneath the hilltop rather than the hilltop itself; fires lit there would be like a beacon signalling their presence to the finman, should he be hunting them.

Jarren and Yenna moved between the fires into the circle.

Talorc and Runa followed. The two apprentices led them to a circle of feathers, stones and shells. The four of them sat within the circle on damp, mossy ground and watched as the ritual got underway.

Skelda lifted a water-skin that sat on the ground before the altar. She pulled out the stopper and emptied its contents into the bowl, before doing the same with two pouches. Finished, she spat into the bowl, lay down the final skin, took two bones from the altar and sat down before it. One by one, the other speys followed, spitting into the bowl and retrieving a pair of bones before sitting down. Brog came last, laying the skull-staff down at her side as she sat.

Closing her eyes, Skelda held her bones aloft and began to sing. Talorc didn't understand the words she used. Grunna had said that in different lands people used different words; these could be foreign words, or words with magic in them.

Skelda struck her bones together, making a clack-clack-clack sound as she struck them again and again. The other speys did the same with their bones, though only Skelda sang. Then Skelda's song ended, and she spoke words Talorc understood.

Ancestors, wisdom keepers,
Spirits at one with sea and sky
Those who rowed the sea before us,
Orkadi of the ancient times
Show us the dark one whom we seek,
Clear of shadows and disguise
We beg, we pray, we cry for vision,
To see as through your long-dead eyes

She spoke and then repeated the verse, and after a few repetitions the other speys took up the chant, swaying back and forth and clacking their bones together. Talorc felt a tug to take out his flute and play along, but he knew better. He wasn't a spey, and this wasn't music. It was magic.

Talorc's head jerked upward. Had he fallen asleep again? He looked about him. Yenna sat on his left, cross-legged and straight-backed, her eyes closed and chin held high as she gently swayed to the chant and the endless clack, clack of bone on bone. Jarren lay curled up in his cloak on the other side of Yenna, snoring softly. Runa sat to his right, glaring at some spey-wife or other. He almost spoke to her but thought better of it.

Those who rowed the sea before us, Orkadi of the ancient times...

Talorc re-crossed his legs, shivering as the damp stole further into him. He couldn't fall asleep again. He had dreamed his whole life of meeting a spey, and now he was present at a speying ritual; the first one to take place - the first sanctioned one, anyway - in hundreds of years. If he survived the Azawan, he would be telling of this as long as he lived. It wouldn't do to say he slept through it.

We beg, we pray, we cry for vision...

Talorc closed his eyes again, just to rest them for a moment.

Dreams of dark eyes and blue-black scales dispersed slowly as Talorc awoke. Before he even opened his eyes, he knew something was wrong.

Runa was moaning, swaying, swatting at the air as if she were attacked by unseen foes. What was wrong? Was the magic making her sick?

He needed help. Skelda. Talorc looked across at the circle of speys and as he looked, one of the spey-wives rose to her feet.

Her eyes glittered dark in the firelight. Moving as if she knew not what she did, she turned and shambled towards the nearest fire. Once there, she bent down and thrust her hand into the flames.

Talorc cried out as the spey withdrew her hand. In it, she

held a burning branch. Turning, seemingly oblivious to the pain she must be feeling, the spey-wife walked towards where the nearest spey sat, chanting and swaying, clacking bones together, eyes closed.

She was going to set the other spey on fire.

Talorc had to stop her. He leapt up, ran forward and came crashing to the ground. Someone had grabbed his ankle. Twisting round, Talorc saw Runa, black-eyed and crawling towards him, a savage grin splitting her face.

He tried to wriggle free but she still held his ankle. There was no time. Talorc kicked out, catching her on the cheek and breaking her hold. He rose to his feet again and ran, but he was too late. The spey with the burning branch in her hand was about to –

A dark shape flew through the air and struck the spey on the face, knocking her and her torch to the ground. Talorc turned and met Yenna's eyes.

'Look out!' shouted Yenna as Talorc was thrown to the ground. His mouth full of blood and earth, he tried to wrestle free of Runa's grip. All about him now were screams and cries of pain. Other speys were succumbing to whatever evil had come to ensnare them.

Runa punched him, making his head ring. Before she could grab hold of him again, he wriggled round to face her. She was a trained fighter, but he had grown up with his older brothers and the ever-present threat of their attacks. He had never won against them, but he had learnt a few tricks.

She struck again. This time he caught the blow with his forearm, wincing as her knuckles collided with bone. He could have struck her then, but he didn't want to. This wasn't Runa attacking him; it was someone else.

But whoever it was, they were trying to kill him, and he had to stop them.

He caught hold of Runa's wrists, holding on grimly while she tried to break free. Talorc looked around again. Every spey was locked into a fight to the death. Jarren was gone; probably fled; he couldn't see Yenna.

He shouldn't have looked away.

Runa's forehead came crashing down against his. Everything was white light and searing, unbelievable pain. Talorc wanted to give up, lie back and let her end his pain; only he couldn't, for now her jaws were probing for his neck.

Animal instinct took over. He found her head with his hands and butted her back. Rolling on top of her, he pinned her down, using some well of hidden strength that perhaps only those facing death possessed. As his vision returned, he searched for Skelda. She could stop this. Where was she? He couldn't see her among the writhing masses.

Could he do something himself? Talorc's thoughts raced as Runa writhed beneath him. He was sure they were under attack by the finman. But how to break the spell, when he knew nothing of magic? The speys should have attacked the finman from the start. Skelda should have listened to Brog.

Brog...

Talorc saw her. She was on her stomach, crawling away from a spey-wife who had hold of her heels. She saw Talorc watching her and shouted something. He couldn't hear her over the mayhem.

Then he saw it.

Her staff. It lay a few arm-spans away from her, its blades and polished skulls gleaming in the firelight. Of course; those blades and arrowheads weren't there for decoration. Battle-magic. She was telling Talorc that if he could reunite her with her staff, she could end this.

But Runa wasn't going to make that easy. She slipped free of Talorc's grip, tightened her knees about his waist and flung him to the ground, hitting his head against a rock. Talorc was only dimly aware of the pain. He had to help Brog end this. Nothing else mattered; not pain, not Runa.

Talorc rolled aside and grabbed the rock as Runa leapt at him.

He swung the rock.

It caught her on the side of her skull. She fell as if she was a stone and lay still.

Talorc got to his feet and lurched over to where Brog was struggling to reach her staff. He sat atop the spey who attacked Brog, remembering how Jed had knocked him down in the field one day and pinned him down like this. Just as Jed had done, he took the spey's wrist and twisted her arm around behind her back, finding the point at which the bones and muscles refused to go any further. Jed hadn't stopped there; he had pulled a little bit further, and a little bit further, testing how far he could go without breaking his brother's arm, while Talorc screamed.

Now Jed was dead. Talorc didn't stop where his brother had stopped. Some part of him feared he was taking revenge on his brother as he ripped the spey-wife's arm from its socket.

He ignored her screams, as did Brog, who kicked herself free, half-crawled and half-ran to her staff and grabbed it, holding it to the sky.

Straight away she began to chant, her words as mysterious as the deep sea. The staff responded, lights sparkling in its myriad eye-sockets. Talorc's skin crawled as if tiny Azawans were burrowing beneath it while the light in those dead eyes grew brighter, and brighter; then the Azawans were not just beneath his skin. They were behind his eyes, in his mind, and Brog was holding the skull-staff to the sky. From the circle of fires there shot great pillars of flame into the sky, and even the dark air was shining...

A great cracking rent the sky and it was over.

No Azawans; no magic. Only the moans and screams of the wounded and dying.

Talorc ran to where Runa lay.

She wasn't moaning or screaming. The Princess of Orka lay deathly still.

CHAPTER EIGHTEEN

Skelda knocked Talorc aside and pressed her head to Runa's chest.

She drew back and held out her hand, letting it hover over Runa as if warming it over a fire. Back and forth her hand wandered, her eyes closed. She put both her hands to Runa's brow and was still.

'Thank the Sea Mother,' said Skelda, opening her eyes and withdrawing her hands. 'No lasting damage.'

Talorc sighed as relief washed over him. If he had hurt her... if he had killed her...

Skelda left and was soon back with her pack, from which she withdrew a collection of bundles made from goatskin and tied with gut-string. She picked out three, spread an empty skin on the grass and laid out herbs from the other three bundles on it.

'Chew the mixture and hold it to her head, here,' said Skelda, indicating the exact point where his rock had struck her. Talorc nodded.

Skelda gave him a long look.

'You did this,' she said.

'Yes.'

'So you could get the skull-staff to Brog. I saw that part. Don't feel ashamed. You did what you had to, and you saved the lives of everyone here.'

'But –'

'I'll be back to check on her.' With that Skelda left to tend to the speys that still screamed and cried among the ruins of their ritual.

Talorc did as instructed, chewing the mixture of herbs before taking them from his mouth and pressing them to Runa's skin, just between her right eye and her ear. In the low light of the remaining fires he thought he could see the skin changing colour as it bruised. Better bruised than dead. Still, her head would hurt when she awoke.

Would it hurt her that he had done it? They were... no, he couldn't say they were friends. He was an orphaned farm boy; she was the future queen of Orka. But she felt like a friend. Even though she was a princess, he felt safe around her, not on his guard as he used to be with his parents and his brothers. He trusted her. And he had almost killed her.

Shivering, Talorc pulled Runa's cloak tighter around her and waited for Skelda to return.

Light was stealing into the cloud-strewn sky when Skelda returned. She seemed more at ease now; the last screams had stopped.

'None dead,' she said, eyeing Runa closely as she sat down beside her. 'Many wounded. This one will wake soon.'

'What happened?' asked Talorc.

'I was wrong,' said Skelda, 'and Brog was right. We should have let her attack.'

'So the finman knew you were searching for him.'

'Yes. It was almost like he was waiting for it. It took half the night for us to gather enough power to start speying. As soon as we did, as soon as we broke through, he was there.' She shook her head. 'He wasn't afraid of us. Why should he be? To have the power to do what he did... we are no threat to him.'

'But what did he do?'

'He possessed us. Not all of us; he took those whose minds were weak, unguarded. These he possessed, turning them on the others. Sister would have slain sister, were it not for Brog. And you.'

Talorc didn't know what to say to that. 'But my mind isn't guarded. I was within the protective circle, but so was Runa. So why was she taken and not me?'

Skelda didn't reply; she only looked at him, as if waiting for him to work it out.

'Yenna wasn't affected either, and she's only a child,' said Talorc, frowning. 'Was Jarren possessed?'

'No.'

'It was only the speys that were possessed. The speys, and Runa.'

Skelda raised her eyebrows. Finally Talorc understood.

Runa, Princess of Orka, was a spey.

Images crashed into Talorc's mind so fast that it made him dizzy. The way Skelda had looked at Runa when she first caught sight of her at Gurn. The way she had watched her since then. Runa crawling towards him, intent on murdering him…

'I didn't expect an attack,' said Skelda. 'I thought I could keep us hidden; I was wrong. And even if we were attacked, I thought the circle would keep Runa shielded. But her own power was so strong, so bright, it made her part of the ritual; so she was there with us, and vulnerable.'

'But how can she be a spey if she hasn't been through an ordeal?'

'Sometimes the Sea Mother creates an ordeal. She weaves it into a person's fate.'

Talorc thought back over all Runa had told him about her life.

I was pulled out of her…

'Runa's mother died giving birth to her. They had to cut Runa out,' said Talorc.

Skelda nodded. 'So her life began with an ordeal. Part of her mother's spirit may have stayed with Runa, speaking to her, nurturing her gift. Did she talk about her mother to you?'

'No, but she took me to her family's burial place. She asked me whether I was telling the truth about the Azawan...'

'But really, she was asking her ancestors,' said Skelda with an approving smile. 'Or trying to, and failing, since the skulls have been silent. Clever girl.'

'Why didn't you say anything?'

'No spey reveals another spey. That has been our most cherished vow since the day our art was outlawed. The princess is waking up, I think.'

'I'm awake,' said Runa, her voice faint. She opened her eyes. Had she heard what they said?

'I'm glad of it,' said Skelda. She put a hand under Runa's head and helped her to sit up. Next she took a small vial from her pack, unstoppered it and held it to Runa's lips. 'Skollish firewater,' she said. 'Drink.'

Runa did as directed, shivering as she swallowed the brew. 'What will happen now?' she said.

'You mean up here, or on Orka?' asked Skelda.

'On Orka.'

'I thought so,' said Skelda. Runa wasn't one to waste time, and talking about this meant they avoided any further talk about her speying. 'We have been broken. Only battle-magic could serve against the finman, and Brog is not powerful enough to locate him alone. I fear the speys have failed.'

'Then it will be war,' said Runa.

'So it would seem,' said Skelda.

'We need to get back to Gurn,' said Runa. Talorc felt a sharp pang of sympathy for her. She wanted to get back up and carry on working; but they all knew there was nothing she could do. Anga had given them four days to find the finman before he went to war. The fourth day was dawning. They had failed.

They stood together. The day had dawned bright enough to see the rippling peaks of Groda laid out before them and the faint smudge on the horizon that was the Skollish coast. The defeated speys sat in groups or else were gathering their things, preparing to leave.

'Thank you,' said Runa to Skelda. It was clear she didn't want to talk about what had happened, or what had been revealed. 'I will see that your pardon is upheld.'

'I'll see you back to Ork,' said Skelda. Runa nodded, and after Skelda had spoken to some of the other spey-wives, she rejoined them and they set off on the path down the hill.

'Wait.'

They had walked in silence all the way down the hill, through the Trowie Glen and to the shore. The wind was blowing away the night's mist, the rising sun bright in a clear blue sky.

Talorc held on to the side of the curragh, looking back at Skelda who stood on the stones of the bay. Runa was already in the curragh, and Talorc had been about to jump in.

'What is it?' said Talorc. He turned and scanned the water but could see no disturbance. There were no other boats out on the sea; people must be keeping ashore for fear of the Azawan.

'This war of your father's,' said Skelda. 'It feels wrong to me. It feels like the finman and his people planned for things to go just this way.'

'Maybe he did plan for us to go to war with the fins,' said Runa. 'That doesn't mean they will win. They went to war with us once before. They lost.'

'They have the Azawan,' said Talorc.

'We have the Orkadi,' said Runa.

Skelda looked away towards the rising sun, the lines around her eyes deepening as she narrowed her eyes. 'There may be another way,' she said. 'One the finman will not expect us to take.'

'What way is that?' asked Runa.

At a wave from the spey-wife Talorc and Runa returned to the shore, the curragh on their shoulders. Skelda looked troubled, glancing repeatedly to the east as she spoke.

'I didn't want to involve her,' said Skelda. 'In this or anything. She deserves to be left in peace. But if the fins win, she will have peace no longer. They will have her again.'

'Have who?' asked Talorc.

'The one who escaped them.'

The old spey-wife sat down heavily and gestured for them to join her. She looked between Talorc and Runa as if struggling to decide whether to share a secret with them.

'I found her out at sea,' she continued, 'east of Calag. At first sight I thought she was a corpse; she nearly was. I treated her as best as I could with what I had, and rowed her back to shore on Calag. I didn't think she'd make it. The girl was near starved, thin as a bird's leg, and what was left of her was covered in layer upon layer of scars.

'It was summer and the weather was kind, thankfully. I made a fire, warmed her and revived her. She didn't know where she was. She was terrified of me and everything that moved, it seemed. But I fed her and won her trust, and in time learnt her story.

'Sariad was born on Narm. As can happen,' Skelda said with a sly glance at Runa, 'she had the gift pouring out of her, even as a bairn. I don't know whether you managed to hide your gift from your father, and I won't ask. But Sariad was not so fortunate as you. Her parents hated speys, like all the good, decent folk around there. So they did what most parents do in their situation; they tried to beat it out of her. There's a belief that a whip made of birch can drive speying from a person.

'They tried, they failed, and when they failed, they took her to a quiet beach and tied her up, to let the waves do what they could not.'

'But the fins found her?' said Talorc.

'Aye,' said Skelda. 'They found her. Took her to Fin Island and one way or another she ended up as a slave to one of their sorcerers, or divers as they call them. A finman named Mordak.

'Mordak hated dries, as they call us, even more than most fins do. He took his hatred out on Sariad, bullying and beating her. He didn't like that she could spey. But what he really hated was that she was a diver. Somehow, whether from birth or from being around it night and day, she picked up fin magic. And oh, did he hate her for that.'

'What is diving?' asked Runa. 'Is it different to speying?'

'Speys talk to skulls,' said Skelda. 'Divers send their minds out of their bodies. The stronger their magic, the further they can go. Most fins have a little of the gift, enough to hear the voices of living sea creatures on occasion, or to sense their presence, for diving is easiest at sea. But some divers can do far more than that. Some can look into the minds of others. Even control them.

'Mordak used magic to try to tear Sariad's gift from her. He tried over many years, in many ways, most of them unspeakable. None worked. She was a few winters older than you are when he finally gave up. Beat her almost to death and threw her from a clifftop. She would have died; she should have died, but the Sea Mother kept her alive and led me to her. Now she lives alone in a quiet place, and she knows peace, for Mordak believes she is dead.'

Talorc and Runa were both quiet. He could see the horror he felt reflected in Runa's eyes as they both tried to imagine what the girl had gone through. Jed and Kellin's bullying didn't seem so bad anymore.

'I don't understand how any creature – even a fin – could do such things,' said Runa. 'Why does the Sea Mother allow it?'

Skelda gave a humourless laugh. 'She guides us; she does not control us. The Sea Mother is a god, but she is just one god. There are many powers between the seabed and the stars, and none of them are all-powerful.'

'Do you think Sariad could help us?' asked Runa.

'Sariad is a diver,' said Skelda.

'So she could use her power to find the finman. Find out what he is doing and how we could stop him,' said Talorc.

'I know she could,' said Skelda. 'All the time they lived together, Mordak could hear her thoughts and she could hear his.'

'You believe Mordak is the finman who summoned the Azawan,' said Runa.

Skelda nodded. 'He is their most powerful diver, and he hates dries. Nothing would please him more than to wipe us out.'

'Where is she?' asked Runa.

Skelda hesitated. She looked to the east again. 'On Fior,' she said. 'In a bone-house on a clifftop.'

'She lives in a bone-house?' asked Talorc.

'She trusts the dead better than the living. I visit her there when I can, and have a man whom I trust bring food for her. Row round the south coast of Fior and you'll see it just before the coast curves north.'

'You're not coming with us?' asked Runa.

'I have work to do among my sisters.'

'But she trusts you. She won't trust us,' said Runa.

'No,' said Skelda. 'But when she looks into your thoughts she will see that I sent you. You have true hearts, each of you. Anger, but no malice. You will win her trust, for you each deserve it.'

'We'll go,' said Runa. 'I'll see that your curragh is returned to you. And thank you.'

'No need to thank me, Princess. I serve Orka, not your father.'

Runa looked offended by this, but chose not to say so. She gave Talorc a nod. They stood and pulled the curragh back into the water.

'One more thing,' said Skelda as they readied themselves to row. 'Sariad doesn't like secrets. Beware of lies you tell yourselves, and each other.' Talorc nodded and they pulled on the oars.

He had the feeling the spey-wife's words were meant for him.

CHAPTER NINETEEN

'This isn't right,' said Runa from behind Talorc.

'What isn't?'

'The sea.'

He looked around. It was mid-afternoon. They were rowing south-east across open water on the way to Fior. After leaving Skelda they had followed the coast of Groda until it veered away south before making for a tiny islet called Switha. There they had come ashore and rested, eating bread, cheese, bannocks and pig-meat from Runa's dwindling supplies before making an offering to the Sea Mother and falling asleep on the sand.

In all that time they hadn't spoken except when they had to. The atmosphere between them had grown steadily more tense; or so it seemed to Talorc. He could have been imagining it. Neither of them had taken more than a few snatches of sleep since they left Gurn the previous morning; maybe Runa wasn't talking simply because she was tired. Or maybe she had guessed that Talorc was keeping a secret from her, and she was angry.

'It's like the sea is dead,' said Runa. 'We should be seeing moon-ducks, terns, cormorants, seals, whales. But there's nothing.'

Talorc thought back to his journey from Odhran to Gurn. It was true; the sea had thrummed with life on those days, or so it had seemed to him. He had noticed that it was quiet today, but had assumed the open sea was just like that some days.

'There are no boats out either,' she said. 'The sea creatures are deserting our waters, and the Orkadi are staying on land.' There was no need to say why. For the hundredth time, Talorc scanned the horizon for signs of the Azawan. Nothing; only the white wings of the waves and the shimmering humps of distant islands. Turning again and looking past Runa, he could see the island that must be Fior in the distance, drawing steadily closer. There was no sign of the Azawan. But it was out there.

'I think it must be leaving Orka to go hunting, then returning here,' said Talorc. 'It's so big, even a village-full of us couldn't be enough for it.'

'That's what I thought,' agreed Runa. 'But no-one knows when it will return, and people are terrified. The sea creatures must know that it has claimed these waters. The ones that can leave are leaving.'

Talorc knew she would be thinking about food supplies across Orka. Food from the fields would keep people alive, but there was no knowing how people might react to being unable to fish because they were too scared to take their boats out. If word had got round about a finman being responsible, people would be pushing for Anga to go to war. If Talorc and Runa didn't return tonight, which was inevitable now, war was certain. Unless they could find Sariad and bring her back to Gurn in time to stop him.

Would Sariad trust them? Not if they were keeping secrets, Skelda had said. Which meant he had to tell Runa his secret before they got to the bone-house. If they went on rowing hard, they should make it before sunset.

He could wait a little longer.

'Runa.'

'What?'

Talorc drew in his oars, laid them down in the hull and turned round on the bench to face her. She squinted her eyes against the light of the setting sun. Beyond her, the cliffs of Fior were close. They would make it to the south coast before nightfall.

'Pull in your oars,' he said.

'We need to get to Fior before dark.'

'I need to tell you something.'

Runa opened her mouth to argue, closed it, and did as Talorc asked.

'I've been keeping a secret from you,' he said.

'Fine. Tell me,' said Runa.

Talorc reached down and tugged off one boot, then the other.

He heard Runa's sharp intake of breath as she realised what she was looking at. His long, finger-like toes. The stretches of pale skin between them, so pale they were almost blue.

He looked up into her eyes.

'Fin-feet,' she said.

'Yes,' he said, matching her stare.

He hated her in that moment. Runa had a secret, too; but her secret allowed her to speak to her mother, her grandparents, all her royal ancestors. To speak to them and know she was loved by them, just as her father and all of Orka loved her. No-one ever kicked her, twisted her arm, beat her, starved her. She was looking at him like he was filth; and compared to her, he was.

Yet as much as he hated her in that moment, he hated himself more. Himself, and his feet. Everything he had suffered was because of them. All the shoves, all the mockery. *Monster.* All the evenings since Grunna's death that he had sat at the quernstones, listening to the family and the villagers talk, with never a single word said to him. He had crawled into a bone-house and tried to speak to skulls; what could be more pathetic than that? If he had died when the Azawan struck on Odhran, no-one in all the world would have known and no-one would have cared. His life would have come and gone like a wave on the sea, and mattered less.

All because of his fin-feet.

'Why are you still alive?' asked Runa.

Talorc didn't reply. So she did hate him. Fine. She could hate him all she liked. He was used to it.

'There's a law,' said Runa. 'Babies born with fin-feet are to be exposed.'

Exposure. By law he should have been left out on the land to be killed by the cold or eaten by eagles. His family had never told him that.

'Their families aren't punished?' he asked.

'They are punished if the child isn't exposed.'

'But...'

Talorc's mind reeled. It didn't make sense. His family hated him. All of them. Except Grunna. They would have liked nothing better than for him to be dead. So why hadn't they exposed him at birth? Why had they risked themselves to protect him?

Whatever the truth was, he would never know it, for they were all dead. They had died, he had survived. Until now.

'Does the law still apply if the baby isn't exposed, and grows up?' he asked.

'I don't know,' said Runa.

A gust of wind blew from the north, rocking the curragh.

'People say that the fins make it happen,' said Runa. 'They put curses on pregnant women. Mothers aren't supposed to go out to sea or even near the shore until their child is born. If a pregnant woman sees a fin in a dream, that means she has been cursed and her child will have fin-feet. The only cure is to slash her belly with a bronze blade, or iron.'

Talorc imagined his father slashing his mother's belly with his iron sword. If only he had done so.

It didn't matter. What mattered was what Runa did now.

'Will you tell your father?' he asked.

'I have to.'

Talorc pulled his boots back on. 'We should keep going,' he said. He took hold of the oars and was about to set them in place when Runa spoke.

'I know what it's like,' she said.

'Having fin-feet?'

'Keeping a secret.'

'Of course you do. You're a princess. You know exactly what my life has been like,' said Talorc.

'You think being a princess means having a perfect life,' said Runa. 'That because I've never gone hungry, because everyone knows my name and no-one – except you – would dare hurt me, I can't complain about anything.'

'Yes.'

'The law against speying was made by my ancestor. Speys have been hanged under my family's rule. And I am a spey.' She took a deep breath. 'I've never said it before. I'm saying it to you now. I am a spey. What do you think would happen if people found out?'

'Your father pardoned –'

'I don't care about the pardon! I care about my people learning I've lied to them, betrayed them since I was born!'

'You say the words "my people",' said Talorc, 'and say you have problems. My people were my family. My village. They're all dead, and when they were alive, they hated me. My brothers tormented me and my mother and father watched and said nothing.'

'Your family broke the law to protect you. They kept your fin-feet secret to protect you,' said Runa.

Talorc couldn't think of a response, which only made him angrier.

'We need to move,' he said. 'The sooner we get there, the sooner we can head back to Gurn so you can tell your father about me.'

'I didn't say I would tell him.'

'You didn't say you wouldn't.'

'He's a lawbreaker too.'

Talorc frowned. 'What do you mean?'

'Don't you understand? He knows about my speying,' said

Runa. Her face softened. 'When I was little, and we went to pay homage at the mounds of our ancestors, I would tell him I could hear people talking. He said I was just imagining it. Then one time I heard my mother's spirit speak. She told me who she was and told me to say things to him. Secrets, memories they had shared, things I couldn't know.'

'Weren't you frightened?'

Run shook her head. 'No. If anything, the world felt less frightening after she started talking to me. It was like I had known she was somewhere close by, but I couldn't see her. When she revealed herself, it was like things had been put right.

'My father realised what was happening. He asked me to say things to her, how he loved her, how he missed her. She said the same things to him, through me. I'd never seen him cry before. I didn't think I ever would. But he cried and cried until there were no tears left in him.'

'And he kept your secret,' said Talorc.

'Yes,' said Runa. 'He said it wasn't my fault, I had been born with it somehow. Then he explained to me about speying and the law against it, and asked me not to spey again, but I knew he didn't mean it. He would have done it if he could. What he wanted was for me to keep it quiet, because I had broken the law; and by keeping my secret, he has broken it too.'

'So you know about my fin-feet,' said Talorc. 'I know about your speying, and I know about your father knowing about your speying.'

'That's right,' said Runa.

Talorc felt the tension dissolve in him as he realised what Runa had done. She had given him power over her father. Power that could save his life.

Perhaps they were friends after all.

'I've tried to spey,' he said. 'I used to sit in the bone-house near my village and talk to skulls. But I'm not a spey.'

'I've always wanted to go into a bone-house,' said Runa. 'I haven't, for my father's sake. I've talked so many times to my own ancestors; I want to speak to the skulls of ordinary Orkadi. Hear their stories.'

'I've always wanted to swim,' said Talorc. 'I wasn't allowed to, in case my feet were seen. I still don't know if I can. But I feel like I could.'

'Well,' said Runa, 'I see plenty of water.'

Talorc glanced left, right, back to Runa.

'You don't mind?' She shook her head. 'But we need to get to Fior.'

'We'll make it,' she said. 'Swim.'

'What if I can't swim?'

'You'll drown.'

After a moment's hesitation, Talorc grinned and pulled off his boots and jerkin. He stood up, seeing himself springing from the boat into the water...

'Careful,' said Runa, grabbing the side of the boat to steady it. Talorc nodded and instead clambered over the side while Runa leant far to the other side to keep the boat upright. Still holding on to the side, Talorc gasped as his legs, his waist, his chest went underwater.

He was in the sea. He grinned up at Runa, who smiled back at him as he kicked his legs to stay afloat.

'Let go,' she said. 'I'll grab you if you start going under.'

Talorc let go of the boat. His arms straightaway responded, moving against the water to keep him afloat. It was as natural as breathing.

Turning, he swam away from the curragh, marvelling at the power in his legs and his feet. His fin-feet. It was hard to hate them in that moment, as he went surging through the sea, faster than he would have ever believed possible. His arms that had been numb from rowing felt as strong as oxen as they propelled him through the water.

Talorc took a deep breath and aimed himself downwards.

It was another world. In this blue world he was no longer

Talorc the monster. He was a sea creature, and all sea creatures were kings. He could fly here, there, out of the water and down, down into the deep blue. The whole vast, endless sea was his to explore, and it was calling to him, welcoming him.

He could stay his whole life down here and be happy. But no; something was pulling him back. He had to breathe. And there was something else: a feeling in the water, like the tone in one of Grunna's stories that told you that some evil was about to enter the fray. The sea was scared. Something was out there that shouldn't be there. Now that Talorc felt it, the feeling was over-powering. He had to get out of the water, or else swim far away.

He surfaced to the sound of screaming.

His head whipped round. Was the Azawan coming? No. It was out there, he had felt it, but it wasn't in sight.

'What's wrong?' he said, grabbing hold of the boat. Runa steadied it as he hauled himself back in, dripping all over the hull.

'You should be dead!' said Runa. 'I thought you were dead! No-one can stay underwater that long.'

'How long was I down there?'

'Too long,' said Runa. Alongside the fear in her eyes, Talorc saw distrust.

'I'm sorry. I didn't mean to scare you,' he said.

'Let's go.'

The rest of the journey was made in silence. Talorc felt his strength strangely renewed by his underwater adventure. He rowed with ease, reliving and wondering at what he experienced. It was a relief that he couldn't see Runa's face, but it was hard to care too much what she thought. There was nothing wrong with holding your breath for a long time. He wondered when he could do it again.

The sun had sunk into the darkening sea by the time they saw

it, crouched above blade-sharp cliffs on the south coast of Fior.
Sariad's bone-house.

CHAPTER TWENTY

The bone-house was just like the one Talorc knew on Odhran. A cocoon of sandstone slabs, with a dark tunnel leading inside. A place to remind the living what life was, Grunna had said. *One brief season. An explosion of thoughts and feelings, sounds and colours and passions that vanish like a flame in the darkness, leaving only the long watch of death ahead.*

Sariad was inside.

'I can see lamp-light,' whispered Runa, who was kneeling down and peering into the tunnel.

'Do you want to go first?' said Talorc.

'You've been in a bone-house before. You first.'

Talorc got down on all fours, summoned his courage and entered the tunnel. It was about three times the height of his body in length, leading from the outside world to the main chamber. He guessed that, as in Odhran, small chambers the height of his waist would surround the main chamber, home to the skulls of southern Fior.

Lamp-light flickered inside. Talorc crawled slowly. He could hear Runa coming up behind him, her pack scraping the roof of the tunnel.

He reached the main chamber and crawled to the left of the entranceway to make room for Runa. She joined him and they both knelt on the earth floor among the seal-fat lamps, taking in the sight of Sariad's home.

Sariad lived within a forest of skulls. The skulls of women, men and children glowed in the soft, flickering lamp-light. They sat among skulls of moles, voles, mice and rats, seals and dolphins. There were bird skulls of every kind; Talorc recognised the skulls of sea eagles and sun eagles, gulls and cormorants and blade-beaks. Some were stacked atop one another, lining the walls, while others hung from the walls in nets of gut-string, fixed to the stone with glue. Attached to the vast web of gut-string were hundred and hundreds of feathers, the skulls staring out from among them.

It was the strangest and most beautiful sight Talorc had ever seen; more temple than tomb. He felt guilty for intruding upon this place. Sariad had decorated her home this way because she felt safe among the spirits of these people, these birds and animals. They were her friends, as he had wished the skulls of Odhran to be his.

He turned to Runa. Wonder and fear passed back and forth across her face like circling buzzards. He was about to tell her that bone-houses weren't usually like this but stopped himself. Sariad was here, listening. They were intruders. The first words spoken should be to her.

Where was Sariad?

She had to be in one of the smaller chambers. In the Odhran bone-house, the main chamber had been empty; the skulls had been in the smaller chambers, or skull-chambers, as he had thought of them. He took a lamp in his hand and crawled over to the nearest skull-chamber and searched the shadows. Nothing.

He moved on from the western end of the tomb to the east, looking into each skull-chamber.

Soon, only one remained.

With Runa behind him, Talorc peered around the corner.

The lamp-light wasn't strong enough here to scare off the shadows. He crawled forward into the chamber.

Sariad cowered in the corner.

Talorc guessed she was three or four years older than he was. Her fair hair was lank, her face thin and she looked at him through startled blue eyes that reminded him of a frightened calf he had once found on Odhran, separated from its herd and bleating for its mother. Faint scars criss-crossed the skin on her face, hands and arms, while one prominent scar slashed her face from hairline to chin. Around her neck she wore a tiny skull on a length of gut-string, while at her side was a skull of a kind he didn't recognise, but seemed familiar; like that of a seal but narrower and with pointed teeth. Her hand clutched a crude weapon made from an eagle's claw glued to a length of wood.

Slowly, Talorc shuffled aside to let Runa in next to him.

Three pairs of eyes flicked back and forth.

The claw-dagger trembled in Sariad's hand.

'You're safe,' said Talorc. Sariad flinched at his words, making Talorc and Runa flinch. She squirmed as if trying to retreat further back into the shadows. 'I'm Talorc. This is Runa. Skelda sent us,' he continued. 'We won't harm you.'

Sariad didn't reply. Her free hand went to the skull at her neck. She stroked it as if seeking reassurance.

'Do you know what is happening in Orka?' said Talorc.

Silence.

It wasn't working. She didn't trust them; he couldn't blame her. There was no good reason for her to trust anyone besides Skelda. The spey-wife had been wrong; she should have accompanied them here. Would they have to go all the way back to Groda to fetch her back here? There wasn't time. King Anga might already have declared war.

'You must miss them,' said Runa. Talorc turned and saw she was talking to Sariad.

'I miss my dead too. All my skulls are quiet. I miss all of them, but I miss my mother most. I used to go and see her all the time. Even when I wasn't talking to her, I could feel her with me. Just a breath of her. But now she's gone, and everything feels wrong. Like the heat of the sun has gone from the world, or the sea has dried up.

'Who is this?' she asked, pointing at the skull Sariad wore on her necklace.

Sariad opened her mouth, closed it again. She took a few

breaths as if to summon the power of speech from some far-off place. 'Dort,' she said.

'A vole?' asked Runa.

Sariad nodded. 'Skull. His spirit fled into the beyond.' Her voice was hoarse, as dry as a bone. 'Can't see him. Can't hear him. I call… he's frightened.'

'I'm frightened too,' said Runa.

Sariad went on fidgeting with Dort's skull.

'You're not alone,' Sariad said, raising her eyes to look at Runa. 'There is a spirit with you. A horse. Worried. Waiting for you… come home.'

'Farla,' said Runa, a smile spreading across her face. 'Tell her I will come home soon.'

'She knows,' said Sariad.

Talorc felt a spark of hope kindle within him. Sariad was talking. Trusting them.

'You come alone,' she said, her eyes darting to Talorc. 'No-one beside you.'

'There was only one person who cared about me,' said Talorc. 'Her name was Pem. She was my Grunna. My family gave her to the Sea Mother when she died.'

'She cares about you,' said Sariad, looking from Talorc to Runa. 'Your spirits touch one another.' She gazed at Talorc awhile then frowned.

'Angry,' she said to him, her voice accusatory. 'Angry at your dead. You hate them. Wish them harm.'

Talorc eyed Sariad's weapon. She clearly preferred the dead to the living. Hating the dead wasn't going to go down well with her.

'Yes,' said Talorc. 'I hated them for the way they treated me. But I can't hurt them. I won't hurt you. I just want to help Orka. The islands are in danger and we need your help.'

Sariad shook her head. 'Others… help.'

'They tried,' said Talorc. 'They failed. We need you. You're the only one who can help.'

Sariad shook her head and looked down at the stone floor.

Talorc and Runa exchanged glances. Runa shrugged her shoulders. She didn't know what to say either.

'I wish we could just leave you alone,' said Talorc. 'You shouldn't have to help. But if you don't help us, you won't be safe here anymore. The finfolk will come.' Sariad flinched at the word. 'The finfolk will take Orka from us. They will enter this place, and they will take you away from here.' She was shaking her head now, sobbing. Talorc hated himself for doing this, but he had to do it. He pressed on. 'Look inside my mind. Look and you'll understand.'

Talorc waited. Sariad went on fingering her vole-skull, looking anywhere but at him and Runa, whispering and muttering to herself.

'It's not going to work,' said Runa. 'She –'

Runa's voice faded. Talorc heard a humming, low and then loud like waves crashing into cliffs in a storm. His mind was awash with pictures, swarming in front of his vision so that he could no longer see Sariad or the bone-house. He saw Skelda, Brog; he saw the rock collide with Runa's skull; he saw Gurn, Criff and Gwynn, the watcher on the shore.

The Azawan.

The seal pup.

The finman.

He heard Sariad's cry of fear as the contact was abruptly broken. Talorc fell backwards, black spots dancing in front of his vision. A headache began to pound at his skull like the swinging of a bone-hammer; it didn't matter. Sariad was speaking.

'You saw him,' she was saying. 'You saw him.'

'Yes,' said Talorc.

'You saw Mordak.'

Sariad had sat silent for some time. It was clear she was wrestling with a decision. Talorc and Runa waited.

'He talked about it. So many years. Didn't believe he would do it,' she said.

'Do what?' said Runa.

'Start a war. The last war, in which the katra – they call themselves katra – take Orka back from the dries. He would sit in his tent with the other divers. They would talk about it. Take the islands back… kill most of the dries… keep some. Every katra dreams of having a dry slave. Keep some of us alive… breed us so they would have dry slaves forever. Punish the slaves for everything the dries ever did to them.'

'Were there other slaves?' said Talorc.

'Yes. Weren't allowed to talk to each other. I wasn't allowed to talk at all, except when he told me to.'

'You were Mordak's slave?' said Runa.

'Yes. He had another slave before he found me. Gave her to another diver. Didn't need her anymore once he had me… but I saw her sometimes. We spoke a few times, even though it wasn't allowed. She said the other wasn't as bad as Mordak. Didn't beat her as much.'

'He wanted you as a slave because you were a spey,' said Runa.

'And a diver,' said Sariad. 'I don't know why, and he didn't either. But I could do fin magic. I could send out my spirit. He didn't understand how I… he didn't like it.'

Talorc shivered as he eyed the scars on Sariad's arms and face. He couldn't imagine how anyone could go through all that and come out sane. Though, he thought as he watched her play with Dort's skull, maybe she hadn't.

'Skelda said you could hear Mordak's thoughts,' said Runa.

Sariad nodded. 'He hated that I could hear them, but he liked it too. He used me to get stronger. He would come at me with his whip... think where he was going to strike... I could read his mind and get out the way. But he sent fake thoughts with real ones. Sometimes covered his thoughts. It was a game to him. Made him stronger, which he liked, but made me stronger too. I learnt to plant thoughts in his mind, to change what he saw.' She smiled. 'I could appear like one of his friends to him, he would tell me things he would never tell otherwise.'

'And it worked?' asked Talorc.

'Not often. It would have worked on other fins; it's easy to create illusions in minds with no magic. Divers are different. We hear whispers of the spell being spoken in our minds. He would ask me to try... when he saw through me, it made him laugh. But then his mood would change. He would ask me again how I dared have the magic of the katra. I couldn't answer. He beat me.'

'But he never found out why you could dive,' said Runa. Sariad shook her head.

'Did he ever speak to you about the Azawan?' Runa asked.

'He loved to talk about the Azawan. It's a legend among them. They say that a diver from the Fire Island summoned it long ago, but it killed the diver. The spell still exists, they said, that will summon it, but it's lost. That's what they believe. Mordak and other divers would drink and talk into the night, talk about how they might find the spell. Mordak swore it would be him. He would use it to take back Orka, then the world, from the dries. I didn't believe he would ever do it.'

'He's done it. The war has begun,' said Runa. 'And we don't stand a chance of winning without your help. We need you to look into Mordak's mind. Find out we can stop him. Otherwise we will all be killed or made slaves.'

'He wouldn't kill me,' said Sariad. 'He would take me as a slave again. I know it.'

'Then help us,' said Runa.

Sariad shook her head. 'I can't.'

'You can, and you must. You knew this might happen. That

he might strike at us, and if he did we would need your help.'

'No.'

'If you don't help us then he will win, and he will come for you again. And take others, too. Other children; and do to them what he did to you.'

Was Runa going too far? The pain in Sariad's eyes wrenched at Talorc. They shouldn't be making this girl suffer anymore. But what Runa said was true. If it wasn't them making Sariad suffer, it would be Mordak.

They waited.

'I will never be his slave again,' said Sariad. A new look came into her eyes. 'I'll help you.'

CHAPTER
TWENTY ONE

'How do you do it?' asked Talorc.

'Different ways. I will use mind-jumping,' said Sariad. 'I move out of my mind, into the mind of the nearest sea creature. Then from their mind into another, and another. Like a flea leaping from animal to animal. Every time I come to a new creature, I sense all the creatures around it. I search their memories for the one I'm looking for. Eventually... eventually I'll find him.'

'But there are so many creatures,' said Runa.

Sariad nodded. 'It can be slow, but it's a good way of moving while staying hidden. There are not so many creatures in the water now, so it'll be quicker than before the Azawan came. And I think I know where he is.'

'On Fin Island?' asked Talorc.

'Yes. If he is alone, and he is not diving, I can get into his mind. If I am lucky. If he is diving, he will probably notice me, or if he is with another diver, the other might notice me.'

'What if he's asleep?' said Runa.

'He doesn't sleep much.'

Talorc and Runa fell silent as Sariad prepared herself. Moving into the centre of the tiny chamber, she picked a selection of skulls from those against the walls and laid them out in a circle around her. She crossed her legs and straightened her back. Talorc noticed that since she had made the decision to help them she had moved differently, spoken differently. Perhaps it felt good to defy the one who tormented her, in spite of her fear.

Sariad took a deep breath, in and out. 'I can do this,' she whispered.

'You can. You must,' said Runa.

Sariad took another deep breath, then another; then she began to sing.

It was a sound unlike anything Talorc had ever heard; except for once. On the beach, on Odhran, in the early morning. She sang the way the way the finman – Mordak – had sung. Deep, rasping – a sound no human should be able to make. But Mordak had taught her. He had taught her his art while he beat her, hurt her, kept her as his slave. Guilt at putting Sariad in danger mingled in his mind with wonder at what he witnessed.

Help her, Sea Mother, Talorc silently prayed. He closed his eyes, imagining a spark of light that was Sariad's mind speeding through the water, from fish to bird to seal to sunshark, all the way to Fin Island.

Sariad sang on. Her song was quiet, soft, wordless, changing only in tone; yet it was powerful. It felt like a claw, pulling on Talorc's mind, drawing him towards hidden, watery worlds; but he resisted. Sariad must swim alone, unseen. The song was beautiful, but frightening too. She could be on Fin Island now. Her mind might be jumping through the minds of finfolk. Any moment she might sense the presence of –

For a moment Talorc's vision blurred. Sariad wasn't singing any more. She was screaming.

Runa was shouting but Talorc couldn't hear her words. Everything faded but for Sariad, who was on the stone floor now, writhing like a fish in the mouth of an otter, screaming and sobbing amid her scattered skulls. She held her hands to her head as if something within tried to pull it apart; some nightmare spawn awakened in the depths of her mind.

A dread presence filled the chamber.

If Talorc had been deaf and blind; if he had been in deep sleep he would have known it. The finman was here. He was every-where. The damp air was his breath; the cold walls were his scaled skin.

Mordak.

Sariad fell suddenly still as Mordak's voice poured from her mouth and rang against the walls.

'Sariad,' he said. His voice was everywhere. 'So long it has been. So long. I have been waiting for you to visit me.

'I wish you had come sooner. You could have been by my side in all this, if you had been faithful. You could have stood with me to watch the Azawan rise from the water. But you hid from me and now you side with the dries.

'Did you really believe I thought you dead, that I didn't know where you hid? Do you think your master to be so blind?

'All would have been forgiven if you had come home. Yet still you may serve me. Serve well and I may be forgiving when I come for you. For now, I have work for you to do.

'Anga went to the speys, as I knew he would. The speys came to you, as I knew they would. Now you will go to Anga. You will be my voice in his hall. You will speak these words to him.

'The war between the dries and the katra begins again. As you waged war on us, in the time of the dark sky, so we now wage war upon you. The islands that you took from us, we now take back from you.

'We offer no mercy; we bring only vengeance. You may not flee east nor west, south nor north. The Azawan shall come for those that try, and they will burn.

'Sariad, my servant, will remain in your court. Every week, she shall pronounce seven names; the names of your people, whom I have long watched. Those seven shall be brought to the beach at the place you call Skate, by noon on the coming Seven-day. The Azawan will come for them, and it shall come again for another seven, the next Sevenday.

'This is how your people shall perish, Anga. The belly of my Azawan awaits every man, woman and child; save for those we shall come to collect, at the very end. Sariad shall be one of them. You shall be one of them. Your daughter shall be one of them.

'These are the first seven.'

Talorc listened as seven names were given. He knew none of them.

'Fail to deliver the seven and an island shall perish,' continued Mordak. 'Allow any to attempt escape and an island shall perish. That is all.'

With that Mordak was gone, as swiftly as lamp-light dispels darkness. Sariad no longer shook but lay with her chest heaving, her mouth hanging open, terror rampant in her eyes. Talorc opened his mouth to offer words of comfort; they died before he could speak them.

He looked at Runa. *Wait,* she mouthed.

Sariad's breathing eventually slowed. She sat up the way Grunna had done in her last years, as if it took great concentration and effort.

'We have to go to the king,' she said.

'When morning comes, we will go,' said Runa. 'But not because he told you to go. We will take you to Gurn and protect you. I swear it.'

'Don't make a promise you can't keep,' said Sariad.

'I can –'

'You can't!' screamed Sariad. 'I am his. I was always his. If I fight him I will fail, and he will punish me. If you fight him you will fail, and he will punish you. We must obey him.'

'I won't argue with you,' said Runa. 'Though I wish you believed me. We leave for Gurn in the morning. Lets sleep while we can.'

'I won't sleep,' said Sariad.

'Very well. Wake me up when the half-light comes.' With that, Runa crawled out of the skull-chamber.

Talorc looked between Sariad and the doorway. 'I don't

think I'll sleep either,' he said. 'I can stay if you like.'

'Leave me,' she said. He nodded and wriggled out of the chamber. Runa was curled up at the far end of the main chamber. Talorc lay down, taking care not to disturb the skulls stacked against the walls. Lamplight flickered on the ceiling and skull-covered walls.

Talorc closed his eyes and prayed to the Sea Mother for sleep, whatever dreams may come. No nightmare could be as terrible as the one he was living in.

The king's chamber fell silent as Runa and Talorc led Sariad in. They had rowed through the day, arriving at Gurn as dusk fell. The guardians at the gate had looked at Runa with unconcealed relief.

King Anga was sat in circle with Derran and a dozen or so other men, some of whom Talorc recognised as headmen or guardians from his days at Gurn before they left for Groda. Had it really only been two nights he had been gone?

'I expected you sooner,' said Anga to Runa, his tone not matching the relief in his eyes. 'You had me worried.'

'We went to Groda with the spey,' said Runa, beginning her story rather than apologising. She told of their crossing, their journey into the Trowie Glen and the ritual on the hilltop. Some of the men exchanged disbelieving looks; she ignored them.

Sariad kept her eyes upon the fire as Runa told the council what Skelda had said of her. She omitted any details of their journey to the bone-house, and Talorc could tell she fought not to hesitate or stumble as she recounted what happened there.

'He spoke through Sariad, using her voice. He told her to give you a message,' she finished.

Sariad finally met Anga's eyes. He nodded once.

'The war between the dries and the katra has begun again,' said Sariad, relaying Mordak's message.

The guardians and headmen stared at Sariad.

'...And an island shall perish. That is all,' Sariad finished.

Mordak's words hung in the air like a reeking smoke.

Every set of eyes went to Anga.

'We proceed as planned,' said the king at last. 'The muster begins in the morning. We meet at Otter Bay two evenings hence.'

'And... and the sacrifices, sire?' said an elderly headman.

'There will be no sacrifices,' growled Anga. 'This finman was right about one thing. We are going to war.'

PART III

CHAPTER
TWENTY TWO

'We're moving.'

All around Talorc, men crawled from under sleeping skins, stood, stretched and pulled on their boots. A few whispered prayers to the Sea Mother. He forced himself to follow suit though cold fear whispered in his ear, telling him to stay nestled beneath his new sleeping skin, upon the warm straw.

One by one the guardians left the lamp-lit store-house that had been allotted to them. The sacks of grain and feed that it housed had been piled high to make room for their sleeping bodies. Talorc waited until he was alone before hurriedly un-covering his feet and pulling on his boots. He blew out the lamp and followed.

Outside a brisk wind whistled through the air. There was just enough light to reveal the squat shapes of the buildings that made up the farm, and the line of men heading away from the farm, down the path through the fields to Otter Bay. Talorc hunched his shoulders and shivered as he went after them. It was autumn but winter's breath rode the wind.

How many of the men and women here today would live to see winter? He feared it would be few. He had tried to get behind Anga's plan to attack Fin Island. Anga knew war; he had fought and bled and killed in the wars of the Skollish kings. Runa supported the plan, and she had grown up training with weapons and listening to the talk of fighting men. Yet it seemed wrong to Talorc. It felt wrong, in his churning stomach and shivering bones.

Was it really wrong, or was he simply afraid? Of course he was afraid; he was terrified. So were the guardians. He had lain awake half the night listening to men tossing and turning, coughing and sighing. At one point he heard a quickly-muffled sob. These were trained fighters; but all they had ever done was train, at Gurn for a moon each summer. This was real. The men must have thought of their families, wondering if they would ever wait out winter or reap the harvest with them again.

Fields gave way to sand and dune-grass. Talorc crested the dunes and looked down on Otter Bay.

There were more people on the crescent-shaped beach than he had seen in one place in his life. Was all of Orka present? Anga had put the call out for every able-bodied Orkadi who could fight to gather here. Talorc had travelled across from Gurn with Runa, Anga and the guardians the previous day. They had come ashore on a beach to the south of the island of Calag and carried their boats across the low-lying island to Otter Bay. Anga hadn't wanted boats sailing round the north of the island, in case they were seen by watchers on Fin Island. Houses and store-houses in the nearby village had been offered to the royal party, while the other Orkadi that arrived had slept among the dunes and on the beach, without fires to warm them.

Talorc had been astonished, as he and Runa wandered among the camps the previous afternoon, at how many people had come. Many more must have arrived late in the evening. Grunna had taught him to count up to dozens, but this was dozens of dozens of dozens of people, gathered in circles upon the beach, their boats lined up from one one end of the bay to the other. Thick fog sat upon the sea beyond the bay, cocooning the camp and hiding it, Talorc hoped, from prying eyes.

'It makes me proud,' said a voice, startling him. Runa came to stand beside him. She was wrapped in a cloak of seal-skin fastened with a bronze broach in the shape of a boar. Its hood flapped in the wind.

'Orka has not seen war for generations,' she continued. 'The dark sky war is more a fireside tale than history to these people. Yet they came. Fishers, farmers, herders. They answered the call to fight.'

And die, thought Talorc.

'Do you think them brave?' she asked. 'Or foolish?'

'I think it wasn't your father that brought us here. It was Mordak. He has us like fish in a net.'

'We are like fish in a net! Orka is the net. We cannot leave. So, we fight. What other way is open to us? Do you have some strategy in mind that you haven't shared?'

'We've been over this,' said Talorc, trying not to let a note of irritation creep into his voice. Runa was spoiling for a fight and he didn't want to give her any fuel. Yet he resented the mockery implied by her words; that Talorc the farm boy could be foolish enough to think his opinion was worth something.

'We have. And you admitted that you couldn't think of any better plan than this. Yes, many of us will die, whether the Azawan comes or not. But at least we have a chance this way. I would rather die fighting than watch my people die before being made a slave.'

She was right. To attack the island was the only chance they had. He couldn't think of another way. But there had to be one. There had to be a better way than this.

'None of us like it,' Runa said, lowering her voice as a group of men passed them on their way to the beach. 'But if you show your fear, people will see, and it will give fire to their own. Fear could spread through our ranks and consume us before we have even begun.'

'That's true for you; you're the princess.'

'And you're Talorc. Everyone knows who you are now. So be as afraid as you like, but don't show it.'

Word went out to head to the boats. There was no rallying speech from the king; he had given his instructions to the headmen last night, to be passed on to the islanders. As the crowds of Orkadi quietly made their way to the lines of curraghs, he caught a glimpse of Anga up ahead, his huge figure easily distinguishable among the mass of people. Talorc glanced at Runa to see her watching her father. The fight between the two of them had raged from when they had arrived at Gurn up until when they left. Runa had claimed she could never be respected as queen, if she had stayed behind when white-haired farmers and scrawny fisher-boys had gone to war. Anga answered that she would never be queen at all if she died today on a finman's spear. Runa made it clear she wouldn't leave him alone until she won the argument, and eventually he caved in.

They threaded their way forward until they caught up with Anga and Derran. Talorc noticed many people looking their way and whispering as they passed. He thought he saw approval in their eyes when they saw Runa standing among them. It made sense, of course, not to risk her life as well as Anga's; but wasn't her life at risk anyway? Like she said, a quick death would be better than slavery. But it wouldn't come to that. It couldn't.

Though it had done for Sariad.

Talorc wondered what Sariad was doing now. Kretta had been given care of her. The smith's wife had pushed out her husband so the two of them could share a house at Gurn. A guard had been posted to watch the door and make sure no-one unknown to Sariad entered, on Kretta's orders. Kretta seemed to understand what Sariad needed to feel safe, and Talorc was grateful for it.

He had looked in on Sariad a number of times before they left. Each time he came away with a heavy heart. She missed her bone-house and her skulls, though she had brought a sack of her dearest companions with her. The vole, otter and bird skulls gave her comfort; but it could never be enough. Sariad didn't believe the war against Mordak and the fins could be won. She believed it was only a matter of time until he came for her. Talorc wanted to tell her she was wrong; he wanted to promise that Mordak would never harm her again. The words never left his throat.

Anga and Derran were waiting for Runa and Talorc at the water's edge. Father and daughter exchanged stiff nods. The condition to her coming was that she remain with Anga; he didn't trust anyone else to protect her.

The king gave a signal which was passed on in silence to each end of the bay. The Orkadi lifted their boats and brought them down to the shore.

It was time.

Talorc, Runa, Anga and Derran carried their craft into the icy water. Screeching gulls scattered as they pushed it out and jumped in one by one. Talorc went last, relieved he didn't stumble and crash into the water. He was getting more used to boats.

Derran and Talorc took the oars, with Talorc at the prow. They rowed in file with the other curraghs out into the open sea. The water immediately became rougher after they left the shelter of the bay. Was the Sea Mother warning them back? Tendrils of fog spun slowly through the sea air.

Runa was scanning the sea over Talorc's shoulder and stroking her sword-hilt. He knew what she was looking for, though they were barely out of the harbour. Were the fins out in their own boats, waiting to spring on them? Would the water start to bubble and hiss, signalling the coming of the Azawan? Whenever Talorc turned and glanced over his shoulder he saw nothing but mist. From the rear, Anga watched Runa, his eyes hardly leaving her.

Talorc could feel the weight of the sword Runa had given him against his hip and thigh. She owned two: one slender and light, one heavier and more powerful. She had given him the lighter one; probably because he wouldn't be able to handle the other.

Her sword hung from her right hip, her dagger from her left. Anga and Runa were similarly armed. They all wore armour of boiled leather; again, Talorc wore Runa's spares. He knew how lucky he was; most of the islanders were armed with heuk-knives and skinning-knives.

'Tell me again,' Anga said.

Runa craned her neck to face her father.

'Again?'

'Again.'

Runa sighed. 'Fins are faster than men. They fight using short spears with flint tips and wear no armour. They can fight in water as well as on land, as they can swim like fish and hold their breath for long periods. It is better to fight them on land than in water.'

'Which is why, if they attack us before we reach their island, we have to make getting onto the island our priority, not fighting back,' said Anga. 'Go on.'

'The best way of beating a fin is to break its spear. After the spear is broken they are more vulnerable, but they still have their teeth, and are still quicker than men.'

'And their tails,' said Derran.

'And their tails,' repeated Runa. 'You have to keep moving, keep your defence up, and wait until you see a clear opening before striking. If your strike fails, move back immediately; never stay in close range.'

Talorc looked over his shoulder again. More mist. The wind had died down. Should he be listening? He had heard it all several times over, as Anga and Derran drilled Runa and the guardians on the grass outside Gurn. Anga had ordered him to join in, since he would be fighting alongside them. Well, fighting might not be the right word. The guardians were going to fight. He was going to die.

Even then, as he had stood with a spear in hand, frantically trying to deflect the blows Runa aimed at him with her wooden practice sword, the war hadn't seemed real. It felt like he had fallen into one of Grunna's stories, one of the long Skollish ones about a clash between two mighty kings, that had taken night after winter night to tell. Now, out here on the cold sea amid a forest of curraghs, it was finally real. The Orkadi were at war with the fins, for the first time since the black sky war. It was from the stories of that war, handed down from king to king, that Anga was instructing Runa. Not since then had an Orkadi stood and faced a finman in combat.

Anga didn't believe that the Azawan would attack. It had attacked Groda the previous night, so the folk from there said. In a strange way, that was good news. Anga believed that the Azawan needed more than a few men in its belly to fill it, so it should now be far out at sea, hunting whales or whatever other meat-laden giants haunted the deep. Of course, the fins might see them coming and Mordak might summon it back. But the mist would hide them, and according to Anga, Fin Island wasn't far away. They should reach it before the sun stole the morning dew.

Wherever the Azawan was, it wasn't close. No steam rose from the seawater. Yet even if they made it to Fin Island, death surely awaited most of their army. The fins must have known that sooner or later an invasion fleet would come. They would be ready.

'What was that?' said Anga.

Talorc looked over his shoulder.

The water was still. He looked back at the king. Derran had ceased rowing; he and Anga were staring past Talorc.

'There's something in the water,' said Anga.

Talorc twisted round again. He scanned the surface of the water.

'I can't –'

The water exploded.

A gigantic grey shape burst from the sea, flipped over in the air and came crashing down on top of the curragh to their left.

Talorc recognised the creature. But this didn't make sense.

They didn't hunt.

Sunsharks didn't hunt.

They were men once. A boat-full of men who got stranded on an island on the way back from a guga hunt. They ran out of food, and so ate each other, killing those too weak to resist. When the survivors returned home, a spey learnt what they'd done and cursed them to drift through the sea as giant fish, their mouths open, always hungry yet never eating.

Another explosion. More screams, men and women crushed or thrown in the water as the breaching shark threw itself down upon them. The shockwaves rocked the curraghs; screams rent the air.

Another shark breached. Another.

This was Mordak's work.

Talorc realised Anga was shouting at him.

'Row! Keep going!' he was shouting. Talorc hurried to obey, though his arms seemed to have turned into sea-grass. Even when he managed a stroke, the boat hardly moved. Derran wasn't rowing. He was shouting at Anga.

'We can't fight off sharks! We'll all be killed!' shouted the guardian over the chaos of screams.

'Some of us will make it! This is our only chance! Row!'

Derran obeyed. Talorc adjusted his rhythm to keep time with Derran and the boat surged forward. Looking around, Talorc saw a few others were moving forward. Only a few, though. The sharks were breaching all through the invading force. Some boats they landed upon and crushed; others capsized as the huge creatures hit the water. Islanders tried to turn and flee, only to crash their boats into others. The water was thick with thrashing and shouting Orkadi.

'They're coming back!' called Runa. Talorc turned and scanned the water through the fog. The sharks were returning; but they were not going to launch themselves into the air.

This time they came like arrows, their fins skimming the surface, aiming themselves at the islanders in the water.

One passed by their boat, close enough for Talorc to look into its eye. For a moment its gaze met his as it sped past.

A group of guardians whom Talorc had bedded beside saw it coming too; only they were in the water.

It came straight at them. They turned and tried to swim away but it was hopeless. The sunshark opened its massive jaws, seized one of the men and tore him in two.

The man's scream turned Talorc's blood to ice as the seawater bloomed red. The shark turned its attention to the other guardians who desperately tried to swim away; with a few thrusts of its massive tail it caught up to them and carried on its slaughter.

'ROW!' Anga was shouting. 'ROW!'

Runa was staring into the water, her mouth agape with horror.

Derran was shouting at the king, hanging on to the rocking curragh with one hand while pointing with the other, back towards Otter Bay.

Talorc couldn't hear Derran. Anga's voice faded to a murmur.

The whole world became a fading dream, about to disappear like water through cupped hands.

There was something else. Something beyond what Talorc could see, hear, touch, taste, smell. A new knowing.

Death was coming for them.

The sunshark burst through the hull of their curragh. Talorc was sent flying through the air by the force of the impact. He saw sky, sea, sky, sea...

He was beneath the water.

As he sank the new knowing exploded out of him. Quick as a diving gannet it surged in every direction, stretching out like the tentacles of a giant squid. He knew without needing to open his eyes what was around him. Broken curraghs, drops of blood; tiny fish, iron swords sinking to the seabed. The sea was alive and every drop of it was singing to him.

Sharks, wreathed in blood. Women, men, their fear battering at him like stone hammers in the hands of giants.

And Runa.

All those other things were present in Talorc's mind, in his skin and bones and teeth and nails; yet only Runa mattered. For as soon as Talorc hit the water, as soon as this new sense awoke in him like the first fiery dawn in the morning of the world, he knew that the shark was coming for her.

Talorc surfaced, gulped air and submerged again. There she was, treading bloody water. Her thoughts swam about her, cascading through the sea to reveal themselves to Talorc. Runa was terrified, like everyone else around her. Yet while the other Orkadi thought only of survival, Runa was hopelessly trying to figure out a way to save her people and resume the invasion. In her mind she saw herself driving her dagger into the eye of a shark. She saw herself clambering onto a curragh, calling out the news of a strategy that could save them. She saw the Orkadi come to their senses, forget their fear and turn the tide of battle on their assailants.

Then her hopes died as she saw death coming for her.

Runa turned to face the sunshark as it sped through the water, its giant mouth agape. Her dagger was in her hand, ready. She dived below the surface, swimming towards the monster to meet it head on.

Closer it swam. Talorc reached towards it with his new sense as he frantically swam towards Runa.

The shark wasn't hungry; not for Runa's flesh, anyway. It ate something else; tiny sea creatures invisible to the eye. Yet it didn't know that. A black cloud fogged its mind, making it forget itself. The cloud was in every shark, confusing them and convincing them that it was human flesh they hungered for.

The shark shot through the water.

Runa drew back her dagger-arm. The water would slow her, she was thinking; she would have to compensate –

But she didn't believe herself. Though she roared defiance at her fate, she knew this was death.

Talorc shared her mind; shared her belief; but then another knowing pushed its way to his mind's surface. It was the kind of knowing that pulled your hand away from the fire; the kind that knows you better than you know yourself.

GO!

His words were a command that shot like lightning through the water. Runa stabbed with her dagger and hit nothing, for the shark had turned away, lancing past her, awash with confusion and anger.

GO FROM HERE! LEAVE US! Talorc commanded all the sharks.

His command shattered the spell that held the sunsharks. As one they halted their attack and swam away as the spell-fog cleared in their minds.

Black spots danced before Talorc's eyes. His lungs were burning. Time to surface again. He kicked out, suddenly deathly tired. Would he make it to the surface?

He made it. Yet just as he emerged from the blood-ridden sea, everything went dark.

He was alone in a vast, dark space.

No; not alone. The darkness was watching him. The darkness was angry with him, and curious to know who he was; how he commanded such power as to break the spell the darkness had cast.

Yet the darkness could not help but reveal a little of itself as it probed Talorc.

It was familiar.

It was the finman.

The boy from the beach. The one who saw the sacrifice.

Yes, said Talorc, fighting to hide his fear. Mordak had him. Be brave like Runa, he told himself. Don't show him you're afraid. *I saw you, Mordak.*

Laughter echoed through the darkness. *Lucky for you I am tired by this spell*, said Mordak. *Lucky for your people I set no armour about it. I did not know the boy from the beach was a diver. Neither did you, but you have been broken open now.*

Go and rest, Talorc. Swim home through the blood of your kin. You have a little time yet before I come for you. The next time you visit my island it will be as my guest.

You will never leave.

CHAPTER TWENTY THREE

At last, Talorc's feet touched sand.

It hadn't been easy to keep pace with the other survivors. He had kicked off his boots on the journey back to Otter Bay, lashing them to his belt, allowing his fin-feet the freedom to propel him through the water. It felt good, though it was small comfort when he looked around him.

The invasion fleet had been an awesome sight. Now it was a pitiful one. They returned to Otter Bay clinging onto the wreckage of their curraghs. Only a small number of boats had survived, and these were filled with the wounded and dying, the strongest survivors manning the oars.

Talorc looked left and right. He was the first to reach the shallow water at the edge of the bay. Quickly he walked out of the water, shook off seawater and slipped on his boots before anyone could see his feet.

Runa was close behind him. She too was uninjured. Wading out of the sea, she shook the water from her hair and clothes. Gone was the cloak with the copper brooch. Talorc could see from her movements how the long swim had tired her.

Talorc and Runa stood side by side, watching as the rest of the survivors appeared out of the fog. Talorc guessed that less than half of those who set out had returned.

'We need to make fires,' said Runa. 'And we need herb-wives to tend to the wounded.'

'I'll go and find a herb-wife. There might be one in the village. You should stay here. Show the people you are alive and unhurt.'

Runa nodded distractedly. Talorc knew she was thinking of her father. In the aftermath of the attack they had found him aboard one of the surviving curraghs with several other injured Orkadi. He wasn't bleeding but his leg was hurt and he didn't have the strength to swim back. Talorc had noticed how it distressed the wounded Orkadi to see their king injured, even if it wasn't badly. There were stories of how the kings of Anga's house could turn into giant boars in battle. If the wounded men and women in the boat had believed such stories before, they didn't believe them now.

Talorc returned alone from the village to see the beach transformed. All of the survivors were now back on the beach, he guessed. They were gathered in clusters around wounded men and women or sat talking in circles around driftwood fires. Talorc spotted Anga limping through the throng with the aid of a staff, shouting orders as Runa trailed behind him. He crossed the beach and caught up with them.

'We should attack again,' Runa was saying to her father's back as he limped through the throng. 'Salvage what boats we can, gather up everyone still able to fight. They won't be expecting it –'

Anga turned and took hold of Runa's shoulder, bringing his face close to hers. 'Do you want to know what I expect, Runa?' he hissed.

Talorc glanced around. Every conversation nearby had ceased. Some pretended not to be listening; others stared openly.

'I expect my daughter, the future queen, not to question my decisions before my people.'

Father and daughter glowered silently at one another. Talorc scanned the faces of the watching Orkadi. A few were watching

Anga with anger in their eyes.

Talorc understood then what decision Anga had made.

He had sent for the seven sacrifices.

Somewhere within Talorc a fire went out, making all the world colder and darker.

Anga turned and limped away. Runa stood and watched him go.

'Runa,' Talorc said.

She turned to face him. 'Did you find a herb-wife?' she asked.

'No,' he said. 'Apparently there's one in a village nearby. They've sent a boy to get her.'

Runa nodded.

Talorc jerked his head in the direction of the water. They left the throng of Orkadi and walked to the shore, where Runa turned to face him.

'He did it?' asked Talorc.

Runa slowly nodded. 'He sent guardians out to find them and bring them back to Gurn. Some should return today, others to-morrow. Tomorrow night they'll be sacrificed.'

'Do you really think he's wrong?' asked Talorc.

'He always told me that being a ruler is the worst fate in the world, though everyone thinks it's the best. Sooner or later you will have to look at your people and decide who lives and who dies. It's an impossible choice, but you have to make it. It's what his father taught him, and his father taught him. Now he has to decide; to sacrifice seven Orkadi, or a whole island. When you think of it like that, there is only one decision to make. But I hate it.'

'I think some would rather he refused Mordak,' said Talorc.

'And some would rather he didn't,' said Runa.

'What would you have done?'

Runa shivered, hugging herself as she looked out to sea. 'Maybe I wouldn't have let it come to this,' she said. 'Maybe I would have killed them all, long ago.'

The party from Gurn left the beach that afternoon. Derran stayed on at Otter Bay to supervise the camp and the return of the islanders to their homes. Local survivors had already begun ferrying Orkadi to other islands, returning to pick up more passengers. Those who could not travel were put up in nearby villages, as well as those too afraid to go back out on the water.

The king limped ahead of the group, unable to help carry a curragh but seemingly determined not to slow them down. They returned to Ork Island the way they had come, reaching the beach at Gurn in the last light of day. In silence they had crossed the water; in silence they walked up the path to the keep.

Haldan the smith was at the gate. It had been decided one man would be needed to stand guard there, despite Haldan's protests. He called to Kretta, who emerged from the house she now shared with Sariad. Both were clearly shocked to see Anga injured but relieved to see them back and safe.

'Are any of them here yet?' asked Anga.

Kretta's smile faded. 'Two. The guardians are with them in the house there,' she said, pointing to one of the dwellings kept for visiting headmen. Talorc realised after a moment whom they were talking about. The sacrifices.

Anga looked towards the house. Talorc knew what he was thinking. Should he go and speak to them now or later? What would they say to him? What would he say to them?

'See that they're looked after,' he said eventually. Without another word he limped away towards the broch. The guardians dispersed to their rest-houses while Runa stared after her father.

'Runa,' said Talorc. 'We need to go and see Sariad.'

It was warm within Kretta and Haldan's house, the peat fire

crackling in the centre of the room, its sweet smoke filling the air. After so much chaos and bloodshed, the quiet, cosy little house felt like another world.

'Sariad?' said Runa as she skirted the fire, Talorc behind her. 'It's us. Runa and Talorc.'

Sariad was sat on the straw in the far left corner of the room, surrounded by a menagerie of skulls.

'Can we sit down?' asked Runa. Sariad nodded and they sat, careful not to touch any of her skulls. Talorc noticed that though she no longer flinched when they came near, her body still tensed as if anticipating an attack.

'You're alive,' said Sariad. 'I'm glad you're alive.'

The last time Talorc had seen Sariad was on the morning of their departure for Calag. It had warmed him to see that Sariad had allowed Kretta to clean some of the dirt off her and wash her matted hair, though doing so revealed further layers of scars which Talorc winced to see. He and Runa had explained the king's plan to Sariad. She hadn't liked it. Even if the Azawan was far away hunting, she warned them, the fins would spot them coming.

'We're alive,' said Runa. Talorc noticed how gently Runa spoke to Sariad. He liked it. 'Many are not. You were right; they knew we were coming.' Runa told her of the shark attack. 'The sunsharks could have killed us all, but they left suddenly. I don't know why.'

Sariad stared past them as if witnessing the tale play itself out among the fire smoke. 'I wish you hadn't gone,' she said, her voice barely more than a whisper. 'But at least they cannot enslave the dead.'

'No-one will be a slave,' said Runa, trying to sound like she meant it and failing.

'But your father is going to obey Mordak,' said Sariad. 'He's going to sacrifice people to the Azawan. I'm not reading your mind,' she added, seeing the worried look on Runa's face. 'I can hold back if I want to.'

'Yes,' said Runa. 'Some are already here. He will give them to the Azawan on Sevenday. Tomorrow.'

Sariad picked up a skull and stroked it while Talorc and Runa watched her. Talorc could see in her eyes that she was remembering when Mordak possessed her and gave her the names of the sacrifices. Did she blame herself for their coming deaths? Was all this his fault, and Runa's, for going to her and asking her to dive for them?

'I don't know how he could have done it,' said Sariad.

'Done what?' said Talorc.

'The spell. Possessed the sharks all at once. I don't know where he could have found a spell to do that.'

'What do you mean, found?' asked Runa.

'Fin magic isn't like speying. Speys learn their spells from skulls. Divers find them. They believe that long ago, all fins were divers. Those fins are called the First Fathers. Every word they said was a spell; whatever they willed, they had only to say it. Fins believe that every spell the First Fathers spoke remains in the sea, like the ripples from a pebble. When a diver dives, he sends his spirit out into the sea, searching for the ripples of those ancient spells.'

'So Mordak found a new spell? One which let him control the sharks?'

'He could already control living things, though not so many, not controlling their movements like that. But yes, he must have new spells now, of course. To do that... and to summon the Azawan.' She shook her head. 'He talked about it for so long.'

'What exactly did he say?' asked Runa, her eyes fixed on Sariad.

'He would sit with the other divers and talk about spells. Eventually he would always start talking about the Azawan. He would tell a story his master told him, and his master told him, and so on.

'The legend was that on the Fire Island in the north, where the ground burns and steam rises from the river-water, an

Azawan once lived deep within the earth. It was the heat from the Azawan that gave the island its nature and name. There were fin colonies there, the story said, and their divers were said to be the most powerful anywhere. Long ago, one of those divers, Katla, found the spell that would summon the Azawan out of the ground.

'Katla succeeded in performing the spell. The Azawan emerged from the earth in a vast explosion. Fire-rivers poured across the island and into the sea. Ash rose into the air, enough to darken the sky, all the way east to Trollheim and south to Skoll.'

'The black sky,' said Runa. 'Our people thought the speys caused it.'

'I didn't know if the story was true, or just another of the legends that the divers told,' said Sariad. 'I suppose it must have been true.'

'So what happened after the Azawan emerged?' asked Runa.

'Katla lost control of it. His mind broke, the spell broke with it and the Azawan disappeared into the deep. Some say that when Katla lost his mind the spell was lost too. Others say that he had already passed it to one of his apprentices, and that it is held by the fins there to this day.'

'Either way, Mordak found it,' said Talorc.

'How?' asked Runa.

'He used to talk about travelling to the Fire Island. Searching the waters for the spell, or if the divers there knew it, taking it from them.'

'How?' asked Talorc.

'By fighting them and eating their brains. That's how divers take spells from one another. He talked about it for so many years but never did it. I stopped believing him.'

They all flinched as the door creaked open.

'Sariad? It's me,' said Kretta, stooping as she entered. She looked between Talorc and Runa. 'The king wants you both in his chamber. He's going to address the sacrifices.'

Talorc lingered at the edge of the chamber as Runa went to stand beside her father.

Anga was sitting in his chair, his crutch leaning against it. Across the fire from him were three men and one woman. Two guardians stood by the door; Talorc guessed they were there in case the sacrifices tried to escape.

The king took hold of his crutch and rose to his feet.

'Orkadi,' he addressed them. 'These last days have been the most terrible I have known. I have seen our people burned alive. I have seen men and women torn into pieces, the sea red with their blood. I have looked into the eyes of a monster.

'I would rather face a hundred of these monsters than stand here before you, and ask what I ask of you.'

Anga fell silent. Was he waiting for an answer or did he not know what to say?

'The thing is,' said a tall, bald-headed man with a crooked nose, 'you're not asking us, are you? You're telling us that come tomorrow you're going to feed us to this creature.'

'A poor choice of words,' said Anga after a pause. 'You are right. I do not ask. I command, as is my right and duty as king. I do not wish for any of you to die. But if I do not do this, the Orkadi will be gone from the world before midwinter.'

'And this way,' said the man, 'we will be gone from the world after midwinter. Which is so much better, isn't it?'

'That's the king you're talking to!' said the woman. 'Show some respect!'

'Why? He's going to feed us to the Azawan tomorrow.'

'I am not happy,' said Anga, his face thunderous. 'I am anything but happy. I have done everything I can to avert this. I led the charge against the Azawan at Skate. I stood face to face with it. I pardoned the speys, the enemies of my ancestors, and let them attack the fins; I led our people in the attack on Fin Island

_'

'And you failed,' said the crooked-nosed man.

The other sacrifices moved away from him. Talorc realised they were expecting the king to strike him. Runa looked ready to do so.

'Yes,' said Anga. The look of fury was gone from his face. He looked defeated, like a broken-winged bird awaiting death in the winter snows. 'I failed.'

'You are not fit to rule,' said the crooked-nosed man.

The look of defeat on Anga's face disappeared as swiftly as it had come.

'My father is fit to rule,' said Runa, stepping forward. 'And you would do well to watch your tongue. You will not meet the Azawan until tomorrow evening; that is plenty of time to teach you some manners.'

'Runa,' said Anga, raising a hand. She stepped back, still glowering at the man.

'You heard the king,' said one of the other men. 'He doesn't want this. He's tried everything. Can you think of anything else he could do? I don't want to die any more than you do, but I'd feed myself to the Azawan ten times over if it meant saving my grandchildren, even for a while.'

'No, I don't know a better way,' said crooked-nose. 'But I'm not the king.'

'I'm not afraid to die for my family and my village,' said the man who had not yet spoken. 'I'm no coward, and besides, I've nothing left to look forward to but rotting teeth and aching bones. But all the same, sire, I'd say no to the fins.' He cleared his throat to spit but caught himself in time. 'If the Orkadi's days are numbered, and if our tale ever gets told, I'd want the senachais to say we refused the fins. That we died fighting, however hopeless it was.'

Talorc could see that Anga was moved by the man's words. He suspected the king agreed, but believed he had to buy time for his people in case a way out presented itself, however slim a hope that was.

'There wouldn't be any fins,' said the crooked-nosed man, 'if Valdar, his ancestor, hadn't truced with them. Everyone knows we could have killed them all and had the islands to ourselves, if his ancestor hadn't been a coward and fin-lover.'

Anga had turned a dark shade of red. The two men stared at one another; the crooked-nosed man seemed to be goading the king to strike him. Talorc wondered if the old man was enjoying this in a strange way; revelling in having the freedom and power to mock a king.

Breaking off from the contest of stares, Anga looked at one of the guardians who stood by the door.

'See that they're well fed,' he said. 'See that they don't escape.'

With that the king limped past the sacrifices and out of the door.

CHAPTER TWENTY FOUR

The wind tried to force them back but they refused.

Anga rode at the head of the party, Runa behind him. Derran had suggested that Talorc not ride with Runa, as people may draw inappropriate conclusions. It had taken Talorc a while to understand what that meant; when he did, Talorc found himself laughing aloud. Surely no-one could ever think that.

So Talorc walked at the rear of the procession, before the guardians and behind the sacrifices, with only Anga and Runa riding up front. They set off into the shrieking wind mid-afternoon. The days were darkening as winter drew closer and the sun rose lower each day. Soon each day would be only a flickering of light between the long expanses of storm-lashed darkness.

From Gurn to Skate, each time they passed near a dwelling, Orkadi would come out to watch them pass. Standing there wrapped in their sealskin cloaks, they stared at the procession; some with sadness in their eyes, others with anger, even hatred. Talorc looked over the heads of the sacrifices, watching Runa's back, praying that the Sea Mother give her strength.

Talorc had slept most of the morning. Rising, he had left the crowded dwelling he shared with the guardians and gone to find to Runa, only to learnt that she had had left to visit the tombs of her ancestors. It hurt that she had gone without him, even though there was no reason for her do otherwise. But with Runa gone, he could speak to Sariad alone.

Quietly entering Kretta and Haldan's hut, he found Sariad sat in the peat-scented, fire-lit room, staring into the fire. He sat down across the fire from her and waited to be acknowledged.

Suddenly she had looked up at him, her gaze as sharp as knives.

'You have awoken,' she said.

Talorc nodded.

'How?' asked Sariad.

'Look and see.'

Talorc held Sariad's gaze as she searched his mind.

'Danger,' she said. 'You have been in danger before, but it was the threat to the one you care for that changed you.'

'But I've seen Runa hurt before. I've hurt her myself –'

'Yet this time you were in the water. It took the water to awaken your magic.'

'So it's true. I have fin magic. I'm a diver.'

A smile hovered around Sariad's lips. 'Yes.'

'Did you know?' asked Talorc.

'When you came here yesterday? Yes. You wear it like a second skin.'

'No. I mean, before. When we met.'

'I sensed the potential. But it was not my place to say.'

Talorc looked into the flames. So it was true. He had magic. But it was fin-magic, to go with his fin-feet.

'Why do I have fin magic?' he asked Sariad.

'Mordak wanted to understand why dries have it. He never could, and neither have I.'

'Perhaps it is a gift from the Sea Mother,' said Talorc.

Sariad laughed. 'Gift?' she said, her expression hardening. 'You call what happened to me a gift?'

'No, I...' Talorc fumbled for words. 'I don't mean what happened to you. But for us to have this power –'

'Power is not a gift,' said Sariad. 'It is a curse. If you don't be-

173

lieve me, ask Anga. Ask him if it is a gift or a curse to send inno-
cent men and women to their deaths. Ask the speys if it is a gift
to have a power that you can be killed for using. Or better yet,
look into my mind. Search my memories and tell me if power is
a gift or a curse.'

'If it is a curse... then why? Why does the Sea Mother curse
us?'

'Why wouldn't she? The Sea Mother is not kind. She does not
love us nor hate us. Neither does she love or hate sunsharks, or
eagles, or finfolk. The Orkadi believe she favours us, yet the Orkadi suffer and die. The finfolk pray and sacrifice to her, yet they
suffer and die just as we do. She is not like us. She gifts us, she
curses us, and we will never understand why.'

'I never understood my mother,' said Talorc. 'She risked her
life by keeping me alive, then acted like she wished I was dead.'

'And mine tried to kill me,' said Sariad. 'Yet I still pined for
her, years after the fins took me. I loved her and I hated her. I
loved and hated the Sea Mother, until I realised that I might as
well love and hate the sea. She is like the sea. She is just there.
Maybe one day someone will take her place. I would like to do
that. I would gift those that deserve it, and curse those that deserve it.'

'Maybe it us up to us,' said Talorc, 'whether our powers are a
gift or a curse.'

'You think I don't understand how you feel,' said Sariad. 'You
have awoken to your power. You can do things no-one else can.
You feel special. The world is shifting around you as you realise you can make things happen, instead of things happening
to you. Everything seems possible. If only Sariad could let go
of the past, you say to yourself, gather her courage and start
searching for ways to defeat Mordak.

'Talorc, I know you have faith in me, and are beginning to
have faith in yourself. But it is not enough. Our enemy is Mordak. He is the greatest diver to have awoken in generations; he is
cruel and cunning and has an Azawan at his command.'

'So you have given up?' asked Talorc.

'I am searching for my courage.' Sariad looked away and Talorc knew it was time for him to go.

'I hope you find it,' he said as he stood to leave. 'Soon.'

At Skate they met the guardians who had been sent ahead. Seven stakes had been erected upon the sand. The burnt broch watched over the bay like a spirit cursed never to sleep.

The sacrifices were led to the stakes, one guardian leading each of the seven. They stood with their backs against the wood as the guardians wound and then knotted thick lengths of rope around them.

That done, the guardians stood back. Anga walked out before the sacrifices.

'I will not speak useless words,' said Anga. 'You know you have the gratitude of our people. If that means nothing to you, so be it. But it is there.'

The crooked-nosed man spat at Anga's feet.

The king gave the man a long look. Talorc guessed he was furiously debating the best response. He could not afford to appear weak by letting such a thing go unpunished; yet he did not wish to be cruel or give in to temper.

'Just promise us you'll beat it, sire,' said one of the men.

'He can't promise that. He can only say he'll try,' said the woman.

Anga opened his mouth to speak when a shout came from the dunes.

Talorc looked up. Orkadi lined the dunes from east to west; men, women and children. The shouting was spreading among them, and a moment later he knew why. Not because he saw what they saw from their vantage point, but because a shudder ran through him, a terrible knowing, as it had done when he touched the sea-wolf; only far, far stronger.

Tendrils of his new sense extended out of his body. Towards the sea they went, where something hammered against them, making him stagger and fall to the ground.

There was shouting and screaming everywhere. Runa was lifting him to his feet, dragging him across the sand. Her heart hammered inside her chest, blood surged through her and her thoughts poured into his. Fear threatened to swallow her but she held out, as always.

'Talorc! Stand up!'

A slap across the face brought him to his senses. He took control of his feet. Runa and he were the only ones left on the beach. The guardians had run for the safety of the dunes. Where was Anga?

Talorc turned round and saw him.

The king stood on the sand between Talorc and the sacrifices. Anga turned and shouted, ordering Runa to retreat. Talorc could hardly hear him over the shrieking wind and the surging waves of boiling, hissing water.

Another slap from Runa. 'Back!' she shouted, and this time he obeyed. They ran for the dunes, climbed up among the waiting guardians and turned to watch.

Somehow Talorc understood that he had to draw his tendrils in close to himself, wrapping them tightly about him as if they were armour. If not, his awareness of the Azawan would overpower him. He would drown in its heat, its hatred, its hunger and fury. So he shielded himself in a way he couldn't explain, any more than he could have explained colour to one who lived in darkness.

It worked. Though the Azawan's presence battered against his mind as it drew closer, it didn't overpower him. Sweating as other Orkadi shivered with cold and fear, Talorc watched the waves come crashing against the bay. He watched those same waves bubble over, smoke rising from them as if the sea were one enormous boiling pot. The waves grew taller and taller, came faster and faster, drawing close to the sacrifices.

The Azawan had come.

Fresh screams erupted as it rose out of the sea, snaking high into the night sky, golden-eyed and glittering. There its head hovered, shifting as the Azawan looked about itself.

At the sacrifices upon the sand. At the terrified mass of Orkadi upon the dunes.

It screamed.

The moment its scream burst from its mouth, Talorc knew with sickening certainty that his armour was not enough. He fell to the ground with the rest of the Orkadi and clung on only a moment before being dragged into nightmare.

He came to with Runa pouring seawater over him.

She helped him to sit up. Looking around, his vision spinning and his head pounding, he saw that the Orkadi were gone. So were the sacrifices. All that remained were the charred, broken stumps of the stakes.

'Where... where is your father?' said Talorc, struggling to speak.

'He went back with the guardians. I said I would bring you back.'

It dawned on Talorc that it was morning.

'How long was I...'

'All night,' said Runa.

Talorc stared at her.

'You looked like you were dead. Your eyes were open, you weren't moving. But you were hot and your heart was beating.' She hesitated. 'There was a spey here. She said she was a herb-wife, but I recognised her from Groda. She said it was the Azawan-scream that did it to you. That it affected you more than everyone else, though she didn't know why. Or, she didn't say why.'

Talorc realised from the way Runa was looking at him that

she knew he was keeping a secret. It was time to tell her.

'I've been diving,' he said. 'It happened when the sunsharks attacked the fleet. I saw a shark heading for you and I just… exploded. I could feel everything going on in the sea. When the Azawan came last night, I could feel it coming before it arrived.'

'An ordeal,' said Runa. 'That's what Skelda called it. When something terrible happens to a spey, and their speying breaks out of them. Maybe it's the same for divers.'

Talorc nodded.

'There's more,' he said. 'When it screamed… do you remember what your father said? About when it screamed at him the last time we were here?'

Runa nodded.

'I went there. Into that place where everything was hatred and torment, pain and fire.' Runa looked aghast. 'But… I wasn't scared. I knew it wasn't real. Mordak was in my mind, twisting and poisoning it. All those things I felt are what he wants us to feel, because he is so full of pain and hatred.' Talorc smiled. 'And there was something else. All that I saw there, I knew it was a dream, or like a story told by a senachai. Only I didn't believe in the story, and I knew Mordak was the one telling it. Instead of paying attention to the story, I looked at him. He was there, Runa, in everything. I could see into his mind.'

Talorc's grin grew wider as he looked into Runa's eyes. 'He thinks he has won. Now that we've given him the sacrifices, he thinks it's just a matter of time.'

'Isn't it?' asked Runa.

'No,' said Talorc. 'Because I know what we have to do now.'

'What's that?'

'We have to go to Fin Island,' said Talorc, 'tonight. I'm going to get us to Mordak, and you're going to kill him.'

CHAPTER
TWENTY FIVE

'What are you talking about?' asked Runa.

'We can do it,' said Talorc. 'The two of us together. We can find Mordak and kill him. Remember what Sariad said. The diver who first summoned the Azawan lost control of it when he lost his mind. If we kill Mordak, the Azawan won't be under his control anymore. It will leave Orka.'

'But how are we even going to find Mordak, let alone kill him?'

'I think he's on Fin Island. I can't be sure,' said Talorc.

'What do you mean, you can't be sure? How could you have any idea where he is?' said Runa.

'Because I saw him. I mean, I didn't see him, but I sensed him. When I was in the nightmare place. He was feeling relaxed, happy that he'd beaten us. It felt like he was at home. So I think he's on Fin Island.'

'And how are we going to get to Fin Island?'

'We'll need to leave now,' said Talorc. 'Row over to Calag. Wait for nightfall if we make it over before then. Once it gets dark we'll make the crossing.'

'Wonderful,' said Runa. 'Since we avoided getting ripped to pieces by sharks last time, we'll go back to give them a second chance.'

'There won't be any sharks. Sariad said the shark spell took lots of power. He won't have them swimming about watching for us when he doesn't know we're coming.'

'He might expect us to attack again.'

'He doesn't.'

Runa was quiet. 'Alright. Say there aren't any sharks waiting for us in the water. The fins are at war. They must be guarding their island somehow, no matter how confident their sorcerer is.'

'Probably,' said Talorc. 'While we're crossing I'll dive and search for fins. We'll steer away from any fins I sense until we find a safe place to land. Once we get there, I'll do the same thing again. We'll search the island under cover of darkness until I sense Mordak. Hopefully he'll be sleeping.'

'Hopefully,' said Runa. 'And then I'll stick a knife in him, and that will be that. It almost sounds like you don't need me.'

'I hope I won't need you,' said Talorc. 'I wish I didn't need you. But if something goes wrong, I'll need someone with me who can fight.'

'And who can murder a sorcerer while he sleeps,' said Runa.

'Am I going alone?' asked Talorc.

'You're planning to sneak up on Mordak. Are you really so confident in your diving already?' asked Runa.

'No. But I have to try.'

Runa looked away. Talorc followed her gaze, across the sand towards the broken stakes.

'We'll need a boat,' she said.

The crossing to Calag took all day. Talorc noticed it was getting easier each time; he noticed too that his muscles looked bigger than before. Maybe if Jed could attack him now, it would be an even contest.

As they crossed the sound, Talorc had ample time to observe each island he passed. He saw the same things everywhere; fields of barley and corn, black and brown cattle, herds of hogs. Some farmers had cleared the fields and brought the harvest in; others left stacks of grain out to dry in the wind. From a distance the lives of the Orkadi looked peaceful, unchanging. But some of the people he saw must have been at Otter Bay. If they hadn't been there themselves, they would at least know people who died in the mouths of the sharks. Their lives could be filled with all kinds of suffering.

Yet they had families. They knew the end of their days was coming, but until then, they would live with people that loved them. When the work of the harvest was done, as they awaited the call to feed the Azawan, they would sit by their hearth-fires, listening to tales in the warmth, eating and drinking and enjoying everything that was good in life. Perhaps they would enjoy life all the more, knowing death was coming.

Did he envy them? No. That life wasn't for him. He knew now that it never had been, either before the Azawan came or since. His future might be death, or slavery, or something else he couldn't see; but it wasn't a home, a family, a farm. The Azawan came, and he had been cut away from that world, as the cord was cut from the belly of a newborn. He had no mother other than the Sea Mother. That could be a blessing, or a curse.

They stopped on the island of Edda to rest and replenish their waterskins. Taking turns to sleep, they kept a lookout, ready to row away if any islanders came by; their faces were too well known. That meant going without food, but it couldn't be helped.

The sea remained calm as they rowed north up the sound between Edda and Calag, before turning northeast to follow Calag's northern shore. Talorc continued to observe the islands, but more and more often he found his eyes on Runa.

She hadn't said a word to him the whole way, but he knew she wasn't angry. Just quiet. Probably thinking about what would happen if she died tonight. If they succeeded, and she lived, would she still want him around?

Runa turned and met Talorc's eyes. He knew a tremor of fear, as if she might have heard everything he was thinking.

'What's wrong?' said Runa.

'Nothing. I'm just thinking about tonight.'

'And?'

'I don't want you to get hurt.'

Runa narrowed her eyes. 'I'll be fine,' she said. 'And if I'm not… my father will find another way.'

'I know,' said Talorc, though he wasn't sure if he did. 'I just mean, well, I appreciate you trusting me enough to come with me.'

'You're risking your life doing this. Why shouldn't I?'

'Because you have a life. You have your father, your people. If you survive this you'll marry one day –'

'I'll marry someone I've never met. A prince of a Skollish clan my father wants to make an alliance with.'

'You… you already know who you're going to marry?'

'His name's Math. I've already met him, apparently, when we visited his court. I was five. I don't remember him, although apparently he cried when I beat him at wrestling. But I'm going to marry him. His clan is powerful. The alliance will help keep Orka safe.' She gave a humourless grin. 'If there is an Orka left.'

Runa took a swig from the waterskin, handed it to Talorc and took up oars again. Talorc did the same, wondering why he suddenly felt so cold.

'You think this will work?' asked Runa.

'I do and I don't,' said Talorc.

After a moment Runa smiled. 'Me too.'

Talorc smiled back at her. They had reached the the north-western tip of Calag, pulled up in a cove and lain down to rest among some dune-grass. Both of them were tired and ravenously hungry. Yet Talorc saw a gleam in Runa's eyes, that said she was thinking what he was thinking.

This could be it. Tonight, they could end the war.

Again, Runa took her dagger from its sheath and ran the edge against her finger. She had lost her sword in the assault on Fin Island. He had made it back with the one she gave him and now it hung at her waist.

'We should sleep awhile before dark,' said Runa. 'But I know I won't sleep.'

'Me neither.'

Talorc went back to watching the evening sky darken. They would wait until it was fully dark before commencing the crossing. The first stars came out and he wondered if they were watching him and Runa, waiting to see if they would survive.

'Do you know any stories about the stars?' asked Runa.

Talorc smiled. 'Lots. My Grunna loved star tales.'

'Tell me one.'

Talorc thought for a moment. 'Well, they say that a long time ago in Skoll, there was a girl, the daughter of a clan chief, who was out among the hills, picking berries, when she met a man she didn't recognise. They fell in love straight away, and she went to live with him in his cave. But when she got there she discovered he was a bear, who could take off his bear-skin and was a man underneath.'

'Like silkies,' said Runa.

'Yes, like silkies,' said Talorc. 'They lived as man and wife in the cave, and had a child. Their son was born as a bear, but he could take off his skin and be a boy when he wanted.

'The family lived happily for years, but one day they were seen by a group of hunters from the girl's clan. The hunters chased the family to a cave, then lit a fire in the entrance to smoke out the bear, whom they thought had kidnapped the girl.

'The bear-man said to his wife that he wouldn't kill her people, but neither would he suffer to be killed by the hand of man. So he took the spear that his wife carried and ran it through his own heart. He fell down dead, and the girl and her son went home with the hunters, to the clan. Her son became chief, and that clan became the Bear Clan, who rule Skoll. The bear's spirit was carried by the smoke of the fire, up into the sky, and became the bear you can see among the stars.'

The story finished, they lay in silence, watching as the star-bear slowly revealed itself.

'I've never heard that story before,' said Runa eventually.

'Did you like it?'

'Math is the prince of the Bear Clan. It reminded me of him.'

'Oh,' said Talorc.

They sat in silence.

'Tell me a silkie story. One I won't have heard,' said Runa eventually.

Talorc thought. 'There's one I always liked, though I don't know why.'

'Long ago in Orka, before the Age of Kings, a young woman, who wasn't married, was crossing from Fior to Ork to visit her friend.

'This woman had got into her skin-boat and set off in the morning, praying to the Sea Mother for a safe crossing, though there seemed little need of it, for the crossing is short and the day was fair.

'As she rowed, she saw a man waving from a skerry. At first she thought he was waving hello, and she waved back. But then she realised she couldn't see a boat, and that this man must be stranded. That's why he was waving; he needed rescuing.

'She rowed over and waited for him to come down to the boat, but instead he called her to join him on the rocks. So she landed and walked up to him, and when she looked into his eyes, she fell in love, faster than her eyes could blink.'

'He was a silkie,' said Runa.

'Yes,' said Talorc.

'And he loved her and took her away, just like in the last story, but people didn't like it, just like in the last story. These stories are all the same.'

'No, this one's different,' said Talorc. 'I mean, yes, you're right, but the ending is different. The boy's father, the Silkie King, comes to see the girl's father. Says his people are not happy about it, and by their law the two must be put to death, and he wants to know if the father will agree to it. He does, and the lovers are led to those skerries. Both their families come to watch. Two silkie men approach the man, take his skin away; they burn it as he screams, then take the two of them underwater to drown them.'

'That's horrible,' said Runa.

'I know. But the thing is, they don't drown. Eventually the two silkie men surface, and when everyone asks where the bodies are, they say that some strange creatures came and took the lovers away from them. The creatures claimed they were Silvers, servants of the Sea Mother, and the two lovers had been chosen to serve her in her caves. The silkies wouldn't disobey the Sea Mother, so they let the pair go, and they were never seen again.'

'What did the Silvers look like?' asked Runa.

'Like dolphins. But they weren't dolphins.'

'I like that,' she said. 'Usually it just ends with the human becoming a silkie and the pair of them swimming off into the sunset together. How many stories do you know?'

'I've never counted. I don't know if I could count that high. Grunna was always telling me them.'

'Was she training you? To become a senachai, like her?'

'Maybe she would have done. But I was never going to be allowed to leave the island. I wasn't allowed on a boat, or in the water, because of my feet. So I couldn't be a senachai.'

'There's no-one telling you that now. If we survive this you could do it. You could build a boat, travel anywhere you wanted with your Grunna's stories. Skoll, the Fangs, Aira, Trollheim.'

'Maybe,' said Talorc. 'If we survive.'

'That's what I would do,' said Runa. 'If my father wasn't king. I would go to all those places.'

'You wouldn't want to live in Orka?'

'Of course I would. But I'd want to see other places, do other things first.' A smile danced about her lips. 'A senachai came to Gurn from Skoll once. He said there is a training school for warriors on an island to the west of his homeland. It is hidden, but if you can find it, you can study there. They say the woman who runs it is a witch as well as a warrior. I think I would like to go and train there.' Runa sat up. 'Do you think it's dark enough yet?'

'Yes,' said Talorc. They stood.

'We're going to Fin Island,' said Runa. 'The two of us. To kill a sorcerer. Are we crazy?'

Talorc took a deep breath and exhaled. 'Lets find out.'

CHAPTER TWENTY SIX

'This is close enough,' said Talorc.

They ceased rowing and pulled in the oars.

'So what are you going to do?' asked Runa, turning towards Talorc and drawing her cloak around her. The air was thin and dagger-sharp.

'I'm going to dive.'

'How?'

'I'm not sure.'

'What?'

'I dived before. When the sharks attacked us… and I think before that, too. It just happened.'

'Right. Well, can you make it just happen now?'

'I hope so.'

Runa rolled her eyes as Talorc turned towards Fin Island and stared upwards.

'Look,' he said.

The children of the night were dancing in the northern sky. They leapt and whirled amid the stars; brilliant rivers of orange and green, yellow and purple and colours he knew no name for. It was the first time Talorc had seen them dance since last winter. It made his heart glad.

He closed his eyes and imagined the tendrils of his new sense, like the limbs of an octopus, wrapped around him just as he had left them at Skate the previous evening. Now he saw them extending themselves out into the water, stretching out, searching for life.

Nothing.

He extended them further, far out into the sea. Was there anything there? In his mind's eye he pictured the water, watched for any glimmer of a life-form; fish, seal or shark.

Still nothing. Was it because the sea was empty, all its creatures having fled the Azawan? He didn't believe it. At least he should be able to sense the water, its ebb and flow, the deep currents, the way he had on the last crossing. He had been in the water himself, that time; but if he tried to swim now he would freeze.

It was no good. Talorc pulled his tendrils back into himself and opened his eyes. Sariad might be able to dive while out of the water but he couldn't. What was he going to do?

He thought back over the time in the bone-house when he had watched Sariad dive. She had simply closed her eyes and sang and it seemed to just happen. She had been trained, though, and he didn't know how to sing like that…

The flute!

He reached into his pocket and pulled out Grunna's flute, remembering the night he had spent under the boat, hiding from Mordak. He had played his flute, the dolphins had come and in the morning his skin was healed.

Talorc put the carved length of bone to his lips, set his fingers in place and softly began to play.

Instantly he felt his tendrils uncurl. They reached unbidden towards the water, and as part of Talorc sat in the curragh, playing Grunna's bone flute, another part of him shot through the sea.

There was no mistaking it. He could feel the currents of the water; he could see the seabed far below. There was movement, too. Life. Quick as thought he leapt forward, into the mind of a seal. Its thoughts were full of fish, and a hungry pup back on the shore, keening for mother and milk. Talorc left the seal, and found nearby the shoal of fish it was headed for. He journeyed on, leaping from dark water to fish to mother seal to dark water again, until he sensed land.

Fin Island.

Wary of danger, Talorc slowed and began to move carefully through the shallow water surrounding the island. He sensed no life-forms other than the ordinary inhabitants of the sea. The way ahead was clear.

Now for the hard part.

Talorc moved his awareness out of the water, up onto the shore. Instantly he felt the sea tugging at him, as if he were a sea creature that could not live on land. He fought the tug, forcing himself forward, back and forth along the beach and then the grass beyond.

Nothing. He sensed nothing alive.

Talorc returned his awareness to his body. He opened his eyes and lifted his lips from the flute. Strange; he had never realised how constraining a body could be, how cumbersome and awkward, like outgrown clothes.

'Well?' said Runa when he turned to face her.

'I didn't sense any fins in the water,' said Talorc.

'Good.'

'And none on the shore either. Or close to the shore.'

Runa frowned. 'You're sure you know how to sense fins?'

'No.'

Runa sighed. 'So what now?'

'They might not live on the south side of the island,' said Talorc. 'It was harder to dive when I tried to move away from the sea, so I can't tell for sure from here. Once we're on the island I could try again.'

'It doesn't make sense,' said Runa. 'They fought us for land even when they lived on every island in Orka. Fin Island is tiny, my father says, so there should be dwellings all across it. Something is wrong.'

'Do you want to keep going?' asked Talorc.

'I'm not turning back.'

They took out the oars again and began rowing, taking care to go as quietly as possible. There was neither wind nor fog to cover their approach.

When Talorc turned and saw Fin Island, he whispered to Runa to go slower. Wincing at every sound, they brought the curragh up to the shore.

The keel hit sand. Stowing the oars, they climbed out onto the pale sand.

'Are you going to dive?' whispered Runa, her hand on her sword hilt.

'Not yet. We'll go inshore a bit then I'll try again.'

Runa nodded. She withdrew her dagger from its sheath. 'Take this.'

Talorc took it. 'Thanks.'

'Don't lose it.'

They headed inshore, Runa going first. The island seemed to be almost totally flat, and Talorc could make out no sign of hills ahead. Above them, the night's children danced through the darkness.

Runa stopped. Talorc came to stand at her side.

Houses.

They weren't made of stone like the ones he knew. In the darkness he could only make out their shape; the houses narrowed from the base and were pointed at the top. Of course. They weren't houses. They were tents.

The Orkadi of old made their homes not from stone but skin. Sealskin, whaleskin even. That was before the sky turned dark and the air grew colder, the winds fiercer.

Grunna had sketched the tents in the ash for him when she taught him stories of the first Orkadi. The fins still lived that way.

But where were the fins?

'I'm going to try again,' said Talorc.

'They'll hear you.'

'Lets move back then.'

They retreated until Talorc was sure he wouldn't be heard. Sitting, he lay Runa's dagger down, took the flute from his pocket and began to play as quietly as he could.

It was harder than at sea, much harder; but he was able to reach out, towards the tents...

Nothing. They were empty. Almost...

Talorc drew himself back, put away the flute and took up the knife again. 'They're empty.'

'Are you sure?' asked Runa.

'No.'

'I'm going to stop asking you that.'

'I can't be sure of anything to do with diving,' said Talorc. 'But I sensed life. There were rats there. I couldn't go into their minds, but I could sense them. If I can sense them, I should be able to sense fins.'

'Alright,' said Runa. 'Lets keep going.'

They passed the cluster of tents, and soon saw more. Talorc dived again; again he sensed nothing but rats, mice, spiders. The same thing happened at the next set of tents, and the next.

'Where are they?' whispered Runa after they had passed seven of the tiny villages.

'They might be gathered somewhere. At a meeting, or a ritual.'

'I don't think so. I think something's wrong,' said Runa.

'So do I.'

'Should we go back?'

'If they've trapped us then going back won't help,' said Talorc.

'You're right. Lets keep going.'

They moved forward more stealthily now, Runa stopping frequently to look about her and listen. The weight of the dagger in Talorc's hand was reassuring.

Stopping to dive, Talorc blew softly into the flute, reached out with his tendrils and saw it.

He didn't just see it. He could hear it, singing like all the whales in the sea; he could feel it pulsing like a great heart that beat for all the world.

Talorc pulled himself back, stuffed the flute into his pocket and picked up the knife. He turned to Runa, who was looking at him with alarm.

'Come with me,' he said, and ran ahead.

Talorc stopped and gazed up in wonder.

It was like the Ancestor Circles on Ork; yet so unlike them.

This Circle towered into the sky. It was made not of stone but of bones; whale-bones, Talorc guessed. Bathed in starlight, the Circle pulled Talorc in like a fish on a hook as the bright dancers whirled through the sky above. Runa was somewhere behind him, whispering urgently, but that hardly seemed to matter.

He entered the Circle. The air around him hummed, spoke to him in voices just beyond his awareness. The Circle knew he was there. It welcomed him.

This was where he could learn to dive.

Talorc turned to Runa, grinning. She had followed him into the Circle and was looking about as if she expected the bones to come alive and attack her.

'What is this place?' she asked.

Talorc was about to answer when he saw Runa's expression change.

'Look out!'

Talorc spun round, cutting at the air with his knife. Too slow. His arm was afire with pain. He dropped the knife; his legs were kicked from under him and he crashed to the ground.

Looming over him was a scaled face; black eyes and rows of jagged teeth.

The fin hissed and lunged at Talorc, its teeth aimed at his throat.

CHAPTER TWENTY SEVEN

Talorc wrapped his hands around the fin's throat.

It hissed and struck at him, scoring his face. Talorc roared with pain as he wrapped his knees around its waist. He pulled it down and to the ground, rolled and brought himself up on top of it.

The fin punched him, making his head spin. Talorc lost his grip and was thrown off the fin and onto the hard earth. The dagger. It was on the grass somewhere. If he could find it....

Too late. The fin had it. Talorc wriggled backwards over the grass as the fin advanced upon him, the dagger in its scaled hand held high.

A kick to its hand from Runa sent the dagger flying.

The fin screeched as she spun out of reach and faced her own opponent again; a spear-wielding fin. The fin used its weapon well; the two of them danced around one another, skilfully striking while evading the other's blows. Runa had only to land a direct blow upon the spear to break it, but the fin seemed to know this. It dodged Runa's attacks rather than blocking them, moving at blinding speed.

And now there were two of them. The fin that had attacked Talorc stalked towards Runa. It retrieved the dagger and held it close, watching Runa, waiting for an opening. The fins were grinning now. They had her.

Or so they thought. As the spear-wielding fin struck at her,

Runa drew back, holding her sword in front of her to deflect the blow. The move left her flank exposed to the dagger-wielding fin. He lunged; just as Runa had expected. She continued to move, spinning round and knocking the dagger from the fin's hand. In the same movement she brought her sword down on the other fin's spear, breaking it in two.

Runa drew back, bringing the two fins together as they advanced towards her, weaponless now, their grins gone. Their was a tight smile on Runa's face. She was alone, but she was armed. She had the advantage.

Or so it seemed, until a fin appeared like a wraith from the darkness behind her. It wrapped an arm around her chest and put a flint knife to her throat.

'Drop it,' said the fin in its harsh, rasping voice.

Runa obeyed. Her sword fell to the ground with a thud.

'Get some cord,' said the knife-wielding fin to the one who had held the spear.

'Why, what do we need cord for? Lets kill them.'

'Not yet. Go.'

The fin hissed and melted into the darkness. Talorc took the chance to study the remaining fins. The one that held the knife to Runa's throat was tall and wore a cloak with scant clothing underneath. Talorc guessed both cloak and clothing were made of fish skin. The other one, who was watching him with teeth bared for any movement, was smaller and wore clothes similarly made, though it wore no cloak. It had amber eyes and wore no boots, showing clearly its long-toed, webbed feet.

The third fin soon returned. It bound Runa's hands behind her back, then Talorc's.

'Bring them to the tent,' said the tall fin. 'They taint this place.'

It turned and walked away out of the Circle. Talorc and Runa followed, the two remaining fins behind them.

They walked north across the island. Talorc almost stumbled and fell several times as he navigated the uneven ground in the darkness. He heard a wheezing sound from behind him that he guessed to be laughter.

Ahead, the leading fin arrived at a tent. It pulled aside the door-flap and ducked to enter. Talorc followed Runa inside.

The tent was as big as Talorc's home. A peat fire burnt in the centre; sleeping places were arrayed around the edges. From the wooden frame hung bundles of dried plants and near the door were stacked spears, hooks and pieces of flint, worked and unworked. At the far side, opposite the door, was a slab of stone with claws and pieces of bone upon it that Talorc took to be a shrine, to the Sea Mother or whatever other god the fins worshipped.

All in all, it wasn't far from what he knew. The fins lived the way the Orkadi of old must have lived.

'Against the wall,' said the bigger fin. Talorc and Runa stood against the wall facing the door flap, between two beds of deer and sealskins.

The three fins faced them. The one who had attacked Talorc bared his teeth and hissed.

'Why don't we just kill them?' it asked.

'Because we need to find out why they are here. More may be coming,' said the tall one.

'Of course more are coming,' said the third, the one who had fought Runa. Their voices were deep and raspy, yet Talorc thought he could detect a difference in tone between their voices. This one and the tall one, he guessed, were female. 'That's why they did it. So they could come here and take our island for themselves.'

'No they didn't,' said the smallest, whom Talorc guessed to be male. 'They did it because they hate us. They fear us,' he said with a grin, looking at Talorc. He moved closer and Talorc tried to stop himself shaking. 'You should fear me,' he said. His breath stank of fish. 'I could kill you before you even knew I'd moved. You dries are so slow.'

'Then why don't you?' said Talorc, forcing himself to meet the fin's eyes.

'Because I told him not to kill you,' said the tall one. 'Yet.'

The male moved back and the tall female came forward. She looked back and forth between the two of them, studying them, sniffing the air. Then she took her knife from her belt and pressed it to Runa's throat.

Runa's eyes bulged but she remained steady.

The tall fin looked at Talorc.

'Tell me now why you came here tonight. Tell me in full and do not lie or I will cut her throat.'

Talorc tried to keep his voice steady. He wanted to plead for her to remove her knife; but he knew one wrong word could be the end for Runa.

'It was my idea,' he said. 'Last night I saw the Azawan when it came to Skate, on Ork Island. I got the idea that the two of us could reach your island tonight, without being disturbed, because your diver wouldn't be watching for us.'

'And what did you plan to do when you got here?'

Talorc glanced at Runa.

'Eyes on me,' said the fin.

'We came here to kill him.'

'To kill who?'

'Mordak,' said Talorc.

'You're lying,' she said. Talorc heard Runa make a tiny sound and he imagined the stone knife sawing through the skin of her neck.

'I swear I'm not lying,' he said. 'I swear it by the Sea Mother.'

The fin held his gaze and sniffed at him, as if she could smell lies. 'You came here to kill Mordak?'

'Yes,' said Talorc. 'Why don't you believe me?'

'Because you must surely know,' she said, watching him

closely, 'that Mordak is dead.'

'Dead? How?' asked Talorc.

'He was murdered by your spy,' said the fin, her eyes not leaving his. 'The one your people sent here all those years ago to learn our ways, learn Mordak's magic and use it against us. The dry-child who sent the Azawan.'

'You mean... Sariad?'

CHAPTER TWENTY EIGHT

'Yes. Sariad,' said the tall fin, spitting the word.

It couldn't be. 'But… I saw Mordak. On the first night of this moon,' said Talorc. 'On Odhran, when he summoned the Azawan.' He had heard Mordak's voice; Mordak had spoken through Sariad; he had spoken to Talorc…

'He was murdered seven moons ago. So was everyone on this island, except us. By your spy.'

'She's not our spy! She's helping us fight the Azawan –'

'Talorc,' said Runa, her voice flat. 'They're right.'

'But… I saw him. I saw Mordak.'

'How do you know it was Mordak?' said the tall fin.

'Skelda… one of our people told us about him. That he was your most powerful diver.'

'And who told Skelda that?' asked Runa.

'Sariad,' said Talorc. 'But we saw Mordak possess her… I heard his voice…'

'And I saw his corpse,' the knife-wielding fin said. 'Moons ago. 'She claimed that he died naturally, of old age. No-one doubted it. On the night of his death watch we gathered at the Ancestor Circle. The Azawan came and I hoped for a moment it was the work of Mordak's spirit; that he had done in death what he did not do in life. I hoped the Azawan would go forth from that place and destroy the ones who took our land from us. Instead it turned on us.'

She withdrew the knife from Runa's throat.

'I thought she was working for your people. But it seems there is more to the story.'

'Sariad was working for herself,' said Runa. 'She presented herself to one of our speys. Told how she had been enslaved, beaten, tormented by Mordak until one day he threw her in the sea. When the Azawan came, the spey sent us to her. She dived, and Mordak took her. Spoke through her. Deliver a message to the king, he said, that he must sacrifice seven Orkadi to the Azawan each Sevenday, until we are all dead or enslaved.'

'But if she is lying,' said Talorc, 'if she controls the Azawan, why is she doing this? Why lie? Why not just use it to kill us all at once?'

'She did not lie about everything,' said the fin. 'Mordak did make her suffer. Perhaps she wants your people to suffer as she did.'

'But why, when it was Mordak who did that to her?'

'Her parents tried to kill her,' said Runa. 'They gave her to the waves for having magic. That's how she came to be with Mordak. Maybe she blames us.'

'But I saw him. When the sharks attacked us. And yesterday evening, when the Azawan came...' Did he know that for sure? Could Sariad have appeared to him as Mordak in his visions? Was she so powerful? If she could summon an Azawan...

'You are a spey?' said the fin.

'No,' said Talorc. He hesitated. What would they think? Yet lying didn't seem wise. 'I'm a diver.'

The fin's eyes widened.

'Who taught you? Sariad?'

'No!' said Talorc. 'I didn't learn from anyone. I don't even know what I'm doing. It just started happening the night the Azawan came.'

'Why you?' said the male. 'Why would the Sea Mother give

the gift to a dry?'

'She gave it to Sariad too,' said Talorc. 'I don't know why it happens.'

'It could be to do with his feet,' said Runa. 'Take off his boots.'

The lead fin thought for a moment. 'Rugi,' she said, 'take off his boots.' To Talorc, she said, 'try anything and you know what'll happen.'

Talorc nodded and the other female, Rugi, came forward. Kneeling, she slipped off his boots and gasped, as did the others.

'Like Sariad,' said the lead fin.

'A spy like Sariad!' said the male. 'Stop listening to them. They're just telling you what you want to hear. They came to see if any of us still live before they move in and take the island. If we let them go then more will come.'

'Maybe you are spies,' said the tall fin to Talorc and Runa, 'and maybe you aren't. You sound convincing, but then, that's the job of a spy, isn't it? And you dries have given us few reasons to trust you.' She moved closer and lowered her voice. 'The safest thing would be to kill you. After we find out what you know.'

Again the knife went to Runa's throat. This time Runa squealed and began to gasp as it drew a tiny nick of blood.

'Talk quickly, boy. No lies this time –'

'That's Princess Runa!' Talorc shouted. 'Daughter of King Anga, descendant of Valdar the Uniter!'

The lead fin's eyes widened. 'Truly? This is the heir of Valdar the Cursed?' A wide grin spread across her face, revealing more needle-sharp teeth. 'Then we can avenge tonight not just the wrong done by Sariad, but by all the dries since they turned against us.'

'Yes, you could,' said Talorc. 'She is my friend, and I know you hate her house and would love to see her dead. So why would I tell you who she is unless everything I'm saying is true?

'We're not spies,' he continued. 'My name is Talorc. My grandparents were Loth and Pem, my parents were Torma and Besk. I grew up on a farm on Odhran. This is Runa. I met her eleven days ago when I traveled to Gurn after the Azawan killed my family and destroyed my village.' He went on, relaying as quickly as possible everything that had happened. Each of the listening fins looked sceptical at times, yet they were all entranced.

'So we came here in secret,' he finished, 'to kill Mordak. And now we know that Mordak is dead, and that Sariad has made fools of all of us. She destroyed your people all at once; she wishes to destroy ours slowly, without revealing who she is. The only questions are why, and how can we stop her?'

'I have another question,' said Rugi. 'Why should we stop her? If what you say is true, why should we care if Sariad kills your people, however quickly or slowly she does it?'

'Because we owe her a blood-debt,' said the tall fin. 'If there is a way to destroy her, we must.'

'Just as we owe this one a blood-debt,' said the male, looking at Runa.

'Then claim it,' said Runa. 'After we have defeated Sariad. Together.'

'We may not have the chance,' said the tall fin. 'You dries may be slow, but you are clever.'

'I will swear it,' she said. 'On my blood.'

'The Sea Mother hears such oaths,' said the tall fin. 'If you break it, vengeance will be hers, upon you and your descendants.'

'I know,' said Runa.

The tall fin withdrew the knife and put her scaled palm to Runa's throat. She touched her hand to her forehead, leaving a smear of red blood there, then leaned in and pressed her brow against Runa's.

'Do you swear that when the sorceress Sariad is defeated, and we wish to claim our blood-debt from you, you will honour our claim, and come to meet us?'

'I swear it,' said Runa.

Talorc and Runa's hands were untied. The tall fin invited them to sit by the fire at the centre of the tent.

'I am Nalga,' she said. 'This is my sister Rugi, and her friend Skeen.'

'Are you hungry?' asked Rugi.

'Yes,' said Talorc.

'They can't eat our food,' said Nalga.

'They don't eat fish?' asked Skeen.

Nalga sighed. 'Do you two never listen? Dries set fire to their food before they eat it. It's called…' she frowned.

'Cooking,' said Runa. 'Fins – I mean, katra – don't cook their food?'

Nalga smiled. 'You can call us fins. We call you dries. No, we don't burn our food. Do the fish cook their food? The birds, the animals? Unlike you, we have not forgotten what we are. But we have fish. You can cook on our fire.'

Skeen reluctantly handed Talorc his knife back. Using twigs supplied by their hosts, he made skewers on which they impaled herring taken from a barrel of salted water. Soon the smell of cooking fish-flesh was making Talorc's mouth water.

Now that the danger had apparently passed he found himself desperately tired, and guessed Runa must be too. Had the danger passed? It seemed the katra were satisfied with Runa's promise to honour the blood-debt. So probably they would leave her alone until then. In which case, could they work together?

And how was Runa going to get out of paying the debt?

'They're ready,' said Runa, tasting her herring. 'Will you eat with us?'

The three katra looked at one another. 'Take some fish from the barrel,' said Nalga to the others.

'I'm not hungry,' said Skeen.

'Do it anyway,' said Nalga. She turned to Runa. 'I know a little of your kind. So should these two, but they never paid attention to their elders. Among your kind, if we eat together, we are friends, yes?'

'Yes,' said Runa.

'Katra eat alone,' said Nalga. 'We eat our fish as we catch it. We store food only in case of times of danger, when the water is unsafe.' Skeen handed a herring each to Nalga and Rugi but took none for himself.

Faster than Talorc's eyes could follow, Nalga lunged at Skeen and bit his shoulder. He roared in pain and hissed at her, baring his teeth, but didn't retaliate.

'Eat,' said Nalga.

After a moment Skeen fetched himself a fish and sat down.

'Hatred for your kind runs deep among our people,' said Nalga, biting into her fish. 'Deeper in some than others. Skeen's mother died giving birth to him. He was raised by his father, who was taken by the sea when Skeen was still young.'

'He was killed by dries,' said Skeen, chewing his food slowly.

'Some will say that of every katra that doesn't come back from the hunt,' said Nalga, 'but we can never know.'

'It's the same among us,' said Runa. 'Whenever someone disappears, people say the fins did it.' Talorc thought of his mother-sister. Had she really been taken by fins? 'But I never heard of any Orkadi who killed a katra. I have never seen one of your people until today.'

'And we do not hunt your kind. It is – or, it was – forbidden, lest the war resume. Yet there can be no war now,' said Nalga. 'We are the last of our clan. If the Azawan takes us, our clan is no more.'

'So lets work together,' said Runa, 'so it isn't the end.'

'What do you propose?'

'We've agreed that Sariad is our enemy,' said Runa, 'and she is using the Azawan as a weapon against us. She used it to almost wipe out your kind, and now is using it against my people.'

'What I don't understand,' said Talorc, 'is why she hasn't just set the Azawan on us, as she did with you? Why has she gone to the effort of deceiving us?'

'What does it matter?' said Skeen. 'We don't have to understand her. We only have to kill her.'

'She's clever,' said Nalga. 'If we're going to beat her we have to understand what she has done so far, and what she might do next.'

'Skeen has a point,' said Runa. 'She is powerful because she controls the Azawan, but she herself is not strong. If we could get to her, and kill her, this would be over. The Azawan would be released from her spell and would leave Orka.'

'We know where she is,' said Talorc. 'It could be as simple as heading back to Gurn and cornering her. But she's a diver. She reads minds. As soon as we're close, she'll know that we know. Even before then, she could dive and find out where we are and what we're doing.'

There was a silence as he realised the truth of what he had said. They were missing from Gurn. What if she suspected that they had come here and learnt her secret? She might already know...

'We can help with that,' said Nalga. She left the fire, rummaged among some skin-sacks and came back carrying two necklaces. Each was made of gut-string, the string glued to a lump of black stone with a jagged pattern etched onto it.

'Death-stones,' said Nalga, reaching into her tunic to show that she was wearing one too. 'They dull your spirit and make you invisible to divers.'

It was all Talorc and Runa could do not to snatch the stones from Nalga's hand as she offered them. Talorc put his around his neck and felt a strange sensation, as if his bones were filling with iron. 'How do they work?' he asked.

'I don't know,' said Nalga. 'But Mordak made all katra keep one, in case divers from another clan should ever attack us.'

'Do katra war with one another?' asked Talorc.

'Do humans?' replied Nalga.

'Thank you,' said Runa. 'So now Sariad won't be able to find us, or hear our thoughts when we go to Gurn. But if she can't read our thoughts...'

'She'll know we're wearing these,' said Talorc. 'She'll know that we know.'

'If we kill her, it won't matter what she knows,' said Runa.

'It's not enough,' said Nalga. 'We can't just plan on surprising her and killing her, as easily as that. Sariad is cunning. She deceived Mordak. She deceived you, and your spey. She deceives everyone. Sariad knows you can dive and that you've disappeared. Even if she doesn't know you're here, she will have made preparations, in case you discover her secret.'

'You're right,' said Runa. 'We need a fallback plan. A way to get rid of the Azawan if we can't get to her.'

'I could dive,' said Talorc. If I got into her mind I could find the spell. Maybe when she was sleeping...'

'It's too risky,' said Runa. 'You know that.'

'I'm willing to try.'

'I'm not willing to let you,' said Runa. She looked towards the ceiling, stopped chewing and turned to look intently at Nalga. 'Would any other katra have known the spells needed to summon the Azawan and to banish it?'

'No,' said Nalga. 'The spell died with Mordak.'

Talorc looked at Runa. She returned his look and he knew what she was thinking.

'When a katra dies,' said Talorc, 'what happens to their body?'

'If the katra is a diver,' said Nalga, 'there is a ceremony within the Ancestor Circle. Every katra attends – or is supposed to attend,' she said, shooting a dark look at both Rugi and Skeen.

'If we'd attended, we'd be dead,' said Skeen, 'and so would you.'

'The clan gathers to pay their respects. The divers chant, and then they eat the dead one's brain.'

'They eat their brain?' said Talorc.

'Yes. In order to retain their knowledge. After that, the body is given to the Sea Mother.'

'And that's what happened to Mordak?' said Runa.

'I don't know what happened to Mordak,' said Nalga, giving the other two another dark look. 'These two decided to skip the ceremony and take the opportunity to swim over to Calag. I saw they were missing and went after them. While I was out looking for them, the Azawan struck. We returned to the island to find everyone dead and Sariad gone. I knew it was her.'

'How?' asked Talorc.

'I never trusted her. I always told Mordak that he was a fool to do so. He cared for her, even though he was cruel to her. I think it was caring for her that changed him.'

'In what way?' asked Talorc.

'He used to hate dries and to dream of beginning another war. But keeping Sariad as his slave softened him. Mordak was so proud of her abilities, although he would never admit it. He'd never had such a capable student. I think she became like a child to him. Mordak went from loathing your kind to believing that katra and dries could be friends.'

'It sounds like you knew him well,' said Runa.

'I did,' said Nalga. 'He was my grandfather.'

'I don't know if you know,' said Runa after a pause, 'about speying.' Nalga nodded. 'If I could find his skull, I could talk to him. We could ask him for the spell to banish the Azawan.'

'Sariad has it,' said Talorc. He was talking before he even knew what he was saying. 'I saw a skull in the bone-house, I thought maybe it was a seal's skull but it wasn't the right shape –'

'She would do that,' said Nalga, her eyes narrowing. 'She would keep his skull, talk to it, torment him even in death with her betrayal.'

'So if we can't kill her, we could take the skull from her, get away from Gurn with it and Runa could spey. Once we have the spell, we can banish the Azawan and Sariad will be powerless,' said Talorc with a grin.

'She'll be guarding it,' said Runa.

'She doesn't know that we know about it, even if she has guessed where we are,' said Talorc.

'So it looks we have our plans then,' said Nalga. 'We will make our way to your keep. We will find Sariad and kill her. If we can't do that, we will take my grandfather's skull. If we fail in that, we die and so do your people. But first, you need to sleep.'

They didn't argue. Nalga pointed at two sleeping places and Talorc and Runa crawled into them, Talorc groaning with delight as he crawled in under the sealskin covering. Soon he could hear the soft sound of Runa's snores.

He wanted so badly to sleep, but he stayed awake, waiting for the others to fall asleep. There was something he wanted even more than sleep.

The Ancestor Circle was quiet.

Talorc stood for a while, watching the children dance through the night sky above him, then closed his eyes. He recalled what he had felt here earlier, when the bone pillars hummed and sang with life. Silently he asked them to sing to him again.

Nothing.

He had slipped out after he was sure the others were sleeping. Now he stood in the centre of the Circle. The katra wouldn't like him going here; this was their most sacred place and, though they had made an agreement, they still saw him on one level as an enemy. Runa wouldn't approve either. But he wasn't going to dive here, desperate as he was to do so; to sink deep into the sea and drift upon currents of whale-song, or soar into the northern sky and dance in rivers of light.

A diver could do such things here; he was sure of it. Even one who knew as little as he did. Yet it wasn't safe. Sariad's spirit was out there, somewhere. But it wouldn't do any harm, surely, for him to sit here and listen to the music of the bones.

The necklace; that was it. It prevented divers from seeing him; it must be deadening his own awareness too. He mustn't take it off.

But just for a moment? It might be his last chance. He would probably be dead soon. He deserved this one chance.

Talorc took the stone in his hand and lifted it over his head.

The bones began to glow. The bones pulsed, they shimmered, they sang to him...

Sariad fell upon Talorc like a hawk from the night air.

She was everywhere, all at once, in the centre and in every far corner of his mind. He was skewered like a mouse upon her claws and could not escape. Vaguely he was aware of his body, thrashing and writhing as she dug deeper into him, white-hot fires of pain coursing through every fibre of his being.

I've been looking for you, Talorc. You're far from home. You've been hiding from me. But the bones tempted you, didn't they, little diver? And now I have you. The voice, the presence was no longer Mordak's; there was only Sariad. He could hear far-off screams and guessed they were his own. Every word she spoke was like a blade slicing into his mind.

That's right, little diver. I don't need to pretend anymore. Though it was fun to deceive you. On the beach, appearing to you as Mordak. I knew you would run home and tell your parents what you saw. When the Azawan came, I knew you would run and tell your king what you saw. But I didn't know you were a diver. Maybe that's what drew me to pick you as my little messenger? Perhaps I should have taken you more seriously.

You have skill, little diver. To send my sharks away; that was real power. I was impressed. But still I let you live. It made being among your people less tiresome, playing our little game, appearing as Mor-

dak in your vision. We used to play games like that, Mordak and I. Maybe I miss them.

But now the time for games is over. You and the little princess are more trouble than you are worth. It is time for you to die.

If you're going to kill me, said Talorc in his mind, tell me the truth first. Why –

Pain consumed him. At some point – he didn't know how much time had passed – he could think again. Sariad was still there. She was listening.

Why are you doing this? Why not just... it was too difficult to form thoughts.

Why not just have the Azawan kill you all? Why the sacrifices? You disappoint me, Talorc. Don't you see? If I kill you all I will have no-one to serve me. If I I threaten the Orkadi with my Azawan, they will obey me but not love me. This way, I can come closer to the centre of power, until your people know me and trust me. Then, when the time is right, all I need do is pronounce the name of the king. He will die, the Orkadi will need a leader, and all the other candidates will be dead. I shall be queen.

Does that feel better, now that you know? Are you ready to die?

I'm not going to die. Talorc had been waiting, letting her relax her grip upon him as she gloated. Now he surged against her, in a way his mind did not understand but his diver-self did. She roared as he struck her, screaming her anger, and tensed, ready to pounce –

Talorc's vision changed. He could see Sariad; she was sat cross-legged against a stone wall, singing in that deep tone she had used when she dove in the bone-house. Her skulls were all around her; firelight danced in her face; she was in Kretta's house at Gurn.

'Sariad? What's wrong?' Kretta's voice.

Sariad's eyes snapped open. For a moment they were full of fury; then they softened, fury replaced by fear.

'Was it him?' said Kretta.

'Yes,' said Sariad, her voice trembling. 'It – it was him. He...'

'He gave you the next seven?'

'...Yes,' said Sariad. 'I'm sorry.'

'It's not your fault,' said Kretta. 'We know how he makes you suffer. I'm with you now. Once you're ready we'll have to wake the king and tell him.'

'But he will be so sad,' said Sariad.

'What do you mean?'

'One of the seven,' said Sariad, 'is Talorc.' Sariad looked straight at him. 'And one is Princess Runa.'

Talorc roared but Kretta couldn't hear him.

The vision was gone.

CHAPTER TWENTY NINE

'You idiot!' shouted Runa.

Talorc opened his mouth to reply but Runa didn't give him the chance.

'What did you think was going to happen? Did it not occur to you that she would be looking for us? Isn't that the reason we're wearing these things in the first place?'

Nalga, Rugi and Skeen stood nearby, a torch in Nalga's hand. Talorc had been torn from his vision the moment Runa thrust his amulet around his neck. She and the katra had been woken by his screams and come running to find him lying on the grass within the bone circle, his eyes rolling back in their sockets, muttering to someone unseen. Runa had seemed scared at first as Talorc came around; then her fear turned to anger as he repeated Sariad's words.

'You would have done it if you were me,' he said, aware of how sluggish his voice sounded.

'No, I wouldn't,' said Runa. 'Don't assume everyone else is an imbecile just because you are.' She lowered her voice. 'Sariad knows where we are now. She'll send the Azawan for us. It could be here at any moment –'

'Not if it's away hunting. Not if she doesn't have the chance to call it.'

'She'll find the chance soon enough,' said Runa.

'And we'll be long gone from here.'

'Really? And where are we going?'

'To Gurn.' Talorc looked at the katra before turning back to Runa. 'I was stupid. I know that. But I was lucky; in more ways than one. I saw her mind again.'

'Just like last time,' said Runa.

'Not like last time. Last time she was pretending to be Mordak. This time it was her, all her. Sariad thinks she's so clever; it's made her careless. She didn't guard her thoughts and didn't bother searching mine, so doesn't know we know about the skull.' Talorc grinned. 'And she does have it. I saw it in her mind. If we go to Gurn we can take Mordak's skull.'

'Well, that's that, then,' said Runa. 'Talorc says we're going to Gurn to ask Sariad nicely if we can have Mordak's skull. Of course, we've been named as sacrifices thanks to him, so everyone who sees us and recognises us – that is, everyone in Orka – will try to take us prisoner and hand us over to my father, so that might be a little difficult.'

'Can you not just trust me?'

'I did trust you. I came here. Look what happened.'

'It could work,' said Rugi.

The others turned to face her.

'So long as the Azawan doesn't find us before then, we could help you get the skull from Sariad and get away before you're caught. She doesn't know there are any katra left alive; she won't be expecting us to help you.'

'Sariad has to sleep,' said Talorc. 'So does everyone else. We just have to sneak in and sneak out again.'

'We're good at that,' said Skeen, grinning at Rugi.

'Not as good as you think,' said Nalga. 'But good enough to get around a few dries.'

'So what do you say?' Talorc asked Runa, raising his eyebrows.

Runa rolled her eyes. 'I think we may as well try it. I'm going to be dead soon either way.'

'Here,' said Talorc.

Atop the cliffs he could see firelight where the guards at Gurn's gate stood watch. On the shore, all was dark. Talorc's night-sight was getting better. He could see far better than Runa, though not nearly so well as the katra.

They brought the curragh into shore, Talorc yawning as he guided Runa. After returning to the katras' tent they had slept until dawn, then eaten before beginning the crossing back to Ork Island. The crossing had taken the entire day, and now the storm that had been building on the western horizon was quickly gathering pace. Moaning winds buffeted their boat and rain poured down as they landed and leapt out.

The katra emerged from the water to join them. It amazed Talorc how little the cold affected them. How similar to his own race were they? How different? They had swum the entire way to Gurn so there had been little chance for talk. He longed to learn everything there was to know about them. If he survived this, he promised himself, he would do so. Though that was unlikely.

'Are you sure you can climb in the rain?' said Runa to Nalga.

'We're sure,' said Nalga with a wry grin, shaking the water from her scales.

Runa took the katras' spears from the curragh and handed them to their owners. They each slipped their spear into a holder on the back of their fish-skin jerkins. Their fine flint knifes had remained on their belts during the crossing.

'This storm is going to break soon,' said Talorc. 'Will you be able to swim?'

'Don't worry about us,' said Rugi. 'Just concentrate on getting out of there alive.' She nodded towards the dim point of firelight.

'We'll get out if everyone sticks to the plan,' said Runa. 'Everyone ready?'

Talorc and the three katra nodded.

'Lets go.'

The katra waded into the water, dived and disappeared out of sight. Talorc followed Runa up the bank and down a path between fields until they reached a meadow. Runa gave a low whistle and within moments a ghostly shape emerged from the darkness.

Talorc smiled as he watched Runa stroke Farla, who butted her head against Runa, licked her and whinnied with joy to be reunited with her companion. Runa laughed and Talorc tried to remember the last time he had heard her laugh.

'Come on, girl. Time to go.' Runa swung herself up onto Farla's back and Talorc followed, seating himself behind Runa.

'This still feels strange,' he whispered, putting his hands around her waist.

'Of all you could choose from, you call this strange,' said Runa. She pressed her legs against Farla's flanks and they set off towards Gurn.

They had landed close to the keep, knowing that the darkness would conceal them. It wasn't long before Talorc could make out the high stone walls of Gurn and the twin guards stood outside the gate, illuminated by torches mounted on the walls. Anga was clearly being more cautious since the sacrifice. Talorc put his hand to the dagger concealed under his cloak.

'Don't do that,' murmured Runa.

Talorc withdrew his hand.

They found and followed the path that led up the slope towards the keep. The guards, one old and bearded and one young and bare-faced, saw them and called out.

'Woah there! Who passes?'

'Princess Runa.'

The guards shifted nervously as they drew closer.

'I wish to speak to my father. Open the gate,' said Runa as they came to a halt.

'Of course,' said the older guard. 'Princess, I'm sorry to say this... I mean, you'll understand we'd prefer not to... but we have to escort you to your father. You and the boy,' he said with a nod towards Talorc.

'Don't worry about it,' said Runa. She dismounted and Talorc followed. 'Thank you, Farla,' she said as she stroked her horse. Runa turned towards the guards and raised her eyebrows as she saw that the older guard had his hand upon his sword-hilt. Her eyes met his and she gave him a quizzical smile. He grinned sheepishly and lowered his hand.

The younger guard opened the gate.

'If you could go first please, Princess,' said the older guard. 'And yourself,' he said to Talorc. They passed through the gate, the guards falling in behind them.

Torches lit the walkway leading to the broch. Two further guards stood at the door to the broch, allowing them to stop any intruders as well as to see anyone entering or leaving the houses. Kretta's house was immediately to the left of the broch.

Runa turned back towards the guards. 'I think your friends can see us from here,' she said with a smile.

'Our orders –' began the older guard.

'Were to guard the gate,' said Runa, her smile gone. 'It is currently open and unmanned. Shall I tell my father that?'

'Lets get back to the gate,' said the younger one. 'Where is she going to run?' he added in a whisper.

The older guard hesitated then turned around and walked back towards the gate. When they had closed it behind them, Runa turned and proceeded towards the broch, Talorc behind her.

Talorc recognised the next two guards. Both of them had lodged in the same house as him at Otter Bay. Unlike the other pair of guards, they had a seasoned look about them. One bore a scar on his cheek and Talorc wondered if they had fought with

Anga on Skoll. That could make things more difficult.

'Kemmin. Aidan,' said Runa, greeting them. They nodded at her, the one called Aidan glancing nervously at his scarred companion.

'It's good to see you back,' said Kemmin. 'We were worried when you disappeared after...'

'Worried that I had run away?'

As they talked Talorc focussed all his energy on one thing. Not looking up.

'No,' said Kemmin. 'I know that's not your way. But Orka's not the place it was.'

'You think I can't handle myself?'

'I've taken plenty of thrashings that say you can,' said Kemmin with a smile. 'May I ask where you were?'

'Why do you ask?'

'Well...'

Don't look up, Talorc repeated to himself. *Don't look up.*

'...And I know you wouldn't run, but folk are scared, everyone is looking for someone to feel angry at...'

Talorc couldn't help it. He looked up.

Rugi and Skeen were climbing down the broch. Their hands and feet gripping the stone; their bellies were flat against the wall.

Talorc's eyes met Skeen's. The young katra jerked his head at Talorc, anger flashing in his eyes.

Talorc brought his eyes back to meet those of Aidan, who was watching him suspiciously.

'What are you looking at –'

The katra fell on the guards, knocking them to the ground.

Talorc and Runa leapt back as the guards and katra fought. This wasn't the plan. Rugi and Skeen were supposed to choke the guards and knock them out without being seen. They would tie them up and hide them in the shadows. But Talorc had given the game away, and each of the guards cried out before the katras' fists silenced them.

'What now?' hissed Skeen, glaring at Talorc as he and Rugi rose from the prone forms of Aidan and Kemmin.

'Get out of sight!' hissed Runa. 'Talorc, get the skull!'

'But how...'

There was no time. The gates were opening. Talorc opened the door to Kretta's house and ducked inside.

Closing the door behind him, Talorc paused, trying to quiet his breath. He could almost hear his heart pounding in his chest.

The embers of the fire had been raked over. It was utterly dark.

Talorc summoned up a memory of the vision he had seen within the Ancestor Circle on the previous night. Sariad had made a nest for herself in the far-right corner of the room. Her skulls were arrayed around her. Talorc tried to hold the picture of what he had seen in his mind. Mordak's skull must be in her sack. Where was it? He couldn't remember. He would have to find it.

Listening, Talorc thought he could hear breathing from each side of the room. It was confusing; the breath of each sleeper interrupted that of the other, but nonetheless he was sure both Kretta and Sariad were asleep.

He dropped to his hands and knees.

Reaching out to feel if anything was in his path, Talorc crawled forward.

He came to the edge of the hearth and stopped. Listened. The sounds of sleeping breath were clearer now.

Talorc turned and edged around the hearth-pit towards the sound of Sariad's breath. She had been sat on a bundle of skins in his vision and Talorc guessed that was where she slept.

He went even more slowly and carefully now. Soon his hand brushed against something cold. He stroked it with his fingers.

One of Sariad's little skulls. Whatever he did, he mustn't break one. Could the skulls speak to Sariad in her sleep? Would they come swooping into her dreams to warn her?

Sariad's breathing halted.

Talorc held himself still.

With a sigh her breathing resumed. Beads of sweat dripped down Talorc's brow. He was shaking. Should he wait until the shaking stopped? No. Runa was - somehow - holding off the guards outside. He had to get out of here soon; he had already taken too long.

Talorc found the skulls in his path, lifted them and placed them on the floor out of his way. He crawled forward and reached out again...

There!

Talorc could feel the sack beneath his hand. The skull within.

Reaching out with his other hand, Talorc delicately opened the sack and pulled out the skull, just as the sound of clashing swords, shouts and then the wail of a horn rent the air.

With a savage shriek Sariad leapt at Talorc.

She knocked him to the ground but he held onto the skull. Nothing short of death would separate them. They tumbled over the earthen floor and Talorc howled with pain as Sariad scratched and bit at him, screaming her fury. She was bigger than him, but he was stronger; she knew how to fight and he knew how to escape.

Kretta was awake and shouting. Red light bathed the stone walls as she uncovered the fire-embers, revealing Sariad's bestial anger as she tore at Talorc with tooth and nail. Gone was the quivering, wretched, broken girl they had found in the bone-house on Fior. Sariad was a creature of fury and hatred and now she had Talorc pinned beneath her. Mordak's skull was wedged between his arm and ribs.

'Sariad! Talorc! Stop it!' Kretta was standing screaming over them. Sariad looked up and met her eyes for a moment. It was enough. Talorc's hands were pinned, but she was leaning in close above him. He swung his elbow with all the strength he could muster, cracking it against her ear. Her grip loosened; he shoved her off and wriggled away.

'She's the enemy!' he shouted as he ran past Kretta and out the open door.

Outside all was chaos.

Guardians had come pouring out of the houses; some armed, some unarmed. Some watched in dismay as Runa fought their comrades; others tried to help her.

Her sword shone in the firelight as she spun and lunged, fending off both guards from the gate. The men were bigger and stronger but her skill was greater. They circled wide, trying to trap her between them.

A voice shouted 'There's the boy! Seize him!'

'Bring Runa down!' shouted someone else.

Talorc reached for his knife and was grabbed from behind. He kicked and struggled but was caught in a head-lock, his arms pinned to his sides, the skull pressing into his ribs. All he could do now was watch Runa, who was now under attack from four guards –

Runa screamed and dropped her sword.

Everyone present fell still and silent as she dropped to her knees.

In that moment Anga strode out of the broch, his jewelled sword held high.

A dark patch spread across Runa's midriff.

From beyond the gate came a shout. 'To the beach! The fins are attacking!'

Everyone present looked at one another, lost as to how to react. All except Anga, who stood staring at Runa, white-faced.

From elsewhere came an inhuman screech that Talorc knew was the cry of a katra.

It worked. The guards forgot Runa; Talorc was released and flung aside as the man holding him followed the others in a dash out of the gate, leaving Talorc and Anga alone with Runa.

The king ran to his daughter and fell to his knees, moaning as Runa collapsed to the ground.

Talorc had to get Runa out of the keep. How to part her from Anga? The king wasn't going to let –

The decision was taken for Talorc as Nalga roared a challenge to Anga.

The king's head whipped round. He rose to his feet as Nalga edged towards him, spear in both hands, mouth open to reveal her needle-like teeth.

Anga unsheathed his sword, tensed and flung himself at the katra with a swing of his sword that could have cloven her in two. She easily evaded, whirling past him and lashing out with her spear, catching the king's forearm.

Enough. They had been given a diversion; it was time to use it - and to get away from Sariad before she came to her senses. Talorc took the pack Nalga had given him off his back and stuffed the skull in. He hauled Runa over his shoulder and ran for the gate.

Farla answered Runa's whistle.

'Can you ride?' asked Talorc.

'Yes,' said Runa, through gritted teeth. 'It's not as bad as I made it look.'

Talorc watched as she hauled herself onto Farla's back. She moved slowly; even if her wound wasn't as bad as she had made it look, it was bad.

'Come on!' she said.

He mounted behind her and they set off. Runa urged Farla on and soon she was galloping up the west road, as fast as she dared in the darkness and rain. The wind howled and shrieked while thunder rumbled in the distance.

'Are you sure you're alright?' shouted Talorc.

'I'm not alright. But I'm not about to die either,' answered Runa. 'Just keep your eyes open for pursuit.'

Talorc turned and looked behind them. He could see the distant lights of Gurn and some other lights that he guessed to be torches taken by the guards to the beach. Very soon they would realise that no invasion fleet was landing.

It seemed they were safe for now. They only had to get to the place where they were to meet the katra. Runa had suggested a headland called the Beak, west along the coast from Gurn. No-one would expect them to head to a place where they could be cornered; they should be safe there for as long as the night lasted. And if they were found...

Talorc heard shouting and the thrum of horses' hooves.

'They're coming!' he hissed. Runa dug her things deeper into Farla's sides and Talorc held on tight to Runa's hips, avoiding her wound as Farla tore down the road, while pinpricks of light appeared behind them and the shouting grew louder.

'There's the marker stone!' said Runa, stopping at a dark lump to the right of the road.

They dismounted. Runa gave her horse a quick stroke and swatted her rump, urging her away. Once Farla had disappeared into the shadows they ran, Runa clutching her stomach, following the winding, narrow path that led up the headland towards the sea.

'Stop!' said Runa.

Talorc halted and stood beside her, looking over the cliff's edge at the surf beating against the rocks beneath. There was no sign of the katra. Of course, they couldn't have got here as quickly.

Runa lay down on the grass, wrapped her cloak around her and closed her eyes.

'What can I do to help you?' Talorc asked.

Runa shook her head. 'I just… need to rest. I'm not dying… until this is over.'

So Talorc stood and waited, shivering and soaking in the rain and the wind, praying to the Sea Mother for Runa to live.

CHAPTER THIRTY

'Talorc.'

Talorc's head whipped round. He had sat down close beside Runa in a vain attempt to keep her warm, his arm wrapped around her shoulder. How long had they been there? It felt like an age. He didn't dare touch Runa's wound, and knew nothing of how to treat it. She was awake, though; she muttered and moaned and shook as the rain fell on her.

Runa was alive. But she was dying.

Three dark shapes clambered over the clifftop.

Talorc breathed a sigh of relief. When the katra had assured him and Runa that they could climb up the cliffs to the meeting place, after swimming through a storm, they had both been sceptical; yet here they were. How did Valdar manage to win a war against these creatures?

No. Not creatures. People.

The three katra gathered around Runa, hissing as they saw her wound.

'We should have done better,' said Nalga.

'You could have done a lot worse,' said Talorc. 'We never would have made it out of there without you.'

'No,' said Skeen, 'you wouldn't.'

'How long does she have?' asked Talorc.

'The wound is bad,' said Nalga. 'She might live if we could get her to a healer, but our healers are all dead.'

Talorc thought of Skelda. 'I know someone,' he said. 'But I

have no way of finding her.'

'The princess has to live,' said Nalga. 'For now.'

The katra hadn't forgotten the blood-debt. Talorc hadn't forgotten either.

'Her spirit is strong,' continued Nalga, 'it will carry her a little further. Do you have the skull?'

'Yes,' said Talorc. 'But –'

'Wait.' Nalga held up a hand and sniffed the air.

'What?' Talorc searched the darkness but saw nothing.

'Dries!' said Nalga. 'They've found you. We need to move now.'

As she spoke Talorc saw a prick of light in the distance. The guards had found their trail. This was it.

'Are you sure this will work?' he asked, already knowing the answer.

'Not if you don't on hold tight,' said Rugi.

'But what about Runa?'

'Not if she doesn't hold on tight,' said Skeen.

Talorc glared at him and nudged Runa. 'Can you hear me?'

Runa nodded. Her eyes opened. 'I heard. They're coming.'

Talorc and the katra stood back as Runa got to her feet, almost falling as she did so.

'I'm fine,' she said, in response to the question in their eyes. 'I can hold on.'

There was no more time to waste. As the torches drew closer and voices arrived on the wind Talorc and Runa followed the katra to the edge of the cliffs. Talorc looked down at the swirling waters and wished he hadn't.

'Hurry!' hissed Nalga.

Talorc made sure his pack was secured tightly upon his back and turned to face Nalga. She turned her back to him; he placed his hands upon her shoulders and hoisted himself up, locking his hands together beneath her neck. Underneath her tunic he could feel the amulet she wore.

They turned to watch as Skeen helped Runa hoist herself onto Rugi's back.

'Don't ask me if I can hold on,' said Runa, her voice pained. 'Just move.'

They did. Talorc's stomach did somersaults as Nalga approached the cliff-edge, turned and swung herself down.

'Quickly!' she called out.

Skeen followed, then Rugi. Runa had pulled her hood over her head; Talorc was almost glad he couldn't see her face. The pain she must be feeling was too much to think about. The only thing he should think about was holding on.

The katra picked their way down the cliff-face as the wind tore at them and the sea surged beneath them. Talorc clung on with his hands, arms and thighs, marvelling at Nalga's strength while worrying for Runa's. But strength wasn't enough. They needed to get out of sight. If they could get beneath the overhang that Runa had described then the pursuit would give up. No-one would guess they had gone down the cliff-face. Then they could climb back up, find a bone-house to hide in and move onto the next stage of the plan.

It had all sounded so simple back in the katras' tent.

The voices were clear now. Looking up, Talorc could see torchlight. If the guards were to look over the cliff-edge now…

Nalga gave a low growl. 'Here,' she whispered. Her breath quickened as she found footholds and moved in under the overhang.

Talorc's muscles screamed as he clung on tighter. Under the overhang, the wind eased and they were protected from the rain. To his right, he saw Rugi climb down beside them, Runa still clinging to her back, Skeen beyond them.

They held still.

The voices above them became clearer. Talorc struggled to make out what they were saying.

Would they guess? Could they know somehow? What if Sariad was with them? She must know what katra were capable of...

The voices grew fainter.

Vanished.

Talorc gave a sigh of relief, just as Runa fell from Rugi's back and plunged into the sea.

He didn't think.

Talorc let go of Nalga and fell. He twisted in mid-air and brought himself into a dive as the sea rushed to meet him.

With a crash he passed from one world into another. He was at home again, his senses exploding into life, the tendrils of his power unfurling and searching the jagged rocks, the pounding water and the seabed beneath. The death-stone cloaked his power but couldn't contain it.

He found her almost instantly. But what good was it? The water tossed her back and forth like driftwood or a dead animal, held under by the immense currents of the stormy sea. He pulled his boots off and kicked out, aiming for her. It was no good. Fin-feet couldn't power him through a sea like this. He went where it willed, and at any moment it might dash him or Runa against the rocks.

He felt another life-form appear in the water, then another, then another. The katra had dived in. They could swim through this; but could they get him and Runa out of there?

The current pushed Talorc to the surface. He opened his mouth to gulp down air and instead gulped salty water. Before he could spit it out he was forced under again.

Something else was in the water.

He sensed it but couldn't see it in his mind. Was it a sunshark? A sea-wolf? Some other servant of Sariad's, come to finish them off?

Whatever it was, it surged through the sea at astonishing speed. Talorc had no chance of escaping it. Even the katra could not escape this. Could he distract it, lure it away from Runa and the katra? They could finish this without him, if they had the skull...

There was no time. It was upon him. It filled his senses and he felt his tunic seized and pulled. As Talorc choked on seawater another presence seized Runa and pulled her away.

The sea went dark.

Salt water plumed from Talorc's mouth as he awoke.

He twisted over and heaved more liquid onto a rock floor. After emptying his lungs of water and filling them with air he looked around him.

They were in a large cave. Runa lay close beside him, her wet cloak bundled at her side, her tunic rolled up to reveal the dark mass of her belly-wound. Her eyes were closed but her chest rose and fell. She was breathing.

Beside them, a roaring peat-fire gave off a sweet smell that soothed his aching lungs. Nalga, Rugi and Skeen sat around the fire. Sat by Runa was an old woman with milky-white skin. She was naked but for the briefest of fish-skin clothes covering her chest and loins. Though she was old, her flesh was tightly-muscled and her bone-white hair shone in the firelight. Her bold, brown eyes followed her gnarled hands as they worked at preparing a herb-bundle.

Sat with them at the fire was the creature that had rescued them.

He was a man; or at least, he looked like a man in some ways. Like the old woman, he had long, fine hair and thick muscles, but his hair, skin and eyes were all silver. He wore a slight smile as he watched Talorc, his bright eyes emanating warmth and kindness. But Talorc had learnt not to trust appearances.

The creature wore, like a cloak, the skin of a dolphin.

Beyond him, around the edges of the cave, were other fires.

Around the fires sat women and men and children. They were purposefully not looking at Talorc. Others had gathered around him, wary parents clutching their children close to them, staring at the strange newcomers with a mixture of curiosity and anger.

One corner of the cave had been painted, depicting a many-limbed, fearsome creature. Candles burned beneath it, on either side of a bowl full of fish; an altar to some god of the deep sea.

Hung from the rock walls were row upon row of sealskins.

Silkies.

'Yes,' said the dolphin-man. 'Silkies.'

Had he read Talorc's mind?

'Did you wonder if they were real?' the dolphin-man asked. 'I know Pem told you silkie stories. Some people think they are just stories. The people of the sea rarely let themselves be seen by the Orkadi; let alone allow them into their homes. Your being here is a great privilege.'

Talorc looked around again. The silkies sat at the fires were looking everywhere but at him. The ones gathered around him did not look friendly.

'As you can see, not all of the people welcome you here,' said the dolphin-man.

'Why not?' asked Talorc.

'Because your kind kill their kind. Before the dark sky war there was friendship between your races. Seals were hunted but never silkies. That all changed, and now they fear and despise you.'

One of the silkie men stepped towards them, waving his hands and ducking his head as he spoke in a strange, guttural tongue. The old silkie woman held up a hand and he fell silent.

'What is he saying?' asked Talorc.

'It is bad enough, he says, that I brought you here; now we are speaking words he cannot understand in his home. He takes this as an insult,' said the dolphin-man.

'How do you understand what he is saying?' asked Talorc.

'It is given to me to speak many tongues. Ogluk is an old friend and ally of mine.' He indicated the old silkie woman. 'She carries great authority among her people, which will hold them back awhile. But soon you will have to leave.' He turned and addressed the assembly in their language, mimicking it with uncanny precision.

'What are you saying?' asked Talorc.

'I am reminding them who sent me here, and threatening them with the consequences of displeasing her.'

'Who –'

'The Sea Mother.'

Talorc stared at the dolphin-man.

'You don't recognise me, do you?' the dolphin-man asked.

'I've never seen you before,' said Talorc.

'Not so close, no. Yet I've stood beside you. I've watched you from close and afar; watched you grow and kept you safe.'

'When?'

'Do you remember the night after the Azawan came to Odhran?'

Talorc remembered it well. Rowing through the mist, seeing a figure that he took to be the finman watching him from the shore. Lying under the boat, the crunch of footsteps on the stones. Playing his flute, closing his eyes, dolphins circling, his skin healing.

This was the watcher on the shore.

'Why?' said Talorc.

'Because I serve the Sea Mother, and she wishes for you to succeed. But I would help you anyway.' He reached out and took Talorc's hand in his cold, silver hands. 'Because I'm Loth. I'm your Grunda.'

Talorc felt the world spinning around him.

'I suppose I shouldn't have hoped you would know me. I thought you might see something in my face. I see a little of myself in yours. A lot of myself, in your spirit. And Pem. You are so like her, though I don't think you ever realised it. And like your father too. You get your worrying from him, and your mother.'

'How –'

'Your father loved the sea when he was a boy. Loved adventures. Torma's favourite thing to do was to take the boat out to some bay we had never visited. We'd get out and go walking and climbing and exploring. He would walk into any home we came to and talk to its owners like he had known them all his life. He would ask them for stories, saying he was looking for new ones to gift to his Mam.

'One day we set out for the western cliffs to take guga eggs. I knew I needn't worry for him, as he was always a fine climber,' he glanced at the katra, 'on account of his feet.'

Talorc's mouth hung open as his mind raced to catch up.

'Aye, your father had the feet like you do. Neither I nor your Grunna minded, we just made sure he kept them secret. He was a great climber, Torma, better than me, and he knew not to take risks up there on the cliffs.

'But a fog blew in, fast as it does on Odhran, without warning. There was nothing we could do but sit there huddled on the ledges, birds squawking and squawling all around us, waiting for the fog to blow off. Only it didn't. Right on the back of the fog came a storm.

'It blew the fog away but it looked set to blow us away too. Or me, at least; wee Torma could hold on better than I could, what with his feet. But the cold and the rain sapped at my strength and I knew I was done for; at any moment I was going to fall. Torma saw it, he cried and cursed me, told me to hang on, if he could hang on then I could hang on, but I couldn't.

'That's when she came.

'I'd always imagined her as a woman. What greater arrogance is there than that; to see the gods as reflections of ourselves? When I beheld her I thought she was a monster. She climbed the cliffs until she was right beneath us, looked each of us in the eye, and told Torma she was taking me. Said to him that his Da had work to do for her, important work. That he would have to say goodbye to his Da.

'Torma wouldn't say goodbye. He wailed and cursed and threatened her, but there was no swaying her. She plucked me off the cliff, pulled me to her and carried me under the sea. I learnt that she chooses people and creatures of all races to serve her as Silvers, and I had been chosen.'

Talorc glanced at the three katra. All were listening intently. Did they believe him? Was this creature mad? Could this possibly be the truth, that this creature was a servant of the Sea Mother, and his Grunda?

Aye, of course I miss Loth, Grunna had said. *But I believe he's out there somewhere, watching me, watching you. I know he loves me still.*

'I've watched you all your life, Talorc. It wasn't easy, given you weren't allowed in the water,' he said with a laugh, 'but I watched as best as I could. The Sea Mother bid me keep you safe and keep you safe I did. And before all this happened,' he went on, 'I saw you walking with your Grunna on the beach. I heard whispers of the stories she told you, felt the fire they kindled in your heart. You were good to her. She remembers it well.'

'What do you mean –'

'I've spoken too long already,' said the dolphin-man. 'The Sea Mother didn't send me here to reminisce.' His expression changed. 'The Azawan is coming, Talorc. It will be back by dawn. It is time to rid Orka of this evil.'

'How?'

'Exactly as you planned. Ogluk?' Loth – for Talorc realised he believed the story, that this Silver was his Grunda – turned to the old silkie woman.

Ogluk shook her head. She spoke some words that Loth translated. 'Her spirit is a boar. It fights; but too much blood is gone.'

'Can we wake her?' asked Nalga.

'Yes,' Loth said after Ogluk had spoken. 'But she will go quicker if you do.'

They all turned to Talorc. He looked at Runa, her hair glowing in the firelight, her eyes closed as if in peaceful sleep.

'She would kill me for not waking her,' he said with a faint smile. He looked at Loth, who nodded his approval.

Talorc turned to Runa and put a hand upon her shoulder. He squeezed gently, then firmer.

Runa's eyes opened and found Talorc. 'Are we dead?' she asked.

'Not yet,' he said, smiling.

'Good,' said Runa. 'I'm not dying... unless Sariad dies first.'

'Can you sit?'

'Help me.'

Talorc put a hand behind her shoulders and helped her up, noticing how she tried to disguise her pain. Loth held the bundle against her chest while Ogluk went to get some cord before using it to secure the bundle to Runa. Ogluk passed Talorc a waterskin with something warm inside it, which Runa gulped down greedily.

'Where is it?' Runa asked as she passed the skin back to Talorc.

He took the pack from his back, unfastened the cords at the top, reached in and took hold of it.

Talorc glanced around. None of the silkies were pretending to ignore him now. Most had left their fires and joined the throng surrounding him. They whispered, pointed, drawn perhaps by the spirit of the famous diver. Rugi and Skeen sat motionless, while Nalga fingered her death-stone.

To the distant music of the raging sea, Talorc lifted Mordak's skull and placed it on the rock floor.

Firelight danced upon it as the assembly silently stared. The white, gleaming skull somehow seemed to know it was being watched.

A child darted forward, reaching to touch it. Nalga snarled and lunged at the child, whose parent pulled the girl away as she screamed in terror.

'Are you ready?' said Loth to Runa.

'Yes,' she said, her eyes narrowing. She raised her hands, flinched and lowered them again. 'Talorc?'

'Yes?'

'Take off my amulet.'

He found the cord around her neck and pulled it off, as delicately as he could, laying it down on her wet cloak beside her.

Runa put her hand upon Mordak's brow and closed her eyes.

CHAPTER THIRTY ONE

'At last,' said Runa, in a voice not her own.

'I must thank you,' she continued. 'Whatever happens, I am glad to be free of her.'

'Are you Mordak?' asked Talorc, his eyes upon the skull.

'Yes,' said Runa. 'Not every word Sariad spoke was a lie. I am Mordak. I was her master, before I became her prisoner.'

'But you are a diver,' said Talorc. 'You were the katra's most powerful diver, and Sariad was your slave. How did she –'

'She was not my slave,' said Runa. 'She served me, yes. But I did not rescue her because I needed a servant. I rescued her because I could not bear her pain.

'Your gift came to you late. Even now, you do not know what it is to be a diver. Sariad was one of the few who needs no ordeal for their power to awaken. She was born with the gifts of both diver and spey. Her own mother guessed it before her child was born; when carrying Sariad within her she dreamed of the things Sariad saw. The deep sea; the past; the dead.

'They hadn't the courage to throw the child into the sea, so instead they tried to beat the gifts out of her. She would run and hide in bone-houses, as you did; her parents would find her and drag her away but, of course, it did no good.

'It was during one of her beatings, while I was diving in what you call the Ancestor Circle, that I heard her cries. I found her, I felt her pain and I decided to take her.

'I took her from the bone-house where I found her hiding and brought her back to live with me. She served me, fished for me and tended my fire, giving me time to attend to my work. All the while I watched her. Studied her. Why had a dry been born with our gift? What did it mean? I saw the hand of the Sea Mother in the child's birth and in her coming to us. I knew there was a purpose to it all.'

'So you didn't beat her?' asked Talorc.

Runa laughed. 'Oh yes. I beat her. I'm not proud if it, but I find it hard to be sorry for it.'

'Why?'

'You can't understand how deeply our kind hates yours. Neither can my young kin who sit listening to me now. Only a diver, one who can sit within the Ancestor Circle and dive into the memories that flow through the sea, can know our pain. You are not yet a true diver, Talorc. I am. I have seen the island city where men and katra once lived side by side. I witnessed the war in which men turned against all their brother races. Most of the races perished, gone from this world forever; the katra who survived crossed the world to escape the dries. Yet wherever we made a home, your kind eventually came and drove us from it; all the way to these islands that we call Nuna, and you call Orka.'

'But Orka was our home first! You tried to take it from us!' said Talorc.

'No. We came here first. Where do you think your people learnt to build circles of stone? This was our home, and we shared it with you when you arrived. But it went the way it always goes with your kind. Times turned hard, you turned on us and because of your metals you defeated us. We made the pact with Valdar and have kept to our island of Doggor ever since.'

'And that's why you beat a child?'

'I told you I am not proud of that, boy. I have cruelty in me, and violence. I restrained myself, but sometimes, after diving and witnessing the suffering of my people, my restraint broke. So she came to hate me, and to do what she did, and I blame myself.'

'I blame you too.'

'You are bold when talking to a skull, boy. You would not be so bold had I still teeth and claws.

'You won't believe me,' continued Mordak, 'but as the years passed I grew fond of Sariad. Yes, even though I beat her. She was a prodigy. As I trained her I saw that in time she would far surpass me. She attained a level of skill no other among my pupils could reach, forcing me to work harder. We delved into one another's minds, played tricks, planting memories and ideas and challenging the other to identify them. We would spar with spears, sending thought-signals to mislead the other. Eventually I had to give up; she was winning every time.

'I had long since forgotten my distrust of her. The days when I beat her were, to me, a hazy memory. You must understand that I was growing old. I wanted to make my mark upon the world before I went to join my ancestors, and saw in Sariad my chance to do so. I believed the Sea Mother had sent her to bring our two kinds together. That was why she had both magics. I thought that through her we might broker some kind of peace. I even dreamed of her ruling the two races, a spey and diver-queen. I told her of how, in the earliest times, the clans of the katra did not have both a chief and a diver; the diver was the sole ruler of the clan. I liked the idea. She liked it too.

We agreed to present my ideas to the clan. Yet Sariad, as she revealed to me after my death, had a different plan. She knew that I carried the spell that would summon an Azawan. I had learnt it on the Fire Isle and dreamed of using it against your kind, but my master forbid me to do so, even to aid our people. I guarded that spell, deep in the locked chambers of my mind. Yet as I grew older, and my mind weaker, I could guard it no longer. Sariad stole into my mind and stole the spell. And then...'

'...She murdered you,' said Talorc.

'And our parents. And all the Nuna katra, but for us,' said Rugi.

'But why the sacrifices?' said Talorc. 'Why did she show herself to me? Why not just kill all of our kind too?'

'Because she didn't just want you dead. She wanted to rule

you. Sariad knew that she couldn't just use the Azawan to terrorise you into giving her the crown. When the Azawan was gone you would turn against her. So she insinuated herself, first with the spey woman, then with you both, and then with King Anga. After that she would begin picking off the people who could challenge her by naming them as sacrifices, slowly, amongst people of no consequence, so none would notice. Over time you would come to rely on her more and more, until when the king was named and sacrificed she could step into his place. Of course, Princess Runa would be dead by then. Sariad would banish the Azawan, name herself queen and none would oppose her. It might have worked, if the boy she chose to show herself to hadn't been you.'

'Yet Sariad is out there,' said Runa, this time in her own voice. 'My father trusts her, and he is hunting me. How can we stop her?'

'I shall give you what you want,' she said in Mordak's voice. 'A spell to banish the Azawan. But it will require both of your powers. You, Runa, must spey so that I may provide the words. Talorc, you must speak them. And it cannot be done here. You must take me to a place of power. One of the First Fathers, the rock pillars your kind call the Spey Kings.'

'Can you not give them now?' asked Runa. 'I may not live that long.'

'You are strong, boar-child. You must cling on to life a little longer. Loth. Ogluk. Nalga, Rugi, Skeen. Help them to reach a First Father. Keep them alive until the Azawan is banished. Go now.'

Runa raised her hand from the skull and opened her eyes. Talorc shivered as the fire spat.

'He's gone,' said Runa, her voice faint and sluggish.

She collapsed.

CHAPTER THIRTY TWO

Ogluk knocked Talorc aside and put her hand to Runa's brow.

The silkie woman muttered words Talorc didn't recognise. Faster and faster she spoke, her speech leaping and twisting, her eyes closed and her expression grave.

At last she fell silent, opened her eyes, looked at Talorc and shook her head. She spoke some words in her tongue to Loth.

'Runa's spirit is letting go,' said Loth. 'She has not long left.'

'Then get me to a Spey King,' said Runa, her voice almost inaudible.

'But she could die if we move her –' said Talorc.

'She will die,' said Loth. 'You know this.'

Talorc looked around the group. All eyes were on him. *Be like Runa,* he told himself.

'Where is the nearest Spey King?' he asked Loth.

'There is one west of here. Close by.'

'We shouldn't use the nearest one,' Nalga interjected. 'Your people will be searching for us in this area.'

'You're right,' said Loth. 'We need to head to the west of Ork. There are two Spey Kings there we could use.'

'But Runa won't make it that far,' said Talorc. 'The water will finish her.'

'Then we will go by another way,' said Loth.

He spoke to Ogluk again, Talorc watching Runa's stomach rise and fall as he did so. They were arguing, their voices growing louder, Ogluk gesturing wildly.

Eventually their voices calmed. Loth turned to Talorc and the katra.

'Lucky for us that Ogluk is less stubborn than most silkies,' he said. 'She has agreed to let us pass through her caves and into the Trowie Tunnels.'

'The Trowie Tunnels?' said Talorc.

'Yes,' said Loth. 'There is a honeycomb of tunnels running from one end of the island to the other. The outer caves mostly belong to the silkies, the inner caves to the trowies. If we use them then we should be able to get Runa to the Spey King in time.'

'Are they safe?' asked Talorc.

Loth laughed. 'Of course they're not safe. But there is no other way.' He stood, slipped Runa's death-stone back around her neck, picked her up and placed her over his shoulder. Ogluk disappeared into a hidden corner of the cave, returning with a shell full of paste. She indicated for Talorc to put Mordak's skull back in his sack and then smeared the paste over the sack.

'It works like a death-stone,' said Loth. 'The skull gives off a magical scent that the trowies will smell; the mixture will dull it. Ready?'

Talorc and the three katra stood. 'How will we find the way?' asked Talorc. 'Have you been through the tunnels before?'

'I am a Silver, Talorc,' said Loth. 'I have gifts that you do not.'

'Is Ogluk coming with us?' asked Talorc.

'The silkies and the trowies do not enter one another's territories.'

'But shouldn't they be helping us?'

'You do not know how lucky we are that they have helped this much,' said Loth. 'It goes against all their ways to intervene in a war between dries and katra, even if the Sea Mother commands it. It is only because Sariad is using an Azawan that they lend their aid. An Azawan means death to all sea-creatures.'

Loth and Ogluk exchanged a last few words before Ogluk came to stand before Talorc. She spoke to him, waving her hands back and forth before touching his brow, then did the same to each of the katra. Afterwards she stood back and a young, bare-chested, black-haired silkie man came forward with a torch in hand.

'We have Ogluk's blessing,' said Loth. 'Now we depart.'

Through dark, dripping, red rock tunnels they followed the silkie man. Their footsteps echoed off stacks and sharp needles of stone as they burrowed deeper into the flesh of Ork Island.

At the end of one tunnel the silkie man stopped and stood aside, revealing a small, natural archway in the stone. Markings had been gouged into the rock above, how long ago Talorc could not guess.

'The Trowie Tunnels,' said Loth. He raised a hand to indicate that the silkie man should stay while he addressed the others. 'Our guide will leave us here. I will take you through the Tunnels in darkness.' He handed each of them what appeared to be a tiny lump of black clay. 'Use this to seal your ears. It will stop you from hearing their music. If you do hear the music, ignore it, or you will be drawn to them, and they to us. Empty your mind and do not speak until we reach the sea.'

With that, Loth stooped and passed into the trowie tunnels. After they had plugged their ears, Nalga followed, then Skeen, then Rugi. 'Take hold of my tail,' said Rugi to Talorc.

He took hold of it, bent his knees and passed through, his back scraping against the jagged stone of the doorway. When he stood, the light of the silkie's torch was gone. There was only Rugi's scaled tail in his hand, and the darkness.

Darkness.

Talorc had thought he knew it. He'd met darkness on mid-winter nights on Odhran, creeping into the skull-chambers of the bone-house. But the darkness under the earth was deeper. It was inside him, trickling through his blood and bones.

Cold came with it. In the cold and darkness and silence, Rugi's tail was his only source of warmth, safety and certainty. It moved from side to side as she walked; he tried to hold on gently, not pulling it this way or that. He walked as quietly as he could, but the soft tread of his feet felt deafening. None of the others made a sound.

On they went.

The path rose and fell, gently. They never had to lower their heads. Talorc imagined grand tunnels, carved over centuries to make elegant passageways for the trowies to pass through. If only he could see what was about him. Somehow Loth could see; could the katra? Maybe his diving powers would help him to see in the dark. If he took off his death-stone... he laughed softly, breaking the silence. He wouldn't make that mistake again.

The trowies were out there. They could be nearby. Wherever they were, he was supposed to keep his mind clear. He returned his attention to Rugi's tail, its undulating rhythm, and to treading softly through the silence.

No good. His thoughts slipped like smoke out of his grasp. Runa. It seemed that it was only by the force of her will that she was still alive. *She will die,* Loth had said. *You know this.* But he didn't know it. Despite all the death he had seen, he couldn't accept that Runa would join his family and the unnumbered dead in the Sea Mother's caves. Runa was too strong. She was Orka's princess; she would be Orka's queen. He imagined her on a distant day, stood tall at the gates of Gurn, the Orkadi gathered to kneel before her and swear loyalty. It was a knife in his chest to think that such a day would not come.

She would be a queen like no other; it was plain to see. Runa would make peace with the silkies and katra, winning their trust and forging alliances that would not break. Over the sea she would go to Skoll, where she would ride with her husband to far-off halls and renew friendships with the Skollish kings and queens. He saw her stood in a great hall lit by many torches, exquisite tapestries on the walls, the light of a hundred lanterns illuminating tables loaded with dripping meat. Throngs of Skollish men and women gazed at her in wonder, or danced to the tunes of the pipes and flute and drum. He saw them dancing, heard the music more clearly as his gaze roved across the hall, marvelling at the fine clothes and ornaments of the Skollish folk.

Then the Skollish folk seemed to shrink.

Their beards grew long, past their knees, while their skin folded and sagged, their eyes growing wider, their noses longer and ears taller. They danced faster and faster as the music in his mind grew louder; Talorc searched his vision for Runa but couldn't see her. He could only see…

Trowies.

They had him.

It was no longer a hall in distant Skoll that Talorc stood in. It was a cavern, the ceiling lost far off in the darkness, so vast he could barely make out the end of it.

The cavern was full of trowies. Men, women and children, all leering at him and laughing at one who could be snared so easily.

Empty your mind, Loth had said, and Talorc had not listened.

Walking among the trows, bearing trays of drinks, were people of his own kind. They were wretched; bone-thin, dribbling, idiot-eyed, some in chains. None looked at him; they kept their eyes down. At a distant table he spied another non-trowie: a woman with hair black as raven-feathers, wearing a cloak of black fur, watching him with a wide smile as if his plight were entertainment.

The music stopped. The cave fell silent.

An old trowie man walked towards Talorc and looked up at him.

'You were not bidden to enter here,' said the trowie man, his lips almost concealed by a thick white moustache.

'I need to pass. Orka is in danger,' said Talorc. He scanned the crowd again. There was no sign of his companions.

'To pass, you must pay,' said the trowie.

'What can I pay you with?' asked Talorc.

The trowie grinned, candle-light dancing in his eyes.

'You can play,' he said.

Talorc looked down. He held in his hand his flute.

'Play,' said the trowie.

'I can't stay long,' said Talorc. Only too well did he remember Grunna and Skelda's stories of the mad ones that emerged from the caves after years of playing for the trows.

'In a hurry, are you, lad?'

'My friend is dying.'

'Well, that's a shame. You wouldn't rather forget about her? Stay here with us?'

'No.'

'Well then. If you're so keen to go. Impress us, give us a good tune, one we've never heard before, and we might let you away early.'

So Talorc played a tune his Grunna had taught him.

The trowies stood. Listened.

They began to laugh. Soon their laughter was so loud that Talorc could not hear himself play. His flute dropped from his lips.

'Terrible. You'll need to play better than that,' said the trowie man, indicating one of the shambling servants, 'or we'll find some other job for you.'

This was all wrong. He had to get away from here, out of the caves and to the Spey King. What could he play for them?

One we've never heard before.

Talorc had an idea.

Once more he pressed his flute to his lips and began to play.

This time, he played his story. He played Sariad sacrificing a seal on the shore. He played the sea-wolf, its pain and his own; and he played the Azawan, fire and death.

He played Runa.

His eyes closed as he summoned his memories and all they evoked in him, and Talorc heard the trowies begin to laugh. But it was a different kind of laughter. They weren't laughing because he played badly. They were laughing at him and his story; the fin-footed farm boy who hoped to save Orka from an Azawan and from war with the katra. An orphaned dreamer who, he understood in that moment, had fallen in love with a princess on the way. Who harboured dreams and hopes hidden even from himself. Of marriage, of unfolding and united powers, a new world of magic and wonder on those islands.

While the truth was, the princess would die. The farm boy would end up alone or dead.

The trowies loved it. Talorc played his last note, opened his eyes and saw that not one of them stood; they were rolling on the cave-floor, lost in their mirth.

He caught the eye of the trowie man who had addressed him. The man gave a nod, just as Talorc was slapped hard across the cheek.

Talorc looked into Loth's eyes. The warmth of the trowie hall was gone; instead there was the cold of the tunnels and, nearby, the roar of the sea. Loth and the katra were staring at him with a mixture of fear and anger.

'The trowies took me,' said Talorc. He was lying on the cave floor, his ear-stoppers gone.

'We know,' said Loth, disappointment in his voice. 'Get up. We're here.'

CHAPTER THIRTY THREE

The Spey King.

The cave mouth faced it over the torrent. Talorc stared up as flashes of lightning illuminated the giant pillar of rock. It could have been a spear of lightning, frozen into stone as it struck the sea. Yet the old story said this was one of the speys who long ago found sleeping giants in the sea, and made them into islands. The speys turned themselves into towers of stone, ready to watch over the islands and the Orkadi forever.

Talorc had seen one Spey King, on the east coast of Odhran. This one was far taller; as tall as the cliffs that half-encircled it. The cliffs were close but too far to jump. Once they were atop the Spey King they would be unreachable from land, should their pursuers find them.

How were they going to get up there, though? The Spey King looked like it could be climbed – certainly by katra, and probably, he guessed, by Loth too, but they would have to cross the water to get there.

Not far up the Spey King, he noticed a gap in the rock where a person could have sheltered in calmer seas. This must be where the young Skelda had faced her ordeal.

'Talorc,' said Loth over the howling wind. 'We need to reach the top to perform the ritual. I will carry Runa. Nalga will carry you.'

'But what about the water?' asked Talorc. 'It'll be too much for Runa –'

'Again, Talorc,' said Loth, 'I am a Silver.' With that he turned, ran and leapt over the water, landing at the foot of the Spey King with Runa still over his shoulder.

'Stop staring and climb on,' said Nalga. Talorc obeyed and held on as Nalga dived into the sea. Before he could even register the shock of the cold they were out again, Nalga hauling them up the Spey King. Loth was already halfway up and Rugi and Skeen soon appeared below them. Talorc clung on to Nalga as the wind and sea lashed them and the rain poured down.

Finally Nalga hauled herself over the top of the Spey King. She lay on her stomach, panting as Talorc climbed off her back, took off his pack and rolled away from her, relishing the feel of the thin, tufty grass beneath him. The sky was still dark, but he sensed dawn coming. Without the night to cloak them they would be found in no time. They had to work fast.

Talorc sat up and saw that Runa was awake. She was sat, cross-legged, facing out to sea, her eyes closed. The strange being that had once been his Grunda knelt at her side, the eyes of his dolphin-cloak staring into the sky. Loth had his hand on Runa's shoulder, whispering words that Talorc hoped were protective magic.

Rugi and Skeen crested the King and stood side by side as Loth turned and addressed them all.

'The sun will rise soon,' he said. 'We must act quickly. Talorc, the skull.'

Talorc opened his pack, reached in and took out Mordak's skull. He handed it carefully to Loth, who placed it on the grass beside Runa and indicated that Talorc should sit to the other side of it.

'What do we do?' asked Talorc.

'Three things. First, Runa and Talorc, I am going to give you a spell to connect your minds to each other's and that of Mordak. Without it, Talorc, you would not be able to follow Mordak's spell. Once that is complete, Mordak will give a spell to Runa and Talorc will speak it.'

'And that spell will banish the Azawan?' asked Talorc.

Loth shook his head. 'It is not so simple. Before you can banish the Azawan, you must find it. Once you have found it, you must join your minds to it. Then you shall banish it.'

Thunder shook the sky.

'Join minds with the Azawan?' asked Talorc.

'You will not be alone,' said Loth. 'Take off your death-stone.'

Talorc took off his own as Loth removed Runa's. He cried out as his senses overwhelmed him. The Spey King was alive and roaring its power beneath him. He could see his companions so clearly that he wondered if his gaze could pierce their skin. Loth glowed like the harvest moon, his dolphin-cloak as alive as the rest of him.

Then there was Mordak. Talorc watched in wonder as lights kindled in the dead katra's eye-sockets, while shimmering scales appeared and disappeared upon the glowing skull.

Runa reached out and placed a hand upon it. A tendril of light shot up her arm and the diver's skull glowed anew.

'Good,' said Mordak through Runa. 'The stone beneath us is strong; but the vessel is weak. Pay attention to the words you hear and follow them exactly. We begin.'

Kneeling behind them, Loth began to speak foreign words, enunciating each one. Talorc and Runa recited them in unison. The pace seemed too slow, almost insultingly so, but Talorc understood why. The power of the spell grew with each word spoken; he could feel it, as if it were a net. One mistake and he would slip out, and they would have to begin again.

The last words left their lips. The first spell was complete.

'Good,' said Mordak through Runa. Yet his voice seemed to come from the skull too. 'Now to speak the words I carried so long, and never dared speak. Do not hesitate; do not give in to fear or become separated, or within the mind of the Azawan you will be trapped and perish.'

With those words, he began.

This time, Talorc did not need to listen and repeat. He spoke the words as Mordak and Runa spoke them. The three of them had bound themselves together. They were one.

Talorc felt his spirit loose itself from his body, untying the invisible ties that held it-

'Look out!' shouted Skeen.

The spell broken, Talorc turned and saw what Skeen had seen.

Firelight in the distance.

The king's men were coming.

'Forget them!' shouted Loth. 'Begin the spell again!'

Talorc forced himself to obey. He closed his eyes and felt for the connection to Mordak and Runa.

Mordak began the spell again. Talorc quickly found himself forgetting the looming threat. The power of the spell was incredible. He was leaving his body again, and could see Mordak's spirit and Runa's beside him. They were speeding over the sea, high above the waves. Down into the water they went, into black depths, shooting forward faster than falling stars. They emerged and slipped back into the depths like brilliant, leaping dolphins of light.

The sea grew hotter.

Together their voices turned wary. Their pace slowed.

The Azawan was ahead.

Before it could stop them they leapt at it, through its skin and into its soul.

It was a world of fire. There was no peaceful place at the heart of this being; only fire, hunger and the rage of a demon enslaved.

They had broken into its soul, and the Azawan knew it.

From the inferno around them formed warriors of flame. Fire-swords sprung up from a forest of limbs as they advanced

and encircled the intruders. Runa was as scared as Talorc was, he sensed; Mordak was cold and calm. They went on speaking their spell.

The flame-warriors leapt at them. A web of light sprung up around them, like a great spiderweb soaked in dew and glimmering in the dawn-light. Fire-swords smashed against it and the warriors screamed, their faces shifting as they did so. Sariad. She was in the Azawan, in the warriors, screaming them on. They attacked again, and again. Talorc felt each blow as a dull thud at first, but as the shield was tested the blows grew sharper.

Yet the shield held. Talorc heard Mordak in his mind, telling them it was time for the spell of banishment. They would release the Azawan from Sariad's grip. He sensed Runa, light as a butterfly. She had only a little life left, yet she held on.

They began the spell of banishment. The flame-warriors roared, and beyond them larger shapes appeared from the flames; Azawans with the face of Sariad, chanting spells, readying to attack.

The flame-warriors struck again. The shield splintered but held. Beyond them, far beyond it all, Talorc glimpsed something else. A memory of what had made the Azawan, something beyond his comprehension, ancient and terrible.

Power suddenly surged through Talorc. He surrendered to it and felt the mouth of his spirit twist into a grin as he gave everything he had to the spell. It would work, the Azawan...

Something pulled at him, a distant pain, and then Mordak was screaming at him to hold on, but it was too late.

Talorc opened his eyes and roared in pain. His left arm felt like it was on fire; he looked down and saw, in the faint light before the dawn, that it was covered in blood.

He turned and forced himself up as Runa collapsed to the ground beside him. The three katra were crouched at his side, their teeth bared. Loth stood tall beside Runa, shouting words

Talorc couldn't comprehend.

King Anga stood on the clifftop opposite. Guardians lined the cliffs to either side of the king, and at Anga's side stood Sariad. She stared at Talorc with undisguised malice while Anga shouted one word, over and over, that Talorc understood.

'Hold! Hold! Hold!'

Some of the guardians were standing with spears or swords in hand. Others held bows with arrows notched, aimed at Talorc.

'In the name of the Sea Mother, I order you to stand back and lower your weapons!' Loth was shouting. They weren't going to listen to him; they were listening to Anga. Talorc could see in the guardians' eyes that many of them wanted to shoot him.

Steam rose from the water. The spray from the towering waves was hot.

'Don't hold your fire!' cried Sariad. 'Shoot him! He's with the fins! They're doing magic to call the Azawan! It's coming!'

'My daughter is there!' roared Anga. 'Hold your fire! Death to any man who fires!'

Runa was on her hands and knees. She was trying to speak, to shout to her father the truth, but had not the strength. There was no time for this. The Azawan was closing in; they had to complete the spell before it arrived. The guardians wanted to obey the king, but they were afraid, and Sariad was egging them on. It would only take one more arrow...

An arrow shot through the air, whizzing past Talorc's ear.

It was the spark that lit the fire. The guardians turned on one another. Anga fought his way towards the man who had loosed the arrow, calling those who would obey him to his side. The sound of clashing swords filled the air.

It was chaos. Amidst it Talorc saw Anga, no longer a man but a wild boar enraged, corner his prey. He swung his sword and cut the man's head clean off.

Anga threw the body into the sea and plunged back into the fray.

Talorc glanced around. The katra were gone. He looked over the edge and saw them climbing down the Spey King. They would cross, climb the cliffs and join the fight, he realised. If they could reach Sariad – where was she?

'The spell!' said Loth. 'Now!' Then Loth went the same way as the katra.

Talorc hesitated. Could he turn his back on men trying to kill him? He would have to.

Runa sat up. He joined her and again they placed their hands upon the shimmering skull.

Runa's life-force was almost gone.

I'm still here, she said in his mind.

Focus, said Mordak.

So Talorc pushed his fear aside and centred himself.

It was too late.

Out of the crashing sea the Azawan arose. Talorc gritted his teeth at the blast of heat it gave off as it soared above him. In the distance, he could see its glittering form stretching away towards the horizon.

It struck Talorc that as terrifying, as full of fury and darkness as the Azawan was, it was an awesome sight. Even beautiful. Perhaps to some it was not a monster but a god.

The Azawan looked down, its head swaying as it took in the sight of them. So tiny and insignificant his kind were to this being. They were not even worth the trouble of eating; yet the sight of them enraged it. How did he know that?

Our minds are still linked, said Mordak. *Now quickly –*

The Azawan screamed.

The fire-world wrapped itself around Talorc. It was not just flame-warriors who came at him now. Within the fires were the nightmares of everyone who heard it. Orkadi men, women and children screamed as their loved ones were tortured, their eyes bled and their skin melted in the fires.

Yet it was different this time. He could see through the horrors as if they were a veil; he could see Mordak's skull and Runa and the flesh of the Azawan itself. Glancing back, Talorc saw that Anga and the guardians were on the ground. These were their nightmares.

Sariad was on her feet, searching for something. Loth and the katra were climbing the cliffs and nearing the top. They were not affected.

Neither was Talorc. He turned, faced the Azawan and submitted to Mordak's urging.

He, Runa and Mordak chanted as one.

Ripples of light sped through the Azawan's body and towards its head as it summoned its fires, while their chanting revealed a web of spell-light around the Azawan. It was caught in the web, and, as Talorc chanted, he turned and saw that the web was linked by a light-thread to Sariad, who had found what she was looking for. A bow.

A few of the guardians were stirring. Skeen neared the cliff-top as Sariad loosed her arrow; it flew past Talorc and glanced off the Azawan. No use watching her. Talorc turned back and saw more and more light streak upwards towards the Azawan's throat as he willed his strength into the chant. It would soon be ready to incinerate them.

An arrow whistled past Talorc's head.

It was working. Talorc could feel the net around the Azawan weakening, unravelling. Then Sariad was there, her power coursing through the net as she gave up shooting and began her own counter-spell.

Mordak responded. His will, his hatred of Sariad fired through Talorc and Runa. The magic filled Talorc, poured through him at such a rate that he thought he would explode, while blood poured from the wound on his arm.

Light ceased coursing skyward through the Azawan. It was ready.

The Azawan opened its jaws wide. Drew back.

It jerked its head sharply. Once, twice.

The web of spell-light around it was gone.

The Azawan thrashed like a puppet pulled back and forth by a god of the sky.

Talorc realised he was no longer chanting. Nor was Runa or Mordak. Then he laughed. He laughed and sobbed and fought for breath as tears ran down his cheeks and his arm went on bleeding and burning.

At last, the Azawan was free.

Amidst all his pain and fear, Talorc found that he felt happy for the Azawan. It was free to leave this wretched place and return to rich hunting grounds full of fat, fleshy whales. Connected by an echo of the joining spell, Talorc knew that the fog in its mind was gone. It was its own master again. At the bid of hunger that must be obeyed, the Azawan turned to go.

But, Talorc realised as the last threads of the joining worked loose, it had something to do first.

The Azawan turned back to face Ork Island. It lunged, high over Talorc's head. He and Runa and the spirit of Mordak turned to watch with savage satisfaction as it snapped its jaws down on Sariad, tore off her torso and pulled away, so quickly that her blood-soaked legs stood for a moment before falling to the ground.

They turned again to watch as the Azawan returned to the water, plunging in and streaking away. Then pain exploded in Talorc's stomach, the ground disappeared, the sea rushed towards him and everything went black.

CHAPTER THIRTY FOUR

Talorc opened his eyes.

He was standing in a cave. Runa was at his side. A massive weight pressed down on the roof of the cave, as if all the sea lay above it.

Stood in a wide circle around them were men and and women with silvery skin and dolphin-cloaks. Loth was there, watching Talorc, a smile upon his face. Sea creatures both familiar and strange swam above them, while in dark, distant doorways, Talorc could make out an assembly of spectres; pale-faced people of smoke and dust. They crowded in close to one another, whispering, staring. There were humans and katra, though they kept apart from one another, even here. Most were strangers, but a few he recognised. Orkadi who had been on the boats when the sharks struck. The villagers of Yarrow.

His brothers. His parents.

Grunna.

Before Talorc and Runa stood the Sea Mother.

She slithered closer to them, her myriad tentacles coursing across the cave floor. Talorc's gaze roved across her, taking in the shoals of tiny, glittering fish that swam about her; the parts of her that were covered in barnacles, in giant starfish and tiny limpets and shrimp. Her face, that was somewhere between that of an octopus and that of an ancient woman, wrinkled and lined with tiny tentacles, wispy hair, wrinkled skin, beaks and lips and sets of darting eyes. Her tentacles danced endlessly, weaving living patterns of light in the air that looked like gateways to other worlds. She shone with her own luminescence; she was both terrifying and enrapturing.

In two of her tentacles she held dolphin-cloaks.

Your journey has reached its end, she said, her voice everywhere and nowhere. *The skins you wear will no longer serve you.*

'Are we dead?' asked Runa. Talorc noticed that the blood from her wounds no longer soaked her clothes. The colour had returned to her skin, the light to her eyes. Was this the purity of death, to exist forever in a state of perfection, the best of oneself?

If he was dead, so be it. To be here beneath the sea with Runa and his family and the Mother of them all, to watch life unfold across the sea until life and the sea were no more, or until his spirit was called to another body; surely he could not be discontent with that. No pain. No struggling. No choices.

And yet, his eyes kept returning to the cloaks.

Not dead. Not alive, said the Sea Mother. She drifted closer. *You have served me well in ridding my waters of the Azawan. In return for your deeds, I offer you these.* She extended towards them the dolphin-cloaks until they were almost close enough to touch, dangling just out of reach.

Talorc stared at the silver-blue skins as she spoke, the dead-and-alive eyes, the bulbous heads and tiny teeth.

Serve me as Silvers, she said. *Move between earth and sea, life and death. Carry my messages, fight for me, watch over my children as Loth watched over you. Weave the strands of fate as I will them. For all you have done, I give you this honour.*

'I have a question,' said Runa.

Ask it.

'Is my father dead?'

Yes, said the Sea Mother.

'Then we refuse your offer,' said Runa.

The Sea Mother was still for a moment. Then black ink erupted from mouth, darkening the cave. Her tentacles beat against the cave floor as she hissed her fury.

You refuse? You refuse me?

'With respect, and love, and in full knowledge of the honour bestowed upon us, we must refuse your offer,' said Runa, glancing quickly at Talorc. 'The past weeks have wounded the spirit of my people and broken the bonds between us. If my father is dead, and I take your cloak, then Orka has neither king nor queen. Those with a claim will fight for the throne, and yet more blood will be spilled on Orka. I must return.'

I did not offer that.

'No,' said Runa. 'Yet if it is in your power then please give it. Otherwise, we will refuse you, join the ranks of the dead and be useless to you. Let us live, and when you need us, we will serve you as Silvers. But give us life first.'

The Sea Mother stared at Runa, her tentacles tensing and loosening. Talorc watched, waiting for her to lash out and snap Runa's neck for her impudence.

Instead, the Sea Mother laughed.

Very good, she said, *very good, child. To bargain with me, and to win. The minstrels of the dead and living will surely sing songs of this day.*

I do desire you as servants. And I can give you life. But I cannot control how long it will last, and when I call you, I must have your oath that you will come. Know, too, that you will not be as you were.

'You have my oath,' said Runa. 'Just give me time to rebuild my kingdom.'

We shall see.

'I want the cloak,' said Talorc.

Runa turned and stared at him.

'What?'

'*You* need to rebuild *your* kingdom,' he said. 'Your work is just beginning. Mine is over. My home is gone. My village is gone. My family are dead and I'm a fin-foot. A dry who can dive. There's no place for me among our people or the katra. This place in-between is where I belong. It's where I've always belonged. I want to be a Silver.'

'But… but I need help,' said Runa. 'The Orkadi have fought one another… we've fed our kin to the Azawan. I'm queen and I've been found out as a spey. The katra want a blood-price from me. Some of the people won't accept me, and the Skollish kings will see our weakness and try to take Orka. I can't do this alone.'

'How am I supposed to help?'

'You're clever. You can advise me.'

'You'll have advisors.'

'By being my friend.'

'You'll have your husband –'

She kissed him.

After a moment that lasted an age, he kissed her back.

As he did so, he realised what he was doing.

He was making a choice.

The Sea Mother's tentacles snaked around them, took hold of them and began to fill their veins with silver-tinged blood.

The silence of the cave was gone. Instead there was the crash of the surf, of cooling water that swirled and struck against the cliffs, cleansing itself of the touch of the Azawan.

Talorc saw a cliff-face. Runa in his arms. The Sea Mother's multitude of limbs about them, climbing the cliff. Death, life, the future, the past, all tangled together in the embrace of a god.

He heard shouts of wonder and terror as they crested the clifftop. By the light of the rising sun, the Sea Mother laid him and Runa down upon the clifftop.

The Orkadi fell to their knees and wept at the sight of her.

As quickly as she had arrived, she departed, leaving Talorc and Runa to rise, uncertain, to their feet, while the wounded men wondered at the truth of what they had seen.

Talorc whispered a prayer of thanks and turned to study Runa. The blood and dirt-stains were back, her hair was wet and wild, her eyes sunken and dark. Yet there was a new light in those eyes, a subtle sparkle to her skin and the faintest smile upon her lips. Two kinds of blood, the blood of a Silver and the blood of a queen, now ran in her veins, and he did not know which he saw awakening.

He looked to the surviving guardians, who had risen from their knees to face Runa.

'Hail Runa, Queen of Orka!' he shouted.

'Hail Runa, Queen of Orka!' they repeated, and bowed with him.

Some bowed lower than others.

The guardians were ready to depart. Messengers had been sent to the nearest village, bringing herb-wives and materials to make stretchers for the wounded and the dead. Other Ork-adi had come as news of the night's events had spread. They gathered around Anga's body, watching as Runa held her father's hand and spoke at length in his ear. Finally, Anga and the others were put onto their stretchers, men quietly vying for the distinction of bearing their fallen king. Word would go out quickly across the islands. The Orkadi would gather for the death-rite of the king and all those who had fallen that night.

The katra were nowhere to be seen. Surely, though, they would return to take what Runa had promised them.

Talorc left the crowd behind. He walked south along the clifftop until he could no longer hear their voices and stood, looking out to sea.

The low winter sun cast all in gold. The sea went on, and on, and he wondered again if it ever ended. Better if it didn't. Grunna believed it was endless, and that upon it all things were possible and existed somewhere. Somehow it was more beautiful that way.

The sea was not at peace – it was ever restless – but he knew it would quickly heal itself of the Azawan's fire and darkness. How could it not? There was no power greater than the sea, and on some distant day he would become its servant. Until then, he just had to go on living.

Far out, he saw a pod of dolphins, cresting and diving, melting into the water like shards of sunlight. Something inside him desperately longed to join them.

'Talorc?'

He turned to see Runa, sat upon Farla's back.

'It's time to go back.'

He looked away, out to sea again. The dolphins had disappeared from sight.

Talorc turned away from the sea, shielding his eyes from the sun as he answered the call of his queen.

THE END

AUTHOR'S NOTE

Authors dread being asked 'where do you get your ideas from?' In my case, the answer is easy. I got the idea from an Orcadian legend, Asipattle and the Muckle Maester Stoor Worm. In the original story, a lackadaisical farm boy named Asipattle defeats a gigantic sea serpent known as a stoor worm, and in return, the king gives him the hand of Princess Gem De Lovely in marriage.

The story is one of many that I tell in my work as an oral storyteller. For ten years I've gathered and memorised myths, legends and folk-tales to tell to audiences in schools, libraries, prisons, festivals and wherever people will listen. It made sense for me to write a novel based on one of these stories, and I'd always felt that there was much more to the story of Asipattle.

Of course, I changed the story a lot. I changed Asipattle's name to Talorc, and Princess Gem De Lovely was politely asked to leave in order to make way for Runa. I studied pagan magic in prehistoric Northern Europe, and brought in creatures from Orkney's folklore that fascinated me; the trowies, the silkies and of course the finfolk.

It is believed that the finfolk may be a dim folk-memory of the Saami people of northern Finland, who could have crossed to Orkney, appearing out of the mist in their canoes. Local legend has it that the finfolk row ships without sails, and live on mysterious vanishing islands, or beneath the sea in a city called Finnfolkaheim. The stoor worm is probably derived from the Norse belief in Jormungandr, the serpent at the bottom of the sea who encircles the world, his tail in his mouth.

As I researched Orcadian prehistory, I learnt about the eruption of Mount Hekla in Iceland in around 950BC, and how the use of communal tombs gave way to individual graves. The eruption would have darkened the sky and caused crops to fail. What would people have thought about that? Would they have blamed witches, as people have so often done?

So I read, and imagined, and wrote the story you have just read. But that's not all; I like to get hands-on with my research. So I learnt scuba diving, and free diving (diving without an oxygen tank), and went beneath the waves in Thailand and Indonesia. Since my finfolk resemble Komodo dragons, I went to view wild Komodo dragons on Rinca Island in Indonesia. And to write better combat scenes, I spent six months training Muay Thai (Thai boxing) in Thailand. Not to mention plenty of time sitting in pitch-black tombs on Orkney.

What Next?

If you've read this far, I'm going to assume you liked the book. If that's the case, I have good news: the story isn't over. There are a couple of sequels (maybe more) on the way. In the meantime, I've got loads of other stories to share with you. I have a weekly podcast, House of Legends, on which myself and some of the world's best storytellers tell the myths, legends and folktales that we love. I'd love it if you subscribed, which you can do at www.houseoflegends.me/podcast

I'll soon start running retreats, where you can join me and some top tutors to work on your writing or storytelling in wild, beautiful places. And if you want to write your first novel – and are absolutely, totally committed to doing so – you can get in touch with me about book coaching at www.houseoflegends.me/contact

I have a readers club, called the House of Legends Club. By joining you'll be the first to get news on the podcast, books, retreats and live events, as well as exclusive discount offers and some creativity and productivity tips to help you with your own projects. You can unsubscribe at any time, and it's quick and easy to do so. As soon as you join, you'll get my free ebook, Silverborn & Other Tales, in which Grunna and Talorc tell stories by the hearth-fire late at night. Find out more at **www.houseoflegends.me/landing-page**

Other than that, feel free to email me to say hello or to talk about sea monsters. I'd love to hear from you. And please do share The Bone Flute on your social media, and leave a review on Amazon. Reviews help me and they help other readers.

Daniel Allison

ACKNOWLEDGEMENTS

I'm lucky enough to have wonderful friends and colleagues who have helped me immeasurably along this journey. Thank you to Feren for curling up on my desk on cold, dark winter mornings; you made writing so much more fun. Thank you to Tom for sharing your knowledge of Orkney and your hospitality. The staff at the Tomb of the Eagles Visitor Centre were kind enough to let me in out of season, show me around and even give me a lift from the bus. If you're in Orkney, and you'd like to see Sariad's bone-house, don't miss it.

Thank you to my beta readers: Claire, Philip, Lally, Ryan, Elisabeth, Peter, Mara, Imani, Suzanne, Rhiannon, Dallas, Renn, Ian, Katie, Annie, Jesse and Bari. Ian, thank you for sharing your knowledge of curraghs and your editing suggestions. Sean, thank you for the coaching that helped me believe I could do this and so much more. And thank you to all of my Thailand tribe not mentioned yet, for the year that changed everything: Liz, Cassie, Pok, Steve, Julia, Aimee, Craig, Alex, Christina and everyone else at Diamond Muay Thai.

A huge thank you to Fay, Sarah and the team at Jericho Writers for believing in The Bone Flute and offering your support. It has been invaluable.

Mum, Peter, Rachel, Paul, Maia, thank you for your support in everything.

Daniel Allison

FREE DOWNLOAD OFFER

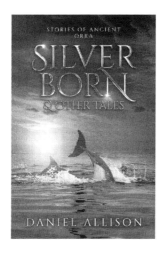

As the winter winds shriek and their family sleeps, Grunna and Talorc sit at the hearth-fire, telling the tales of ancient Orka. Stories of trowies, silkies and even the mysterious Silvers.

I'm offering Silverborn as a FREE ebook exclusively to members of the House of Legends Club.

Get my FREE ebook at www.houseoflegends.me/landing-page

COMING SOON
From
Daniel Allison

Finn & The Fianna
A New Retelling of the Celtic Legends - available 2020

The stories of Finn MacCoull and his warriors were once told at every fireside in Scotland and Ireland. After centuries in obscurity, this collection brings the tales soaring to life again.

Within these pages are Diarmuid, whom no woman can help but love, and Ossian, a warrior-poet raised in the woods by a wild deer. There is Grainne, ancient ancestor of Iseult and Guinevere; and Finn himself, whose name was once a byword for wisdom, generosity and beauty.

Enter a world of feasting and fighting, battles and poetry, riddles and omens; join Finn and the Fianna in their never-ending quest to drink deeper and deeper of the cup of life.

'A master storyteller whose words are visions... this is Celtic myths & legends at their fantastic best!'

Jess Smith, Author of Way of the Wanderers

Stay up to date on Finn & The Fianna - join the House of Legends Club at www.houseoflegends.me/landing page

HOUSE OF LEGENDS PODCAST

If you loved the Bone Flute, you'll love House of Legends. It's a weekly podcast on which I tell my favourite myths and legends; the kind of dark, weird and brilliant stories that inspired me to write this book. I also use the podcast to keep readers up to date with what I'm working on and my upcoming live events.

You can listen on my website at
www.houseoflegends.me/podcast

BOOK COACHING WITH DANIEL ALLISON

From first thoughts to final draft

Are you ready to write your first novel? If the answer is yes, and you are seriously committed to making your dream a reality, I would like to offer you book coaching. Whether you have an idea or a first draft, I can provide you with support, feedback and accountability to help see you through to the finish line.

Contact me for details at www.houseoflegends.me/contact

ABOUT THE AUTHOR

Daniel Allison is an author, oral storyteller, podcaster and book coach from Scotland. The Bone Flute is his debut novel, inspired by the myths and legends that he tells to audiences throughout the world. Daniel has lived in India, Nepal, Uganda and Thailand and is currently living in Edinburgh while writing the sequel to The Bone Flute. He loves cats and hates celery.

You can keep up to date with Daniel by subscribing to his podcast, by writing to him via his website or by joining the House of Legends Club at www.houseoflegends.me/landing-page

Printed in Poland
by Amazon Fulfillment
Poland Sp. z o.o., Wrocław